**Praise for the Novels
of Lydia Joyce**

Whispers of the Night

"Tantalizing, spellbinding, sizzling, and captivating, this novel lures readers into its depths, making them never want to leave. Joyce hones her skills as an erotic romance author of the finest caliber in a tale as dark and seductive as rich, decadent chocolate." —*Romantic Times BOOKclub*

"Ms. Joyce takes [a classic romance] theme and places it in exotic locales. . . . It makes for a fun and interesting change of pace. Readers who enjoy exotic locales will want to check out this dramatic story." —Romance Reviews Today

The Music of the Night

"Danger, deception, and desire all come together brilliantly in this sublimely sensual historical romance."
—*Booklist* (starred review)

"Complicated, challenging, sexy, and altogether adult."
—All About Romance

"Joyce spins a tale that is . . . mesmerizing and fascinating. . . . Dark, intense, and with a surprise ending that will leave you breathless, her latest Gothic makes its mark on the genre."
—*Romantic Times BOOKclub* (top pick)

"Refreshingly different from the usual romance book offerings . . . intelligent writing . . . an excellent example of what a talented writer can accomplish if they choose not to follow the pack."
—*The Romance Reader*

continued . . .

The Veil of Night

"Intelligent. Passionate. Filled with dark secrets and illuminating love. This is what romance is about!"
—Robin Schone, *USA Today* bestselling author of *The Lover*

"The next great romance author has arrived, and her name is Lydia Joyce. *The Veil of Night* is a stunning debut from a young writer who possesses remarkable maturity and style. Every page is charged with sensual energy and confident grace. It is a gorgeous, complex, absolutely riveting novel. If there is only one new author you will try this year, it must be Lydia Joyce."
—Lisa Kleypas, *New York Times* bestselling author of *Devil in Winter*

"A lush, erotic historical Gothic romance, with just the right dark and mysterious hero and a strong heroine who can match him. Anyone who has ached for the Gothics of the past shouldn't miss this book!"
—Karen Harbaugh, author of *Dark Enchantment*

"A powerful love story, compelling and beautifully written."
—Alison Kent, author of *Deep Breath*

"Beautiful. . . . The prose is lyrical, and the characters' thoughts are expressed in a mature and insightful way. . . . Impressive. . . . The author pulls it all off with considerable aplomb."
—All About Romance

Voices of the Night

Lydia Joyce

A SIGNET ECLIPSE BOOK

SIGNET ECLIPSE
Published by New American Library, a division of
Penguin Group (USA) Inc., 375 Hudson Street,
New York, New York 10014, USA
Penguin Group (Canada), 90 Eglinton Avenue East, Suite 700, Toronto,
Ontario M4P 2Y3, Canada (a division of Pearson Penguin Canada Inc.)
Penguin Books Ltd., 80 Strand, London WC2R 0RL, England
Penguin Ireland, 25 St. Stephen's Green, Dublin 2,
Ireland (a division of Penguin Books Ltd.)
Penguin Group (Australia), 250 Camberwell Road, Camberwell, Victoria 3124,
Australia (a division of Pearson Australia Group Pty. Ltd.)
Penguin Books India Pvt. Ltd., 11 Community Centre, Panchsheel Park,
New Delhi - 110 017, India
Penguin Group (NZ), 67 Apollo Drive, Mairangi Bay,
Auckland 1311, New Zealand (a division of Pearson New Zealand Ltd.)
Penguin Books (South Africa) (Pty.) Ltd., 24 Sturdee Avenue,
Rosebank, Johannesburg 2196, South Africa

Penguin Books Ltd., Registered Offices:
80 Strand, London WC2R 0RL, England

First published by Signet Eclipse, an imprint of New American Library,
a division of Penguin Group (USA) Inc.

First Printing, March 2007
10   9   8   7   6   5   4   3   2   1

In memory of Grande—and the
people in our lives we may not always like
but still will never cease to love

Acknowledgments

Special thanks to Emma Gads, yet again, and to Robin Perini, who helped me whip this book into shape. And eternal gratitude to the support of Anne Bohner and Nancy Yost—thank you both for the faith that got me here.

Prologue

Maggie shivered, wrapping the sooty shawl tighter around her thin shoulders as she hunched behind the brute bulk of Johnny.

Fog pressed down upon the city, smothering it, pulling the smoke down from the chimney pots to swirl in the streets under the weight of the brown and breathless sky. It was a black fog, a killing fog, and Maggie and the other chavies had coughed up soot every morning that week when Johnny kicked them awake. That morning, Moll had coughed up blood.

Dawn had been an unfulfilled promise, a slight lightening from tomb-black to dirty gloom, extinguished mere hours later as maids lit the morning coal fires in grates across the city and the smoke floated up and settled back down again, great snowflakes of soot falling with the drizzle. The bobbies strolled along their accustomed patrols swinging their bull's-eye lanterns even at ten o'clock; by two, the lamplighters were at work, their progress marked by a trail of dirty, sulfurously glowing orbs that illuminated nothing but more fog.

Now, Maggie judged from the pinching in her stomach that it must be gone past four, and the premature dusk had slipped into an unnatural night. Johnny stood at the base of a streetlamp against the parapet of the bridge, shining his thief-lantern's unshuttered light into the thick brown soup, where it was sucked into nothingness, and nothing shone back.

She was scared, more scared than she'd ever been. Because Johnny wanted a man dead, and he wanted Maggie to do it.

Her wrist already ached with the weight of the pistol, her free hand keeping her shawl closed tight to conceal it. She had watched Johnny slot the rounds into place in the doorway—the gun was new, the shine of the metal dulled with soot, and so large that Maggie had to steady the barrel with one hand so that she could make her short fingers stretch to reach the trigger.

"That Danny's a blooming mean bugger," Johnny had growled, enjoying her fear, "but all me lieutenants got to do their part, eh. It's the initiation, it is, and there ain't no excuses, even if yer are a chit."

Maggie did not want to be his lieutenant, but he didn't give a body a choice—if he asked, you could either be his lieutenant or his rival, and she knew what happened to his rivals. A gun on a bridge or a knife in a doorway, and some other poor chavy on the other end of it, who didn't want to kill anybody any more than she did . . . She should have stayed out of pickpocketing. That was boy's work. Then Johnny never would have discovered her talent with locks, nor would she be here now, lying in wait for a man she hardly knew. But even this was better than the hell many of the other girls were living. Maggie's mind shuddered away from the pulp that had been made of Sally's face that week, first by a john and then by

Johnny—and, almost worse, the mute, dead acceptance of it in her eyes.

"I think I hear sommat," Johnny hissed, and he slid the cover over the lantern so that the utter, stifling darkness wrapped around the streetlamp they stood under, shrinking the world to a circle of no more than twice the length of her outstretched hands.

Maggie gripped the gun harder, keeping it under the cover of her shawl. Even in the choking darkness, the city teemed, and the last four approaches had been false alarms.

Someone was drawing near on foot, and whistling. Maggie knew the tune—an aria, her favorite aria from an opera that had just opened two nights before. The whistler's rendition was playful, even cheerful, and his heels hit the pavement with jaunty crispness. This could not be the man she was meant to kill, not someone who whistled arias.

The man stepped into their gritty orange ball of light, and Maggie saw the neat moustache, the eye patch, the hair that was flaxen under a felt hat.

"Do it!" Johnny snarled, grabbing her by the arm and wrenching her forward.

Maggie raised the gun. She saw surprise on Danny's face, exultation on Johnny's. And she saw other faces of people who were not there, bruised and empty and in pain—Sally's and Little Thom's, Moll's and Long Jenny's, Fat Billy's and Sweet Polly's. And then she swung the gun and pulled the trigger. The report reverberated against the walls of fog, deafening her as the pistol jumped and jerked back against her hand, and Johnny's eyes went wide at the new, round hole in his forehead.

He fell back, hit the parapet of the bridge, and went over. Maggie gasped against the pain in her wrist. The pistol dropped to the ground with a leaden clatter, and she ran the three steps to the parapet and looked over. But the fog had already curled back, swallowing the brief disturbance of Johnny's body as if it were no more than a rock tossed into a void. There must have been a splash below, but Maggie did not hear it.

In a day or two, one of the scrawny mudlarks with their dragnets and leaky boats would find the body downstream and pull it from the river, turning it dutifully over to the authorities after stripping it of everything of value. It might eventually be identified, or it might not, but whatever else happened, Johnny was gone for good, and his chavies were free.

Free. Maggie backed away from the edge, and her heel struck the dropped revolver, sending it skittering a few feet across the filthy cobbles. She picked it up—wincing at the weight on her sore wrist and switching it quickly to her other hand—and started to toss it after Johnny. But then she hesitated and slipped it back under her shawl. A pistol was worth too much just to throw away.

"I thank ye kindly, me colleen."

Maggie turned quickly to see Danny still standing where he had stopped when she raised the gun. He was wearing a smile under his moustache like another man might put on a hat, as false as his lilting accent.

Maggie was shaking inside, but she tipped up her chin and looked him squarely in the face. "Yer owe me, Danny O'Sullivan."

His smile did not change. "I could use a girl wi' that kind o' spirit, to be sure."

"I don't want to be used by nobody," Maggie said. "I want to be let be. Me an' mine. We don't need no scurf nor no kidsman. Not Johnny, not you, not nobody."

"Sounds fair t' me," Danny said, shrugging. "I'll be sure t' let you know when we're even again."

"We won't never be even. Yer owe me yer life," Maggie countered.

His single blue eye twinkled. "Ah now, but Maggie, me colleen, here, even lives can be bought and sold like day-old fish on a costermonger's barrow."

With that, he brushed by, and a few seconds later, the fog swallowed him.

And Maggie shivered.

Chapter One

Four years later

Charles Crossham, Lord Edgington, took the steps of the gilded Baroque staircase two at a time, seething inside even as he kept his expression carefully schooled in an icy neutrality. How could Millie have dared to destroy five months of his planning in a single fit of pique? She might not know that his was the hidden hand behind Lily Barrett's debut, but her interference was still intolerable. He strode down the East Gallery, the cold marble clicking under his shiny boots, and flung open the door to her sitting room, planting himself upon the center of the pastel Aubusson rug that overlay the carpet before her hearth.

Millie jumped at his entrance and looked warily over the top of her novel at him as he fixed her with his coldest stare. She was ensconced in her favorite chair, a delicate thing of cream silk nestled near the filtered light of the lace-swathed window, which glowed with the chill winter light.

"I heard what you did at the Rushworths' ball," he said.

Her gray eyes went wide. "What did I do?" Her voice

was a trifle breathless, her hands gripping her book so that its spine creaked in protest.

Charles gritted his teeth that she could even ask such a question, her false, fluttery little display grating against his raw nerves. God, but he wanted to take her and shake some sense into that self-centered little brain of hers. "You humiliated Miss Barrett," he said instead—lightly, for he knew how to best handle his sister after four years of being the head of their household. "You single-handedly destroyed her chances for a successful Season."

Millie relaxed slightly, waving a graceful and negligent hand. "Oh, that. Miss Barrett—or whatever her name really is—has no upbringing and no connections; she does not belong in our circles. Colonel Vane might claim she is a poor relation, but we all know she is someone's shame, and all I did was say it aloud so we didn't have to pretend anymore. You should be grateful. To display her at the most fashionable London balls degrades us all."

"Lily Barrett is none of your concern," Charles said, keeping his tone flat even as he boiled inside.

Millie pressed her lips into a little moue of irritation. "She's such a dull, nervous little creature. She was farmed out in the country, and that is where she belongs. Why do you care about her? I'd be half inclined to suspect she was your shame, dear brother, if only you were old enough." She smiled at her own wit.

His shame! Charles smothered a snort. His sister was closer to the truth than she could imagine. Charles had a sudden temptation to let his sister know precisely how close to accurate her jab was.

But no. That would only anger her, and as satifying as it often was to rile his sister, Charles wouldn't risk his enterprise on such a gamble.

"You will undo this," he told her simply, calmly.

A stubborn crease appeared between her eyebrows. "Or what?" She shook her head, sending her ash-brown curls bouncing.

She was digging in for a fight. Charles suppressed the urge to grind his teeth. After her last scrape, he'd gone so far as to deny her food until she agreed to use her allowance from her grandmother's bequest to make it right. She had held out for four days until she collapsed, at which time the doctor had made it clear that enforcing Charles' dictum any further would put her health in mortal danger. Though Millie had eventually conceded after additional, less extreme privations, he wished for no repeat of that battle.

"Do you want me to think of something?" he demanded.

"I suppose not." Millie smiled slightly, though her expression had an edge. "I don't understand why you must always pick fights with me. I certainly have no desire for us to be in conflict."

"Don't try to manipulate me, Millie," Charles said impatiently, recognizing her gambit. "I am not our dear, departed papa."

"I don't need you to remind me of that," she snapped. After a moment of silence, she changed tactics yet again. "Why do you want me to make up to her? You know no girl like that could ever pass for one of us."

Charles allowed himself a frown. "You are very certain of that."

She rolled her eyes. "Of course I am, sweet brother. Someone like her . . . why, she is nothing like us! She is made of"—she waved her hands vaguely—"different stuff. Baser stuff."

"Coarser, inferior stuff?" he suggested. The idea

amused him darkly despite the situation, given exactly how much *stuff* his sister and Lily Barrett shared.

"Exactly. Don't you think so?" she pursued.

"I am not, perhaps, as wholly convinced as you," he said.

Her green eyes narrowed with thought, and Charles wondered if she had any idea how transparent she was when she attempted to be devious. A wager. He was certain it was going to be a wager. It always was, with Millie.

"I don't want to argue with you, Charles dear," she finally said. "I hate when we're at odds. So why not settle this straightforwardly? You believe that someone like Lily Barrett could pass for one of us. I believe that it is pointless to try, and so shunning her now is an act of mercy to the poor thing. If you can prove to me that I am wrong, then not only will I apologize profusely to your Miss Barrett, but I will also have Mamma sponsor her in a formal debut, with a court presentation, a ball, and everything." She beamed, certain that she had baited a hook he could not resist.

And it was very, very tempting. Such an arrangement was far more than Charles had hoped for—far more than he had been able to arrange with his quiet, behind-the-scenes string pulling. All he would need was a pretty and talented actress, unknown in his circle. And Charles, of all men, knew where to find women who yearned for the stage.

Charles nodded decisively. "I will hold you to all your promises," he warned.

Millie settled back in her chair with a feline smile, at ease again, convinced she had scored a coup against him, no doubt. "I wouldn't expect any less from you, dear brother."

Charles snorted and turned to leave as she lifted her

book again. He paused with a hand on the gilded door-knob and looked over his shoulder. "And Millie?"

"Yes, Charles?" She glanced up from her novel, raising her eyebrows in smug inquiry.

"I also learned about the wagers you lost at the Ferrers' ball and paid off your debts yesterday. I have spoken to Mother, and she agrees that gambling more than one's pocket money is a vulgar habit in a girl. You won't be seeing your allowance again until I have been recompensed for both the sum and the trouble that you caused me." Charles paused, as if just thinking of an alternative. "Unless, of course, you would like to discharge your debt through an appropriate act of kindness to Miss Barrett."

Millie's smugness dissolved instantly, and she snarled, reaching behind her back and yanking out a violet needle-point pillow, which she flung at his head in answer.

Charles caught it easily and dropped it to the floor. "I suppose not," he said mildly.

He left, shutting the door behind him, his footfalls echoing in the East Gallery as he retraced his steps. The ranked generations of his family watched him coldly from their gilt frames. In the expressions of the young Crosshams burned the light of their decadence, their smiles full of self-indulgent satiety and their eyes sharp with avarice and lust. The same people in later portraits were ravaged by jaded dissolution, their limbs gout-thickened and their bitter expressions periodically softened by the misty look of those who float the hours away in a dreamy haze of laudanum, opium, or absinthe. Their gazes seemed unrelentingly hostile as they bore into his back—he, who balked against everything the family had ever been or stood for. Everything he had been raised to be. Taking care of Lily Barrett was just one act of defiance among many.

That task, at least, was simple enough, even if Millie had thrown a barrier in his way. All Charles needed was a moldable, pretty young thing from a sufficiently disgraceful past with a certain talent for acting to play the part of a country squire's daughter. Any Edgington male knew exactly where to get that:

The opera.

Maggie stepped into the grimy alley as the stage door shut with a final thud behind her. Sally unfolded her arms and pushed off the wall she had been leaning on. Maggie scanned the alley reflexively. It was empty except for them. Dusk was falling fast, and a fog was rising from the river and mixing with the soot that sank from the chimneys in the heavy air. Already, it swirled around their ankles when they moved.

"Well? What'd he say?" Sally prompted.

"Nofing." Maggie couldn't keep the bitterness out of her voice. *I should've blown Danny's brains out on that bridge, too, when I had the chance*, she thought viciously. For two weeks, Danny O'Sullivan had been sending her word through various messengers that he wanted to talk and she had ignored them all; she knew that Danny never just "talked," especially not now that he'd absorbed or destroyed every other gang of any size in London. Walking from Billingsgate to St. Giles used to involve passing through the territories of a dozen scurfs. Now, there was only one, and he was the worst of them all.

So Maggie had kept her head down, avoiding his bruisers' favorite haunts, and in retaliation—or warning, as Danny's retaliations tended to be deadly—he'd had her blacklisted. He hadn't told her so, of course, but he didn't

have to. When she'd been sacked from her singing gig at
The Mermaid's Dance for upsetting an important gentleman and no one else would take her, it didn't take much
figuring to know who was behind her sudden disgrace.

Maggie sighed, rubbing her eyes tiredly with the back
of her hand. "Mr. 'Awkins didn't even want to see me,
and when I pushed in anyways, 'e turns around and says
'e ain't got no room for another burlesque singer. I says
I'll do anyfing, and 'e says there ain't nofing that's
enough to make up for making certain gennlemen angry."

"Anyfing?" Sally's deep blue eyes shadowed with dark
ghosts of the past. "Maggie, you ain't never—"

"Don't you tell me what I've done and what I ain't,"
Maggie snapped, turning her back and walking quickly
toward Tottenham Court Road. She heard Sally's footsteps behind her, easily matching her short stride. "We're
running out of blunt, Sally. 'Arry ain't 'ad no copy work
for days, and Nan keeps getting soused instead of staying
with the barrow, and I ain't seen Frankie in a week. We're
already behind on the rent. If I don't do somefing, old
Widow Merrick is going to throw us all out, and then
we'll really be doing anyfing anybody asks us to 'cause
we won't have no choice no more."

They reached the street, and Maggie stalked down the
crowded pavement toward Church Lane. She heard a
snuffling noise, and she knew Sally was crying. She tried
to steel herself to the sound, tried to stay angry.

"You ain't never 'ad to sell yourself afore, Maggie,"
Sally said. "You don't know what it's like, all those men,
huffing and puffing on top of you—"

Maggie stopped and whirled to face her friend so suddenly that Sally nearly collided into her. Traffic streamed
past them on either side, but Maggie ignored it. "I ain't
selling myself to all comers in the Haymarket, Sally. I am

trying to make a business deal, eh! And I am out of ways to try an' sweeten it except throwing meself in as a little treat."

"I won't let you do it for me—"

"Then are you going to keep me from doing it for Moll? Or 'ow 'bout little Jo?" Maggie asked savagely. "Do they deserve to live on the street 'cause of your high-and-mighty ways?"

Sally was crying in earnest now, tear tracks making clean streaks in the dirt upon her scarred cheeks. "Moll and Jo are Nan's problems, not yours. You're me best friend, Maggie, and I can't stand to see you doing this to yourself."

Maggie wanted to cry, too, but she didn't. She couldn't remember how. It had been too long. "You know I can't just let them down like that," she mumbled, pulling Sally's angular frame against her in an awkward hug. "We been together for years. They're me family, too."

"Maggie's chavies," Sally agreed softly. A porter with a crate on his back spat a curse at them as he squeezed past, and she sighed and let go as Maggie turned to continue down the street. "What are you going to do now? That was the last theater within five miles of Church Street, even counting the penny gaffs."

"I'm going to go to the one singing place where Danny ain't got no say," Maggie said firmly. "The opera. Perle sent me a note, said she'd heard of me problems and got me an audition. You'll see. It'll all turn out right. Better, even. With me as an opera singer, just think of all the blunt we'll have!"

Her voice rang with confidence, but inside, she recognized that declaration for what it was—a surrender, an admission of defeat, a hopeless, last-ditch effort to leap at a dream that could never be hers. Her voice had not been good enough for the opera four years ago, and nothing had changed since then. But what else could she do but try again? There was nothing open to her anywhere else.

She would audition again, she would fail again . . . and then she would disappear, to Southampton or Leeds or somewhere so her taint wouldn't drag down the chavies with her. It was the only thing she could do for them, and it wasn't nearly enough.

Chapter Two

Covent Garden. The site never failed to impress Charles with its incongruities. The soot-encrusted, classically detailed mansions that surrounded the flagged piazza were beginning to decline from impoverished gentility to outright poverty, overlooking a teeming mass of people so quintessentially British that the buildings' Italian-inspired lines were rendered ludicrous. St. Paul's Church rose on one side, the false front of its portico austerely and inappropriately Roman, while three parallel arcades ran down the center of the square, overflowing with all the noise, chaos, and waste of the wholesale vegetable and flower market.

There was no reason to stop there, for his carriage could have easily brought him around the corner to the front of the Royal Italian Opera. But the tumult of the market had always attracted him, now more than ever since his own life had become so unseasonably staid and stifling with his father's death.

Charles opened the carriage door and stepped lightly onto the pavement without bothering to lower the steps. The layered detritus of packing straw and discarded produce squelched damply beneath his boots. Half a hundred stalls sprawled before him in the open square, belonging to those sellers who had neither the volume nor the value of goods to afford a coveted place along the arcades. Their tables were three-quarters empty so late in the day, but still the market thronged with wholesalers, green grocers, porters, costermongers, street Arabs, and flower women, the entire strata of the lower orders exposed for the examination of the idle scientist.

Charles wove between the stalls and into the heart of the market, down the gallery between two of the arcades. This time of year, there were no fresh vegetables with good Middlesex mud clinging to their roots, but there was still no shortage of goods to be had. Onions, turnips, and potatoes stood bare to the crisp air, still dusty from their storage bins; forced fruits had been coddled into succulence for the tables of the rich; and the travel-battered produce of warmer climes sprawled in frostbitten piles across the stall counters. Bristling in the chilly air, cheap hothouse flowers nodded their heavy blossoms as Charles strode past, their leaves and petals carefully glued and wired to withstand the most jarring wagon ride or overheated parlor.

The Floral Hall glittered dully ahead of him in its iron-and-glass intricacy, and Charles dodged a woman carrying a basket of apples on her head to duck inside. Here, in the warmth of the conservatory, the exclusive purveyors of the rarest and most expensive flowers laid their wares, and well-heeled ladies perused their displays with elegant deliberation, placing orders for their next dinner party or ball. Charles returned the nods of two—the Countess of Rushworth, accompanied, as always, by her pale and sharp-eyed daughter, and Mrs. Algernon Morel, who was surely up to no good. But he stopped only at his favorite vendor's booth to buy his usual boutonnière, a discreet and very expensive orchid with some incredibly unpronounceable name that he happened to like. Then he passed through the building out onto the street and turned to face the fresh white facade of the rebuilt opera house, still eerily pristine amid its grimy neighbors.

He climbed the steps quickly and pushed into the lobby. Mr. Larson waited for him, as promised, talking desultorily with Sir Nathaniel Dines and Lord Gifford. Dines and Gifford shared with Charles a dilettante's interest in the arts, though once a particularly acerbic lady had remarked that they made better patrons of the opera girls than the opera. The baronet nodded as Charles approached.

After a round of greetings, Mr. Larson respectfully ushered the gentlemen into the opera house proper, guided by a nondescript clerk with a small, shielded lantern. They stopped at the center of a row of orchestra seats a third of the way from the front, not so close that they would be eye-to-ankle with the singers but close enough to see anyone on stage with perfect clarity. Charles wondered, not for the first time, what it would be like to see an entire performance from here, at the level of the stage instead of looking down on it from the Edgington box. He sat between Mr. Larson and Dines, leaning back against the plush velvet of the seat.

Only the center section of footlights upon the stage was lit, and it cast the ship's rigging, ready for the first scene in that night's performance of *Tristan und Isolde*, into a fabulous labyrinth of rope and sail. Across the house, Charles could make out the faint silhouettes of the hundreds of seats that seemed not so much empty as expectant.

Charles usually relished these moments, when the air was hushed with anticipation and the stage was an empty shell waiting for someone to step out upon it and reveal herself to be the next great voice of the opera . . . or just another girl with no talent and unreasonable aspirations. Today, though, he was preoccupied with his plans for winning the bet against his sister.

"Miss Crossham wrote me an interesting letter yesterday," Lord Gifford mentioned, leaning past Dines to speak to Charles. A tall, raw-boned woman stepped out onto the stage. She looked like a middle-aged laundress. Charles dismissed her instantly as utterly unsuitable to the opera or to his own purposes and did not bother to pay attention to her audition.

"I suppose she told you of our little argument," Charles murmured, not bothering to keep a tinge of disgust from his voice. Millie had no discretion, nor would she circumscribe her correspondence to ladies now that she was out of the nursery.

"She seemed quite irritated by it," Gifford agreed.

"I received one as well, rather more tart than yours, I'd wager," Dines put in. "She took me to task for my part in the affair. She seems to think that if I hadn't defended the girl so vigorously, she would not have been so impelled to cut her down, and your little clash might have been avoided." Dines wiped his monocle with a spare handkerchief and screwed it into place, then winced at the appearance of the woman on the stage and affixed it to his lapel again.

Charles suppressed a frown. As convoluted as it sounded, there was some truth to Millie's assertions. Dines' supercilious ways excited an emotion that could well be called loathing in Millie, and any position he took would usually be vigorously opposed by her out of obstinacy—or principle, as she airily named it. Dines knew full well the effect his actions had on her and had, no doubt, exploited the situation for his own amusement.

There was a time that Charles himself would have found it vastly entertaining, too, but the memory of the mean conditions in which he had found Lily Barrett washed away any thought of humor.

Dines gave Charles a sideways look, as if reading his mind. "Everyone already knew what Miss Barrett was, Edgington. The pretence was mildly diverting at first, but she is so very stolid that everyone had long tired of her before the Rushworths' ball. Millie only wanted to relieve us of the burden of having to continue pretending past the point that it was any use to anyone."

"Why do you care so much?" Gifford put in. "You act as if she's your former whore. Are you trying to get her safely wedded and bedded to some empty-pocketed wastrel before her condition becomes obvious and you're stuck providing for her brat?"

Charles snorted. Dines was much better at causing scenes and scandals than preventing them, and he had never shown the least flicker of empathy for anyone in all the years Charles had known him. It was a shame Christopher Radcliffe hadn't been there. Or Faith Weldon. They knew how to talk sense into Millie—and they knew that however transparent a pretence, it would be accepted as long as no one went about poking holes in it. Lily Barrett's pretty face, good temper, and respectable dowry made it likely that some younger son of a gentleman would have overlooked her absence of a past to court her.

The current singer was cut off by Mr. Larson and left the stage with an awkward, old-fashioned curtsy. Dines paused as another woman stepped forward, replacing his monocle as he surveyed her. This time he left it in. The new woman—girl, really—was a buxom blonde thing, pretty and with curves in all the right places. She called out the piece she was to sing, and Charles winced at her broad Cornish accent as Dines' lips curved upward subtly. Dines had a weakness for innocent country lasses. Charles preferred sophisticated women of a certain experience, himself, for any but the shortest association, though he had been too busy recently with the affairs of his estate to devote effort to such a time-consuming pursuit. Personal preference aside, that girl was too rough even for the more mercenary purpose he now had in mind.

The girl began to sing an unremarkable little popular air, and Dines made an expression of distaste. "If your sister's behavior bothers you so much, old chap, why not do something about it?"

Charles grimaced. "With Millicent, that is far easier said than done."

Dines tilted his head, and the distant footlights gleamed dully off his monocle lens. "Oh, come now, Edgington. She is only a woman. All you must do is find a weakness and apply a little strategic pressure."

"What would you recommend?" Charles asked curtly. "I find brutality upon my own relatives distasteful."

"It is well-known that Miss Crossham has a certain affection for gambling," Dines said, shrugging negligently. "Why not simply bet her?"

Charles laughed. He couldn't help himself. "Too late, man. She already bet me herself."

Dines' head snapped sideways, the eye behind the monocle invisible in the light from the stage. "Has she? What were the conditions and the stakes, if I might ask?"

"If I prove to her that some clodhopper or guttersnipe could be accepted into society, then Millicent will make certain that Miss Barrett is welcomed back into our circle by having my mother sponsor her debut." Charles said the last with some satisfaction.

"And your interest in her well-being remains concealed," Dines put in. "Clever."

Gifford shook his head, whether in admiration or disbelief, Charles could not tell. "She has been begging for a social secretary for months, has she not? I would have merely suggested a kind of bet under which bringing in a secretary of sufficiently low background and casting her in the role of impoverished decency would have sufficed. You are too ambitious."

"Millicent could beg herself sick, but she knows I'd never give her a secretary," Charles retorted, dismissing the possibility out of hand.

"And what, may I ask, do you forfeit if you lose?" Dines asked, his tone falling into ennui once more.

"Millicent didn't bother to make a counter offer, except that it is assumed that I will require no apology from her," Charles said.

Dines gave a bark of laughter. "For a girl who loves to wager, she certainly is terrible at it."

"A fact you have not been lax to exploit," Charles said coldly. Half of Millie's debts from the Rushworths' ball had been to Dines.

Dines shrugged, smiling without a hint of remorse.

"So, have you come to the opera this time to go hunting for your clodhopper?" Gifford asked.

"Or guttersnipe," Charles agreed.

"How about that one? She's pretty enough," Gifford said, nodding to the blonde.

Charles grimaced. "She looks like a milkmaid."

"There will be plenty of others today," Dines said. "With luck, surely one of them will be suitable."

Charles turned his attention back to the stage. "Millicent believes in luck. I believe in planning."

Dines seemed to find his comment unaccountably amusing. "As do I, old chap! As do I."

"I'm ready," Maggie said firmly. Her stomach churned, but she steadfastly ignored it. It could only churn because it was not empty, she told herself. Because of her own resourcefulness, the pinch of hunger had not turned to a bite for nearly four years now, and Maggie intended it to stay that way.

Perle Blanc stood—posed—in the light of the single gas jet at the door to the dressing rooms. She always seemed to be on an invisible stage, and Maggie often wondered if her imaginary audience followed her even when she was alone. The opera singer tossed her flaxen curls and laughed throatily. "*Oui, ma chérie*, but of course you are ready! Do not worry yourself—all of us started out as yer are." Her voice slipped into cockney on the last three words, her French accent falling away like a dropped dressing gown as she treated Maggie to an arch look.

Maggie smiled—both at her friend's attempt at humor and at the trust that her reference to her real origins showed. But Perle was wrong: They were not the same, for Maggie knew that neither her voice nor looks were a match for the curvaceous soprano's. "Fanks," she said, her *th* slipping into an *f* in her nervousness. Perle held up a warning finger, and Maggie amended, "Thank you," in her best imitation of upper-class tones. Maggie might not be a great singer, but she was an excellent mimic.

Perle nodded, accepting everything she meant by those words. "You must sing your very best. Mr. Larson is looking for another soprano for the leading roles."

"I don't care about singing lead." In fact, the lower her profile, the better. The longer it would take for Danny to discover her new job and to try to spoil it.

Doubt flickered over Perle's face and disappeared again. Maggie knew why—Mr. Larson had more than enough decent singers in the chorus already. He was looking for a new prima donna. And Maggie already knew she would not be it.

No, she told herself sternly. *I ain't giving up that easy.* There would be a way for her. She just had to find it.

Perle shook her head as if to clear it. "Now, we haven't long, *ma petite*. Give me your hat. Are you sure you would not like to borrow a prettier dress?"

"Perle, you're half a foot taller than me, and you've got them curves"—Maggie waved her bonnet expressively before handing it over—"where I ain't got nofing. I'd look like a right fool."

Perle snorted and began to hustle Maggie toward the wings. "I do not see why you did not bring something more showy to wear. Something from your dance hall act, since you always dress like an old crow otherwise," she grumbled.

"Believe me, Little Peg's costume wouldn't do much to impress Mr. Larson," Maggie retorted. They reached the back of the line of hopefuls, and Maggie stopped, her nervousness returning all at once. Beyond the three women and the scrawny boy, she could see the immensity of the opera house, resplendent in crimson and white.

It was so much grander than any place she had ever performed before, much grander even than it had been before it had burned six years earlier. In front of the stage, the plush seats marched back in rows of silent witness circumscribed by the intricately decorated galleries of the boxes, all under the chandelier that glittered dimly in the shadows of the ceiling. In the center of the house was the royal box, surmounted by an enormous crown and trailing crimson draperies. The would-be opera singer who stood upon the stage looked lost—her voice sounded lost, thinning and disappearing in that vast space.

The dim, dirty roughness of the working part of the opera house, even in its new incarnation, was as familiar to Maggie as her little flat, for every backstage of every theater had a fundamental sameness to it. Some had high ceilings and space for vast crowds of performers, and others were small and cramped. But they all shared the same darkness, made dangerous by props that somehow never have any place to be except underfoot and in the way; the same ropes that crisscrossed the ceiling, supporting lights and scenery, controlling backdrops and curtains; and the same smell, a mixture of greasepaint, oil, and sweat.

Maggie had spent many evenings hiding in the opera house's wings as a child, ready to take on any little task the performers needed as they hurried on and off the stage in return for a penny or two and the privilege of watching the opera from behind the scenes, the energy of the production humming through her as the music danced and soared and throbbed. It was how she had met Perle ten years ago, when she'd been a mere slip of a child and Perle had still been dusting the cockney from her speech and singing the roles of the page boy and the saucy maid. Only once in all those years had she set foot upon the opera house's stage itself, and then Mr. Larson had told her what she had always known—that her voice was adequate and quite dramatic but no match for the divine instruments of the singers of the Royal Italian Opera Company.

Damn you, Danny, she thought for at least the thousandth time that week. *What did I ever do to you?*

The girl on the stage finished singing and, after a muffled word from the house that Maggie couldn't understand, stumbled off the stage, looking stricken. Then the stagehand called Maggie's name. Perle gave her hand one last squeeze, and Maggie took a deep breath and stepped out onto the stage and into her future, whatever it might be.

Charles looked up as a small, shawl-wrapped female entered the stage. He watched without interest as she crossed it, expecting the theater urchin to do some sort of adjustments to the lights or the scenery before the next audition. But she turned squarely to face the house, and the footlights revealed features with the definitiveness of adulthood, radiating a force of character startlingly unexpected on such a small body. She was no urchin but a woman, another singer to audition for the opera.

Her eyes and hair were black, her skin fair, even slightly sallow in the brilliant stage light. Her features were regular; on another woman, they would have been pretty. But such a word was insufficient to convey the effect she had upon a watcher, for what Charles was struck with, above all, was her strength.

There was a defiant boldness in her stance as her gaze ran blindly over the seats in the house, seeking her audience through the glare of the footlights—a brazenness, even. She stood forward, poised on her toes as if she were prepared to act at the slightest warning, whether to attack or to flee, Charles could not guess.

She stepped out onto the apron, her black shawl slipping down her shoulders to reveal a severely plain brown calico dress.

"Shall I begin?" she called out.

Charles was startled to hear that her accent was flawlessly upper class, though he would swear that she never had been a lady. He sat forward involuntarily.

"Go ahead, love," called out Mr. Larson.

"Who is this girl?" Charles hissed.

Mr. Larson looked at a tablet in his clerk's lap. "Margaret King, sir," he said. "It says she auditioned once before, four years ago, but I don't remember her. She must have been a child then, at any rate. She says she's had a dance hall act since then, and Perle Blanc vouches for her reliability."

Dines' eyebrows shot up, and Charles knew why. Perle Blanc was the opera's unchallenged leading soprano, as great as La Grisi and Madame Viardot in their heydays, and as preoccupied with her own ego and dignity as any prima donna ever had been. How would a common dance hall singer at least half a dozen years her junior be intimate with her?

The girl was now staring in their general direction. "I will be singing Odabella's entrance from the prologue of *Attila*," she announced.

Charles' interest was piqued even more. *Attila* hadn't been played in London for years, though it was at least by Verdi—these days, an opera by someone other than Verdi was hardly considered an opera at all. More unusual, though, Odabella's part was hardly a choice for a woman looking to portray herself as either ingénue or sophisticate, the two flavors of femininity currently most popular in the opera.

The woman closed her eyes for a moment, breathing deeply as if preparing herself, and when she opened them again, her expression had changed to one of piercing intensity. Without warning, she began to sing, the first note emerging with a clarity and force that sent a chill up Charles' spine. He could believe that she stood on a bat-

tlefield, that she was a woman who had faced down the
Hun's hordes with a sword in her hand and a snarl on her
lips. And now, in defeat, she still stood proud even in
front of the barbarian king himself, scorning women who
hid behind their men and did not rise to defend their
homes and their children. She was an excellent actress, a
perfect actress.

Exactly what he was looking for.

Objectively, Charles knew that this Margaret King's
voice was nothing noteworthy—that she had to slow for
the most difficult passages, that she was slightly weak in
the middle of her range—but his gut still clenched reflexively as she glared out at the invisible Attila. He didn't
want it to end, and as the words of Attila's reply came automatically to the forefront of his mind, he stood without
thinking, knowing exactly what he could do to prolong it.

Maggie reached the end of the section, her voice ring-
ing out defiantly before she fell into silence. She blinked
and realized that her hands were clenched into fists, one
raised above her head, and her shawl had slid off her
shoulders to puddle on the floor. She was about to reach
down and pick it up when a rich male voice rang through
the emptiness.

"Bella è quell'ira, o vergine . . ."

The voice rolled on, Attila's response to Odabella's
challenge. The singer wasn't a professional—Maggie
was certain of it—but it had a stirring quality despite its
roughness that sent a shiver over her as it filled the house,
making it reverberate in sympathy. Frozen with uncertainty and confusion, she stared at the black wall beyond
the lights as the singer approached, his voice brimming
with confidence as he declared his admiration for
Odabella and announced that he would grant her a boon.

Maggie hesitated. Was this some sort of test? She gave the reply even as she peered blindly ahead, trying to make out the form of the singer. *"Fammi ridar la spada!"* Give me back the sword.

"Take mine!" Her Attila was moving closer—his voice was louder now, and she just could make out the shape of a figure a few feet beyond the reach of the footlights.

The words of the aria came automatically even as Maggie stared at the approaching man, unable to tear her eyes from him. She swore her vengeance, her determination to kill him with the sword he had given her. Just as she reached the last line, the man vaulted lightly onto the stage. No longer a shadowy shape, he stood gleaming in the footlights, a stranger in an immaculate black frock coat—tall, powerful, his skin ever so slightly bronzed with a healthy glow that no true Londoner had ever boasted of.

Who was he? she wondered wildly, staring into his shadowed eyes and fighting the feeling of being cornered. Where was Mr. Larson, that he was allowing the man to leap onto his stage?

The man took up his lines easily where she had left off, striding toward her like the king Attila was supposed to be, full of unconcious arrogance that she doubted was assumed.

Reflexively, Maggie lifted her chin, her entire body tensing, holding her ground through sheer will alone. She was not acting now. Whoever he was, he was a man of power, while she was no one at all, and she knew that no good could come to her from his attention.

But the Attila hesitated as he admitted how the fierce warrior woman had touched him, and then he stopped in front of her, so much taller that she had to tilt her head back to meet his eyes. Then, confessing his wounded heart, he took her hand . . . and knelt in front of her.

It was all Maggie could do not to jerk her hand away and flee. Her street-honed senses jangled a warning—*this is not safe, this is not right!* But she wouldn't let herself move. She could not allow herself to give in to her weakness. For somewhere in the darkness of the house sat Mr. Larson, holding her future in his hands, and she would face down anything rather than risk her last chance.

"Thank you for your time."

The words came floating out of the blackness, bored and indifferent. Mr. Larson. Maggie heard his words but could not tear her eyes away from the man who knelt before her. The manager probably didn't even recognize her, but she knew his voice from all those years that she had lurked, just another shape in the wings, just another insignificant figure waiting to scamper to do his bidding.

"You have promise," the voice continued. "Your dramatic portrayal is superb. But your vocals are just too rough, and though you sing like an Odabella, a Lady Macbeth, even, you are so short that it would be hard to put you in such a role. Maybe with some training, you might have what I am looking for despite your lack of stature. As it is, though, I would recommend that you return to the dance hall or go into the theater."

The man at Maggie's feet was still staring at her so intently that the words hardly registered. There was a slight jolt to her gut, but the dizzying sickness she had expected was simply not there. She was too numb to feel much of anything.

Amber, she thought vaguely. Or brandy. In the glare of the footlights, she could see the color of the man's eyes clearly. He stood, and she had to tilt her head up again to look at him as he loomed over her.

"Come with me. I may have an amenable arrangement for you," he said. His speaking voice was much like his singing one—dark and resonating, with a rough edge that rasped like a warning across her ears.

I've got nothing to stay here for, she thought, swallowing hard. *Nothing more to lose.* So she nodded once, tightly, and let him draw her into the obscurity of the wings off stage left, away from where the rest of the auditioning singers stood, waiting to be called upon—away from where Perle waited for her to return.

Once in the darkness, the man did not stop but led her onward, moving so surely that she was convinced he knew the opera house's hidden face as well as she. They emerged in the hall by the dressing rooms, deserted now, the single gas jet flickering fitfully, sulfurously in the dimness. He eased his grip upon her hand, and Maggie stepped away, out of his grasp.

He smiled. Maggie thought it was meant to be reassuring, but that very realization made her only more wary, for his mouth did not seem much accustomed to the exercise. Her eyes rose from his lips to take in the rest of his face. He was very handsome, she realized with a small, warm sort of shock. She had been so preoccupied with the signs of authority and wealth that little else had registered. His features were perfectly regular, his teeth straight and white, his light brown hair thick and glossy with pomade, and he glowed with vigor that made Maggie feel tired and worn next to him though she knew he must be at least half a decade older than she. He was far too sleek to be trusted, she decided, sleek like a fish that sliced silver through the water for an instant before gulping a struggling beetle off the surface. And at that moment, she felt rather like a bug.

He was looking at her with a piercing kind of attention, taking in her face, her stature, her slight figure. She saw approval in his expression, colored by an undercurrent of something more intimate, and she backed away even as her skin buzzed a little in instinctive reaction to his regard. She trusted neither gentility nor attractiveness. The first, she had learned, was often a lie—as for the second, Danny was handsome, and even Johnny had been good-looking in his way.

"I brought you back here because I wish to speak to you," the man said, apparently realizing that she had no intention of breaking the silence.

"Speaking ain't no crime," Maggie muttered, falling in her anxiety back into the chaunting of St. Giles. She bit her lip at her lapse.

The man looked pained. "I never intimated that it might be." He paused, surveying her again, and Maggie wasn't sure whether she wanted to back away or step nearer. "I must say that I was impressed by your acting ability."

Maggie's stomach tightened a little even as she forced herself to reassume a more refined accent. "But not my singing."

"It was quite competent as well, but I must admit that it was not the primary subject of my admiration," the man said.

Maggie raised her chin in recognition of his honesty. "Mr. Larson seemed to be of the same mind."

He crossed his arms over his chest, leaning one shoulder against the plastered wall. Maggie did not quite believe in his show of ease. There was still too much tension in his shoulders, too much intensity in his expression. "But you heard what he said. Perhaps with some further training—"

Maggie laughed, cutting him off. "*Further* training. I

never had a day of it—it is and will always be beyond my scant means."

The man cocked his head to the side, still watching her. Maggie returned his look stare for stare, pushing down her uncertainty and the tautness that formed deep in her center in response to his disconcerting attention. Men like him did not pay attention to girls like her, not if they meant anything good by it.

"It does not have to be," he said finally, as if confirming her thoughts.

Maggie narrowed her eyes at him. She should leave now. And yet . . . what other hope did she have, of anything? "What do you want in return for teaching me?" A girl could only earn that kind of money on her back or in the type of work that could get her transported or hanged. She'd reached the point where she would take the former, and gladly, if it would get her a place out of Danny's way, but as for the latter, she was far from desperate enough for work capital yet. She'd been taken up once already. There was little chance of leniency if she were arrested again, and Leeds was a better fate than Australia.

The man raised an eyebrow. "I teach nothing. I am a connoisseur and a patron, not a teacher."

He was toying with her. Mocking her. He had no intention of offering her anything. Maggie pressed her lips together hard and turned away, walking toward the stage door with movements made jerky by suppressed frustration and despair. She had no time for games with a dangerous man. She needed to be applying herself to earning safe, ready money . . . somehow.

The prickling awareness at the back of her neck told her he was still watching, and she had not gone more than three paces when she heard his step behind her.

"Wait," he ordered. His voice cracked with authority,

as if he could not imagine that one such as she would disobey his command.

She hesitated with her hand on the door. She could slip
through into the chaos of Covent Garden—but he would
surely follow and, if he was inclined, chase her all the
way to Church Street. Setting her jaw, she turned back to
face him. He carried himself much like so many of the
Tory lords, full of self-importance and the indefinable
gravity of a man who had many weightier concerns than
whatever activity currently engaged him. But his face was
incongruously young, open, and almost soft with the ease
of his pleasant life. Even the youngest of the street Arabs,
toddling behind their raucous brothers, did not have that
kind of air about them, and Maggie wondered suddenly if
there was a particular kind of youth that only the wealthy
could afford.

"What do you want?" she demanded. "Just tell me
straight out, with none of your fancy talk."

His lips twisted slightly at her bluntness, but she just
folded her arms over her chest in conscious imitation of
his earlier pose, feeling her heart beat fast under her hand
at her own daring.

"Fair enough," he said imperturbably. "The proposi-
tion I offer is simple, though somewhat unorthodox. If
you enter my protection for a certain length of time, I will
provide for you, pay you fairly, arrange for you to be
trained both in a lady's deportment and an opera girl's
singing, and in return, you shall participate in a little charade lasting no longer than a week in which you will pose
as the lady you shall have learned to be."

"Your protection," she repeated suspiciously. "I won't
take no hand in anything that might make trouble for me."

"I assure you that this will make no trouble for anyone
in the world. I merely wish you to indulge my whim in

this matter, and know that it is nothing more." He said the words with the same deliberation that he had said everything, and Maggie had to swallow her bark of laughter at such a sober reference to his *whim*. Instead, she said nothing, simply looking calmly back at him as he watched her, trying to draw out a fuller explanation.

His brows lowered at her silence, and his expression took on a distasteful edge. "Your parading as a lady shall win a wager, if you must know," he added curtly. "For that reason, it is in my interests that you get the best education possible."

Maggie did smile then, slowly. She wasn't entirely sure she believed him, but if he meant something more sinister, why come to her at all? There were many trusting country beauties walking the Haymarket who would easily step into a carriage only to disappear forever, with no one the wiser. Nor could she think of a likely scenario of how a man like him might have become acquainted with her less legal talents, which she had abandoned years ago. Even if he wasn't telling the whole truth, it might not be very far off.

"What's your name, then?" she demanded, testing his earnestness. "I don't do business with strangers."

His jaw clenched for a moment, then relaxed. "Lord Edgington," he said, with a small, smooth bow—to their future partnership, however unequal, Maggie was sure, for she could not imagine that he made a habit of bowing to girls like her.

Lord Edgington. She knew that name in connection to the opera. She relaxed fractionally. The baron was a frequent patron, taking an interest in all the workings behind the scenes as well as the public productions and, of course, a few of the singers. Not quite trustworthy, perhaps—no man of his standing could ever hold himself accountable for his treatment of someone like Maggie—but as reliable as could reasonably be expected.

"What are the exact terms, sir?" she asked, softening.

"For the period of your . . . refinement . . . which will last no less than one month and no more than three, I will provide you with a small house in Chelsea, food and servants, a suitable wardrobe for your role, daily lessons, and a stipend of one pound a week," he said flatly.

Maggie's hold tightened on the doorknob. A pound a week. She could pay off the back rent and save up a tidy little sum. With twice as much, she might do practically anything. Would he swallow it? "Two quid a week, no less." Her voice almost shook as she said the words.

The baron's expression darkened, and for a moment, she thought he would refuse her outright. "I am not in the habit of negotiating with those I seek to employ, but in the interests of peace, I am willing to compromise. Two pounds a week—but only if you come with me immediately."

"I have to stop by my flat, sir," Maggie protested. "To tell the chavies . . . the others where I'm going to first."

"My carriage is waiting. I will drive you there." He stepped past her, so close in the narrow corridor that Maggie caught a whiff of cologne and expensive cigar smoke from the black superfine of his frock coat. Her heart sped up—scents like those, rich scents, had always meant danger, the association irrevocably intertwined with the memories of dipping a hand into an unguarded pocket or snatching away a handkerchief left carelessly peeking from its home. Adrenaline and fear made a familiar, heady mixture, and she clasped her suddenly itching hands in front of her as he reached around and opened the stage door. *I don't need the edge no more,* she told herself, mingled memories of Newgate and Johnny's body tumbling over the balustrade replaying in the silence of her mind. *I don't want it.*

"After you," Lord Edgington said impassively, holding the door open, oblivious to her reaction.

Maggie squared her shoulders and stepped out to face a new chapter in her life, whatever it might bring.

A future, she assured herself as her boots crunched down on the filthy flagstones. *Security.* And, since it was the one thing inextricably linked to everything good and safe in her mind, *Money. More money than I ever had in my life.*

Chapter Three

Charles watched the woman from his seat across from her. She had not retrieved her shawl, and neither did she wear a hat, but she was veiled by the shadows in the carriage so effectively that she might have been muffled up to her chin. Only a smudge of a pallid face was visible, marked by her dark and wary eyes. She fairly radiated distrust, and her tension did not remind him of a frightened rabbit so much as some small, swift predator—a feral cat, perhaps, or something even more wild, like a sleek mink.

Was this a mistake? Could such a creature forget her skittish, untamed ways and be transformed into a convincing facsimile of a lady? When she had stood upon the stage, she had seemed capable of anything, but now, in the closeness of the carriage, he wondered if she were even capable of hiding her edginess for two minutes together, never mind exercising all the skills and graces that came naturally to women of his sister's class. Why did the recognition of such essential differences make her more interesting to him? He enjoyed the company of sophisticated women, not ignorant gutter girls.

Her steady, unblinking gaze was disconcerting, and he

broke away and looked out the carriage window at the increasingly shabby, tumbledown houses that they passed. It was approaching his tea time: the sun was setting above the grimy streets, though it would be hours yet before any lamplighter approached this region of the city. Already, the streets were filling up, charwomen and day laborers trudging home from their work, pursued by the costermongers who hawked everything from hot dinners to cheap trinkets to tiny bags of coal. The streets here were barely wide enough to permit the carriage to pass, and the wheels straddled the gutter that ran down the middle, overflowing with a foul effluence that he could smell even with the windows tightly shut.

The carriage stopped in front of a shop that seemed no more or less disreputable than any of its tired neighbors, bearing a dirty pasteboard sign in the window that read MERRICK'S OLD CLOTHES, the name she had given for the location of her flat. Charles looked at the girl, but she only continued to stare at him.

"I am coming with you," he decided. He did not trust her shuddered gaze. She could slip into any one of the houses or shops and disappear into the warren of back gardens and alleys, ending their association before it was truly begun. For some inexplicable reason, it was very important to him that she did not, that she was the girl he used in his plans, not someone else.

Though he scarcely knew her, he was certain that she represented something rare, something that was perhaps even precious because of its rarity. He found himself increasingly interested in this strange girl, and already his private claims to a merely academic curiosity rang false in his own mind.

"You aren't needed," she said roughly. She reached for the door. Charles caught her small, thin hand, and she flinched at his touch but did not jerk away. He opened the door and knocked the wrought iron steps into place, still keeping his hold upon her. He stepped down and pulled lightly so that she had no choice but to follow or actively resist.

She followed, and he could feel a slight tremor through her grip.

"I want to come," he said simply, ending the argument before it had well begun.

The woman looked at him as if trying to read his mind, and then she shrugged, withdrawing her hand firmly from his grasp. "It won't hurt nothing." Her voice was beginning to slide back into cockney rhythms. That had to be trained out of her.

She slipped into the nearest doorway, to one side of the main entrance to the shop, and Charles followed. The street's denizens were backing up around the carriage, which sat like a black cork in the middle of the street. Some pushed past, but many stopped to watch Charles and the girl as if they were a Punch and Judy show, snarling the people behind them in the growing crowd. "Maggie's got herself a gennleman," Charles heard one woman say. "A right nob," another agreed. Those phrases and others like them rippled back and forth through the assembling crowd as more faces appeared in the windows of the buildings on either side of the street. Charles felt exposed, an interloper in a world that did not belong to him. The feeling was novel, for he was used to every place being where he belonged simply by the virtue of his presence, and he did not like it.

"Your carriage driver should move on, guv'ner," the girl—Maggie—muttered softly. Then, turning to the watchers, she said in suddenly broad tones, "Leave us be, eh! I've got some business wif 'im!" There was a general shuffling of feet, and to Charles' amazement, the crowd began to disperse obediently, with even a few muttered apologies amid the grumbling.

Who was this woman?

Any questions would have to wait, for she unlocked the door then, a small silver key disappearing into her skirts as she pushed it open. Charles gave his driver Stephens the order to circle around until he should come out again, and he followed her inside.

A grimy landing greeted them, scarcely deep enough to accommodate the side door to the old clothes shop and no wider than the narrow stairs that slid upward into shadow. The dingy, fading dusk crept through the narrow fanlight above the door to turn the steps into a pattern of lines and shade. There was a grating sound as the girl locked the door again behind them. Without a word or glance, she slid by, the space so narrow that her skirts brushed against his legs, and he caught the scent of the raw tang of lye soap in her hair. He had the sudden impulse to grab her arm and pull her against him, his blood quickening reflexively at the urge. He wondered how she would react. He wondered why he wanted to—there was nothing of the sophisticated sybarite in her manner, much less the innocent debutante who so often sashayed with disingenuous calculation into his path.

But she was past before he could make up his mind, mounting the stairs ahead of him. Charles followed, the worn treads gritty under his sleek boots.

They climbed past the shop on the ground floor and stepped out onto the next. Here, the hall widened for a passageway that permitted access to the second flight of stairs stacked above the first. Charles found himself confronted by a pair of scanty lace curtains on either end of the corridor, each barely broad enough to be stretched

across the windows they were meant to shade. Maggie
led him down the hall to the next landing, their feet sending up a low cloud of dust along the tattered runner that
had been salvaged from a more impressive rug. The walls
were papered in a particularly hideous shade of green,
and on either side of the single door along the long wall
was a picture, roughly framed, of some muse or nymph in
a style Charles dimly recognized from the prints the street
stationers were always waving about. To his amazement
and horror, there was even a hall table lurking under the
stairs, a battered affair of pine stained dark in imitation of
mahogany, complete with a dusty cut-glass bowl for calling cards and a small square of a mirror, wedged against
the underside of a step so that it reflected back no part of
even the shortest visitor higher than the shoulders.

"Who lives here?" he asked in bemusement as Maggie
started up the second flight stairs.

"Old Widow Merrick," she replied without glancing
back. "Our Moll does for her. Mrs. Merrick fancies herself a lady, brung down in the world by her misfortune
not to marry up in it."

Charles paused for a moment at her words, their unin-
flected tone belied by the dry humor of their meaning.
Maggie had reached the second floor by then, and he took
the steps two at a time to catch up. Another flight of stairs
continued up at the opposite end of the narrow passage—
"To the garret flats," she said shortly when she turned to
see him looking at them—but Maggie stopped at the farthest of the two doors along the hallway and fished in her
skirts again. This corridor was all bare boards and white
plaster, and the hall table's place under the stairs was
taken by a handbarrow, which earned a frowning glance
from Maggie as she unlocked the door.

Charles had no time to reflect upon that reaction, for

the door swung open, and he was met by a flood of light and a cry of "Maggie!"

The girl passed over the threshold, and Charles followed warily, still blinking against the glare as the unbalanced door swung shut behind them.

As his eyes adjusted, his first impression was of chaos. They stood in a mean, windowless kitchen, its smoke-discolored walls decorated haphazardly with various labels and advertisements that someone had thought pretty and had pasted up. He found himself under the unexpected scrutiny of dozens of pairs of ink eyes, from those of bouncing babies disporting in the Extra Suds of a patent soap to pert ladies intent upon extolling the virtues of Blake's Blacking for All Iron. A stunted stove against the opposite wall mercilessly radiated heat, while a small deal table surrounded by mismatched chairs, a long kitchen dresser, and a child's cot completed the furnishings and so crowded the space that it would have felt close even without the five none-too-clean bodies that filled it. Charles had never been in a room that was so very poor before, the aura of poverty clinging like a miasma to everything, dirtying even the raw-scrubbed tabletop. It smelled of stale sweat, old food, and clammy linens, and Charles kept his lip from curling up in reaction only with effort. Instead, he crossed his arms and leaned against the door frame, schooling his expression into the bored indifference that was as familiar as an old coat.

" 'Oo's this?" demanded a redheaded youth. He had leapt to his feet when Charles entered, and now he was staring at the baron with narrowed eyes as his hand slid toward his coat pocket and the weapon undoubtedly concealed there.

Charles' heart sped up, and he tensed as a spike of

adrenaline shot through him. Would this be the ignoble end of the last of the ignoble Barons Edgington? Somehow, it seemed only too appropriate. He kept that thought to himself and gave the youth a thoroughly contemptuous, thoroughly aristocratic smile, taking satisfaction in seeing the boy waver even before Maggie spoke.

"Leave him be, Frankie," she said. Whatever the boy was, he was not her lover, not with the tone she used with him. Charles found that obscurely pleasing.

Scowling, Maggie looked around the room in the light of the Argand lamp that flared upon the table. She gave Charles a look over her shoulder and then gave a little shrug, as if he were just one more thing than she could manage right now. "Where's Nan?" she asked the three people gathered at the table. "The barrow's in, and the soup's still on the stove." She sidled between a chair back and the dresser and glanced in a tub that sat upon it. "An' only 'alf the bowls are washed!" She turned back to face the people at the table, but they were all staring fixedly at Charles. Frankie was still glaring, though less certainly now, and the brown-haired boy was watching with interest while the expression of the girl was steeped in distrust.

"I washed the best I could, I did." That small voice came from the cot, where a little girl stood leaning over the bars that came up to only her chest while a very small child of indeterminate sex sat sucking its fingers at her side.

"Oh, Moll," Maggie said, her expression softening abruptly. "It ain't—isn't—your place to do your sister's job."

The little girl nodded but still looked crushed.

"Nan is in the bedroom. Asleep," said the brown-haired boy, his accent a startlingly refined contrast to his surroundings. He wore a neat suit in the sober ditto style, clean and cheap, and his hair was arranged carefully and modestly with macassar oil, giving him the appearance of a very young and very poor clerk.

"Drunk," added the scar-faced girl beside him, never taking her wary eyes off Charles.

"Rouse her, then," Maggie ordered. The girl started to rise, but Maggie immediately motioned her down again with a sigh. "Never mind. She's just trouble when she's soused, and I got somefing to tell you first."

"Oh, you don't say," sneered Frankie, his hand straying toward his pocket again.

"Frankie," Maggie repeated patiently, as if it were a frequent refrain. She pulled up the remaining chair and sat, looking Charles over as if he were an unfamiliar, hair-triggered weapon that had appeared in their midst. "He's a toff by the name of Lord Edgington. He wants to win a wager, so he's to become me . . . me patron for a while in return for a little innocent confidence work."

"Maggie . . ." the scarred girl warned, her expression tight.

"Don't you worry yourself," Maggie said, her words going thick. "It ain't swinging work. Nor none of that kind, neither, love," she added when the girl's concern didn't seem to lift.

"If you're sure, Maggie . . ." the scarred girl said.

"I'm sure," Maggie said shortly.

Frankie gave Charles an attempt at a scathing look, slightly hampered by his lingering discomfiture. "I reckon I'm not wanted 'ere. 'Ere's a tanner I come across today, though maybe you don't need it with this toff giving you as much blunt as you could wish for. I'm off to the beggarmaker." With that, the freckled youth pressed a coin into Maggie's hand and left the flat, still scowling at

Charles. Maggie gazed after him for a moment with a slight frown on her face, but she turned quickly back to Charles.

"I've got to pack now." She gave him a tight smile, the first he'd seen from her. "Don't you worry, sir. It won't hardly take a minute. Sally, come on."

The scarred girl and Maggie stepped into a side room, taking the lamp and leaving the kitchen with only the light that passed through the open doorway. There was a squawk from within, and a pretty girl—the negligent Nan—came stumbling out, blinking blearily and scraping a mass of black hair from her face before setting to work scrubbing the bowls and banging them together as noisily as possible.

A quietly spirited debate was coming from inside the other room, most of it in a patter so fast that Charles could catch nothing. The clerk-boy stood, clearing his throat awkwardly. "I'll get the barrow down," he said vaguely to the air, and he sidled past Charles, out the door, and into the corridor with a muttered, "Pardon, your lordship."

Maggie and the plain girl emerged again, bringing the lantern back with them. Maggie was slightly flushed with some emotion Charles could not identify, and she carried a compact bundle in her arms. Charles could not help but think of his sister's boxes and trunks that accompanied her wherever she went, even upon the shortest trip, and compare them to the pitiful contrast Maggie's bundle made.

Maggie must have read something of his thoughts in his face, for she raised her chin and said, "I'm ready, sir," before edging past him proudly and out of the tiny flat.

Charles gave her a tight-lipped look and followed.

*   *   *

Maggie stood in the doorway as Lord Edgington's black carriage rounded the corner carefully, the far wheels splashing into the gutter and out again. The matched blacks stepped high, contemptuous of their surroundings. Harry had already taken the barrow into the street—he shoved it, limping, into the next doorway down so that the carriage could pass.

The carriage stopped just as the baron stepped out of the stairway. Maggie edged past him to lock the door again, and he went suddenly still, the cessation of movement almost more alarming than if he reached for her.

"Excuse me," she muttered, slipping the key back into her hidden pocket. She of all people knew how pointless the gesture was, but Widow Merrick felt safe behind her cheap locks.

Lord Edgington frowned at her. "I expect you to demonstrate more respect in the future."

Maggie stared at him, baffled. "What do you mean, sir?"

He gave her a sharp look. "You really do mean that, don't you?" He gave a sound that was halfway between a snort of disbelief and a bark of laughter and stepped forward fluidly to open the carriage door. Maggie waited.

"Well?" he asked, nodding toward the interior of the carriage.

Maggie blinked. He meant for her to go first, as if she were a lady. She looked at him askance, raising her eyebrows, and stepped inside, dropping against the squabs so that he could enter behind her.

"You might as well begin learning your role now," he said, his broad frame blocking the light from the doorway briefly as he stepped through. "To the Chelsea house, Stephens," he added to his driver before shutting the door behind them.

This was the first day that Maggie had ever ridden in a carriage without the purpose of thievery or a confidence game, in vehicles that had smelled either of mildew or a disguising coat of cheap paint. It was strange, unnatural, almost, to sit against luxurious velvet and to know that she was there for more-or-less honest purposes. The carriage started off as the baron sat, and Maggie found that his presence was no less unsettling than it had been the previous trip—perhaps even worse now that she knew that he had judged her and had already found her wanting in some way. She twitched the curtain aside half an inch, so that she could watch the passing shop fronts without being seen—and so that she did not have to watch him.

"I hope I haven't caused any trouble for you."

Maggie turned at the sound of Lord Edgington's voice. His tone was studiously bored, but his eyes were keen. Were the words a kind of peace offering?

"No trouble," she said, and hoped that it was true. It would be a matter of hours before Danny got wind of something as big as this . . . but then what could he do? Maggie was eluding him, moving into a world in which he had no power. So far, at least.

Maggie thought of the baron standing in the kitchen of her flat and filling it up in a way the eight chavies never had. She felt an unaccustomed jolt of shame. She had been so proud of how far she'd come, that she had left behind the flash kens, the flophouses, even the rented rooms and now had a whole flat with her own furnishings. . . . But she realized that those achievements, to her so vast, amounted to almost nothing to a man such as him. She was ashamed of Widow Merrick's ridiculous hall mirror and the pathetic poverty and dirt of her own flat. Ashamed of Frankie's roughness, of Harry's frayed cuffs, and of Nan. Poor Nan.

"She isn't always like that, you know," Maggie found herself saying abruptly.

"Who?" Lord Edgington turned his attention to her with an expression of polite inquisitiveness on his face.

"Nan. She isn't always like that. She isn't usually like that." Maggie pulled her bundle harder against her chest. "And it isn't all her fault. Things have happened to her that shouldn't have happened to nobody. Anybody," she corrected.

"I don't see as it's any of my business," he said, but his air was distantly inviting, as if he were vaguely curious, if only to pass the time.

"I saw the way you looked at her," Maggie retorted, irritated by his offhand manner. Of course Nan wasn't a concern of his—none of the chavies were. They weren't a concern of anybody but her. "You looked at her like she was something the dustman forgot to haul away. Well, she isn't. She's a good girl, mostly, and she loves her sister and her little boy and would do anything for them. But some days, the world is ugly and full of memories, and the gin palaces are always aglitter with light and laughter . . ." She trailed off into silence, dropping her eyes to where her fingers pinched and worried at the shawl that surrounded her small bundle. She was talking to a real nob, a man who had never known and could never know what she meant. His world always glittered, and it wasn't cheap mirrors or colored glass, either, but real jewels and crystal. The rich drank wine to savor the moment. The poor drank gin to forget it.

"You speak like someone who understands," the baron observed.

Maggie looked up again. He wasn't looking at her like an interesting object, an amusing toy anymore; he seemed to recognize, perhaps for the first time, that she was a breathing, thinking person. She decided he deserved an honest answer. "I may not be a model of temperance like Harry, but I've got no love for the bottle. I've seen too many people ruined by it."

"I meant about the memories," he said, and for a moment, the unruffled smoothness of his expression took on a strange edge.

"Oh," Maggie said, as inevitably the memories came washing over her, all the bruises, all the sicknesses, all the deaths she'd witnessed—and, surmounting them all, the one death that she had caused.

"Am I right?" The smoothness was back now, so that Lord Edgington did not look so much like a baron but like a portrait that a baron would wish committed to posterity.

"Nan's memories aren't mine," she said, shaking her head.

"Better?" he pursued.

"Different," she corrected, wanting to end that line of questioning. "I'm not Nan, so they can't be compared."

"No, you certainly are not Nan." Was that a hint of humor sparking in his eyes, scarcely seen by the light of a passing gas lamp? And the look that lingered there, as if it had been left behind when he wiped his expression clean—why did it make her pulse speed up and the frigid air of the carriage suddenly seem too hot and close?

The carriage stopped then, and Lord Edgington pushed aside the curtains. "Ah. We have arrived," he observed.

He opened the door and leapt lightly down, holding out his arm to Maggie. She was struck again at how young he looked, how pristine, and she wondered why that appearance of youth made him no less frightening. She took his arm, the fabric of his sleeve smooth and thick under her thin glove. She felt a flutter in the pit of

her stomach as she stepped down and looked at the house.
To her objective judgment, it was stolidly middle class, of
no great size, almost suspicious in its sheer ordinariness,
flanked as it was by rows of houses distinguished by their
wrought iron area-railings and balconies on the otherwise
identical façades. Yet knowing this did not keep her from
feeling a kind of hushed awe that this residence would be
her own for at least a few months—and, if she were honest with herself, she also felt more than a little trepidation, knowing what must be expected of her, to earn such
a place.

*For a house like this and two pounds a week, he's
bought me five times over,* Maggie told herself firmly. *I
ain't never balked at the boldest dodges, so why should I
balk at something most any down-on-her-luck needle
worker has done to get some bread and tea?* But that did
nothing to still the fluttering in her stomach.

Without a word, Lord Edgington led her up the stairs
to the stoop, their shoes smudging its meticulously
whitened surface. The brass knocker had been taken
down to show that the master or mistress of the house was
not in residence, but the baron rapped sharply upon the
door.

There was silence for a long moment, and then came
the sound of footsteps approaching and the chain being
drawn back, and then the door opened to reveal a slender
woman in an attractive late middle age and the starched
white apron of a servant whose dirty work was done for
the day.

"My lord!" she said, her expression amazed. It was
hard to tell if it was a greeting or a mild blasphemy. "I did
not expect to see you so soon after . . ." She looked down
at Maggie and seemed to catch herself. "Oh. I see. I am

sorry, my lord, the house is not ready for . . . visitors."
She trailed off again.

"Margaret King, this is Mrs. Pershing, the housekeeper," Lord Edgington said, his tone chilly. "She has
been a loyal associate of the family for many years. You
can trust her implicitly. Mrs. Pershing, Miss King is here
as a part of a foolish bet involving Miss Crossham."

The housekeeper stood aside, looking more worried
about the baron's arrival than Maggie's appearance. "I
wish you had sent some notice, my lord, for the house is
all shut up. There are dust sheets over all the furniture,
and I haven't aired most of the rooms or changed the bed
linens in a month, nor yet do I have a maid or a cook."

"It shall be sufficient to ready the bedroom for Miss
King tonight," Lord Edgington said negligently as he
stepped into the hall and stripped off his overcoat, handing it to her. "And send out for a late supper. You may discuss the need for further domestics with her tomorrow—
the usual number will suffice, of course. And send to
Mme. Rochelle for a full wardrobe and tell her that Miss
King is to be a sweet, genteel ingénue and is to make
none of her own decisions."

"Yes, my lord," Mrs. Pershing said, looking not in the
least surprised by any of those remarkable declarations.

She took his coat and hat and, after giving Maggie no
more than a cursory glance as she relieved her of her bundle and gloves, retreated up the stairs.

Her indifference solidified what Maggie had suspected—this was a house accustomed to hosting women
of questionable background, of whom Maggie was
merely the latest. Well, then, it was settled. She was willing enough, and Lord Edgington would let her know
when he wanted . . . that. And that was that.

"Mrs. Pershing will give you a proper tour belowstairs

in the morning," the baron said, nodding to a door under the stairs that presumably led down to the kitchen. "I will show you the rest of the house while she is readying the bedroom."

"All right, then, sir," Maggie said, even though it had not been a question.

The baron opened a door in the hall and motioned Maggie into the dark room beyond. Hesitantly, she stepped through. He reached above her, and Maggie shied away instinctively, stepping into the room. There was a momentary hiss, and then a gaslight sconce sprang to life beside the door, revealing the shape of a round table in the center of the room under a white sheet, with a delicately proportioned seating group shrouded in the bay window.

"The morning room," Lord Edgington said laconically. An odd feeling crept over Maggie, almost a kind of amazed skepticism and a dawning delight. A room made just for mornings, to be all hers, at least for a while—a place for breakfast, early teas, and morning domestic duties, utterly superfluous and as large as her entire three-room flat in St. Giles. She walked around it slowly, touching the furniture through the sheets, hardly daring to believe that it was real and frightened of the price that such a house must bear—afraid that everything that she was could not be enough to pay it. Lord Edgington's presence by the door, dark in his sober frock coat, his hair and eyes terribly golden in the gaslights, seemed suddenly oppressive.

"You may take off the sheets, if you wish," he said with his devastating indifference.

Maggie glanced down to where her hand rested against the covered tabletop. Mutely, she closed her fist around the cloth and pulled it gently off. It came, whispering and sliding across the slick wood to settle in billows upon the green carpet. Mahogany shone darkly in the dimness of the single gas jet. A feeling of unreality settling over her, Maggie turned and began to pull the sheets from the rest of the furniture, moving with increasing speed as her amazement mounted. In moments all the sheets lay crumpled on the floor, exposing slick wood and plush upholstery, all rich and astonishing to her even though she knew that they were not fine enough to be even the castoffs of the baron's residence.

A dark doorway led to the back room of the ground floor, and she stepped toward it with a look back at the baron. He inclined his head in permission, so she entered, groping along the wall for a light fixture. The shadow of the baron entered behind her, and a moment later, the room was washed in light as he turned on the gas to the sconces that flanked the fireplace.

It was the dining room. Without waiting for permission, Maggie pulled the great sheets from the long oval table and the desk against one wall, then stopped to stare, breathless and still only half believing. She raised her eyes to find Lord Edgington staring at her, a distantly quizzical expression on his face belied by the too-intimate shadows in his eyes.

"It is mine," she explained, incapable of giving those words the incredible significance they had in her mind. "For a little while, at least, it is all mine."

The baron's expression did not change, though his gaze grew even more intent, making Maggie's mouth go dry. "The parlor is on the first floor, running the entire length of the house." The words were disjointed from the message his eyes were sending her, strangely dry.

Giving herself a mental shake, Maggie stepped out of the room's second door and back into the front hall. Her feet were soundless upon the encaustic tiles—she realized that she was falling back into the habits of a thief; on some level she still had not fully accepted that she had a right to be in a house like this.

She started up the stairs, forcing herself to step solidly, noisily onto each tread. She could feel Lord Edgington's presence close behind her. The back of her neck prickled. On the first floor waited the parlor; on the second, the bedroom, and when they reached that, she knew what would come next. She turned the corner at the landing, where a gas jet glowed on the wall. The unlit upper hall was wreathed in shadow, but the darkness was Maggie's old friend, and she advanced without hesitation as her eyes adjusted to the gloom. There was only one door on this level. Maggie opened it and went in.

Only a glimmer of light spilled in from the stairway. Maggie took three steps inside and stopped, peering into the depths of the room for the fireplace and the gas jets that would flank it.

She heard the baron's uncertain entrance behind her, and she turned to see his broad black silhouette pause against the lighter gray of the doorway. He took another step, straight toward her. Could he really not see her? He seemed so all-powerful that the possibility of such a limitation made her feel obscurely relieved. She held her ground, curious to find out if he would lurch into her before he realized she was there. The baron started forward again, and he must have seen her at the last instant, for he pulled up sharply, seizing her shoulders to keep from running into her.

"I did not see you," he said. No *Pardon me*, no inquiries about her condition—just a simple, bald statement of fact. He was so close that Maggie could feel the pressure of his legs through her narrow skirt, could almost feel the heat of his body inches away from hers, and his hands were a vise upon her shoulders. It would happen now, right here. She could feel it. Her heart sped up, the rushing of blood loud in her ears, and she tried to swallow to wet her suddenly dry throat.

"I know," Maggie said, her voice coming out hoarsely. "I was wondering if you were going to trip over me before you stopped."

His gripped softened, shifted, but he did not let go. "Did you want me to?" Again, there was a sense of disjointedness in his speech—a note in his voice behind the cool words that told her that he cared little what her answer was at that moment. Her breath stuttered in her chest.

"No. It would have hurt," she said. What was she supposed to do? Was he waiting on her?

"I will pretend that you meant that it would hurt me." His hands tightened again, but not painfully, and he pulled her toward him. Maggie resisted her impulse to wrench free as warmth twisted low in her belly. She came up against him, his body startlingly solid, large, and warm against hers. She shuddered a little as the feeling in her belly intensified, recognizing the sensation as something she had always run from before. But there was nowhere to run tonight. Her last chance for safety was . . . here, as unbelievable as it seemed at this moment. In this man's arms.

"Maggie," Lord Edgington said, as if trying out the name. "I am wondering something myself. I am wondering what you might do if I did this." And with that, he lowered his mouth toward hers.

Chapter Four

M aggie jerked back instinctively as a jolt of alarm ran through her, but before the baron could react, she corrected herself, tilting her face up toward his and angling it so that his rather blind movement came into contact with her lips.

His mouth brushed hers off center, landing half on her cheek, and she froze at the touch, its strangeness taking her by surprise even though she had braced herself for it. The next attempt was far more than a brush, moving squarely over her mouth as he covered it with his own, deepening the kiss instantly as she instinctively surrendered what he demanded of her. His touch was so hot, so soft and yet hard at the same time—impossible to fight in both its insistence and its sensuousness. The contact seemed to shoot through her, from their joined lips to her center and back through all her limbs, a twisting, shivering sensation that made her mind buzz and her skin tingle.

Was this what a kiss was supposed to be? The thought came feebly, as if from far away. She had been kissed before, usually when she was too slow to miss a drunk's lunge and rough, slobbery smack upon her mouth, but nothing had prepared her for this. The movements of his mouth and tongue whirled through her brain, the rhythm seizing her body in its grasp and fusing it to his will.

I don't know how to do this, she thought, panic welling up. *I'll mess it up, and he'll think I'm no good, and he'll want to go back on his bargain. . . .* Her hands closed spasmodically on the smooth fabric of his frock coat.

The baron pulled away, breaking the kiss. Maggie's breath came fast, as if she'd just run up a flight of stairs, and her head spun, her senses jangling in confused reaction. *I did it wrong. I did do it wrong, and now he's going to send me away.*

But he said nothing, and she realized that he was panting in the darkness, too, his chest moving under her hands where they still crushed his superfine coat.

He still wanted her. Maggie didn't know whether she should be terrified or relieved. After a moment of conflicted confusion, she realized what was expected next, and she raised her hands slowly to the top button at her throat. But instead of loosening it, she just stood there dumbly, staring at the shadow of the man in front of her.

Was this the right choice? Was it her only choice? If she changed her mind now, would he let her go, or was it already too late for that? Heat still thrummed through her nerves, muddling her mind and making her thoughts swirl sluggishly, around and around. She'd spent half her life keeping herself from such a fate . . . and yet she hadn't lied to Sally, for it wasn't the same as selling herself in the Haymarket, not at all. It had seemed so clear, then, on the street in front of Mr. Hawkins' theater, but now she did not trust her own objectivity, for part of her very much wanted this to happen for reasons that had nothing to do with her future beyond this night.

Your mum was a whore, she told herself savagely,

wrenching open the button. *Why should you think you'd be any different?*

Her fingers moved quickly. The second button came free, then the third and the fourth, her hands brushing against the baron's firm chest in the narrow space between them. He was so close to her, a mere thought away, and she could almost feel the need pulling his body taut as it did her own.

He reached out and closed his hand around hers. For a heart-stopping moment, she thought he meant to halt her, but when he pushed her hands away, it was only so that he could loosen the buttons himself. The heat of his touch sent a twisting thrill through her, her heart speeding and skin heating where she felt the pressure of his fingers through her corset.

Yet even as her body thrilled to his touch, his action struck deep in the portion of herself she kept apart, a demonstration in more absolute terms than words ever could express of the gulf that lay between his world and her own.

But that small pain was soon pushed into a dusty corner like so many others, brushed away by the heat of the baron's hands so near her skin, the expectation that he sent curling slyly through her center to settle low in a dull, hopeful ache.

The last button came loose. Maggie closed her eyes as the baron flattened his hands against her stiff corset, sliding his palms across its quilted fabric to push her bodice open and down, across her shoulders. The motion transformed fluidly into an embrace as he pulled her firmly against him. Her arms trapped now at her sides, she met his kiss fully, ready and yet still unable to defend against the hot, hard movements of his mouth against hers. He tasted of brandy, smooth and rich. He tasted of wealth. He freed one hand and lifted it to rest upon the naked skin above her corset, and even as pleasure rippled through her from his touch, she could not help but shudder away from his large hand so near to her throat.

But then his hand slid lower, finding the edge of her shift and following it, slipping under its gathered neckline and pressing lower, into the narrow space between her small breasts and her corset. Her eyes snapped open, and she swallowed a gasp, the movement constricting his hand and pinning it against her flesh. She could feel the texture of his thumb, subtly rough, against her nipple, which hardened so suddenly that it sent a little jolt of reaction through her core. Before she could say anything, he began to move his thumb across her breast, caressing it urgently as he kissed her harder, and pulling her thin and making her senses dim to everything but him.

He tightened his grip, crushing her to him, and a surge of alarm shot through her. She shouldn't be doing this. He was just too large, too strong, too powerful for her to trust. She was nothing to a man like him. He might hurt her, kill her, even, and few would ever know and fewer still care.

Don't be a ruddy idiot, she snapped at herself before her fear could crest into hysteria. *You made your choice. It's too late now.*

The baron pulled back for a moment, and Maggie forced herself to relax against him and tilt back her head in invitation. He lowered his head again to hers, but instead of resuming their breathless embrace, he brushed his lips softly, titillatingly against hers, once, twice, three times, so that her senses were stretched with wanting him before he took her mouth hard.

Heat sizzled across her skin and jolted inward, so that her center burned in a throbbing sympathy to his rhythm.

Her limbs seemed suddenly heavy, her joints loose, and she sank against his strength. As if that were a signal, the baron began pressing against her, urging her downward.

She stood for a moment in sense-battered confusion before she realized that he meant for her to lie down. A hollow tightness in her belly seemed to jump as her knees gave obediently. He lowered with her and kissed her again, shifting so that he loomed above her as she sank onto the floor. The rug was soft and thick under Maggie's palms, and as she allowed herself to be pushed back into it; she could smell the faint odors of dust and wool even as the baron's scent, the baron's taste, swam dizzily in her head.

He knelt between her thighs, and though she knew his weight was on his knees and elbows, she felt as if she were being pressed into nothingness beneath him, her singing senses consumed by him. Between them, his hand brushed her thigh; he grabbed a fistful of her skirts and pulled them upward. She felt a breath of cold air against her naked flesh. Did she want this? How could she? How couldn't she?

He kissed her neck, sending her thoughts into disarray, and all she could do was to cling to the lapels of his coat as he loosened his fly and maneuvered himself between her knees. She tightened her thighs involuntarily against his approach, yet he kept coming, the width of his hips levering them apart. She had the sudden vision that he was a wedge that would spilt her in two, and she had to bite her lip against a whimper even as the heat inside her roared up in welcoming anticipation. She couldn't breathe—her corset was too tight, it bit into her, made it impossible to think. And then he was there, his erection pressing hard against her opening, pressing and then inside, in a sudden jolt that was pain and pleasure and yet transcended both.

Charles was yanked out of his libidinous haze by the resistance of a barrier where no barrier should have been.

A barrier. She had been a bloody virgin.

I can't stop. I damned well don't want to stop, he thought even as he jerked out of her though his erection throbbed for release. "What in hell do you think that you're doing?" he snarled down at her.

"What?" the girl blurted. She started to wriggle against his weight, which did nothing but intensify his frustration.

"You were a virgin!" he said. He swore as she wriggled again, and he started to roll away.

Maggie's grasp on his coat pulled him back. "No—don't go! I'm sorry I'm no good," she blurted. "You're right—I ain't done this before, and if I ain't doing it right, I'm sorry."

Charles stared down at the pale oval of her face in the darkness, sickened by her words and what they said about him.

"I'm sorry," she repeated, the words somewhere between a plea and an angry outburst. "Give me one more chance. You can't send me away now. I know I can do better."

He had the sudden urge to shake her. She had initiated this encounter as an innocent—well, at least a technical one—throwing him in the role of, what? Seducer? Despoiler? Whatever it was, it tasted bitter. He pulled away from her, standing, his lust abruptly quenched. Or so he told himself though, damnably, parts of him still had no urge to end their dalliance so soon.

"Get up," he said harshly, finding the key to the nearest gas jet and twisting it to summon light and chase away the desire that still pulled his body as tight as a bowstring. He had to get control of himself.

The flames flared orange, then yellow, bathing the room in a warm glow, and that was almost worse, for when he turned back around, the girl was sitting up with her skirts in disarray about her calves, her expression bewildered and defiant and her eyes still smudged with passion as her hair fuzzed wildly around her head and her bodice hung open to her waist, revealing her painfully plain corset beneath. Devil that he was, it only made him want her more.

"I am not leaving," Maggie said, her chin rising in seeming belligerence even as her voice trembled, her dark eyes wide. "I gave you what you wanted. It isn't my fault you decided you made a bad deal."

The meaning of the words took a moment to register—*what he wanted.* He looked around the modest parlor, and with devastating clarity, he saw the house as she must have and as what, in fact, it had been until his inheritance: a quiet, discreet place for the Baron Edgington to keep his mistress. What could be more logical, more natural than to assume that he could require such a duty of her?

"Sit," he ordered, pointing to the vague shape of a sofa under its white sheet. "And for God's sake, fasten your dress."

She stared at him for a long moment, then clambered to her feet and crossed warily to the sofa, perching on its edge. She made no attempt to button her bodice.

Charles busquely fastened his trousers, then placed himself squarely in front of her and glared down. She was so small and disheveled, so confused and distrustful that he felt resentfully as if he were being forced into the role of monster.

"You can't tell me you didn't want this," he found himself saying, a defense couched in an accusation.

Maggie simply looked at him mutely, and he couldn't help but wonder . . . had she? If she had been the one to kiss him, he could lay the blame at her feet. But as it was, he had kissed her, and she had responded as he had expected her to, and then she had unbuttoned her dress—in invitation, he had assumed then, but perhaps just in obedience.

Damnation. Now the little beggar girl was staring at him as if he had just killed her mother. She was so simple, so ignorant, so ordinary in her ugly brown calico dress and clumsy coif. Lovely enough in her way, certainly, but so common. He didn't know what he had been thinking, there in the dark—if he'd been thinking anything at all except that there was someone undeniably young, female, and willing in his arms, and he'd been too preoccupied with running his family's estates to have found himself in a similar position in several months. It wasn't his fault. He'd done what any man in his position would do.

"I thought—" He broke off. She didn't need to know what he thought. "Margaret. I have no expectations of anything from you except your excellent performance as an actress in the role that I, as your benefactor, set before you and your hard work in obtaining the skill necessary to fulfill that role."

"Oh," she said then. Though she did not blush, the monosyllable contained worlds of mortification. "But you kissed me. . . ."

Charles raised an eyebrow. "I found myself alone in the dark with an attractive young woman. It seemed like the thing to do. Just because I make no other demands of

you does not mean that I will ignore an opportunity or
deny an invitation."

"Oh," she said again, and he saw a flash of calculation
in her eyes before her gaze dropped—to his waist, where
his open frock coat provided inadequate cover for the
erection that seemed oblivious to the change in both his
activity and his state of mind. "I didn't think it was . . .
bad," she said, experimentally, or so it seemed to Charles.
She looked back at his face with a look of such manufactured coyness that he couldn't help a snort.

"If that's the most enthusiasm you can muster, I think
I'd prefer the company of Madame Palm and her five
daughters tonight."

Her face shuddered instantly. "I am trying!"

"I don't want you to try!" he shot back, exasperation
making him pettish. He looked at her, sitting on the sofa
and staring sullenly at him, and he made a realization.
"You don't believe me, do you?"

She made a face, then muttered, "No."

"Why not?" he demanded.

She looked even more uncomfortable. "You're a toff,
and I'm a dance hall singer. And I did tell the truth. It
wasn't bad."

"You certainly know how to charm a man," Charles
said, stung into irony.

The girl just looked at him—stupidly, a vicious part of
him wanted to say, but her hooded eyes were too alive
with consideration for him to lie even to himself. "I know
nobs," she said finally. "They're honorable enough to
other nobs, but they happily let a poor, honest greengrocer's family go without their supper because they just
got to have enough ready money to make a bet at the
Ascot. That greengrocer wouldn't pass the time of day
with the likes of me, and it don't take a wit to know what

that makes me to a nob. I don't know why you'd care about what I wanted."

That bit more deeply than her previous comment, and though Charles wanted to flatly deny its validity, her words had a touch of truth in them. He never would have tried to kiss a simpering debutante just because he found himself alone with her and a randy itch, much less take her virginity upon an old Turkish rug.

Something of his thoughts must have shown in his face, for the woman shrugged, her eyes shifting away in discomfort. "I'm not saying you might not be right in your ways," she said. "Anyone at all would say you're worth ten of me, at least." She was quiet for a moment, then her gaze rose to meet his face again. "You were right, if it makes a difference. I did want it. I just don't know whether or not I should."

Charles cleared his throat. He could kiss her, take up right where they left off. . . . But they weren't in the dark anymore, and he would have to face her again the next day—see her regularly, in fact, until her performance was done, and he wasn't sure he wanted to turn their uncomplicated business relationship into anything more intimate or significant. He didn't even know anything of this girl except her desire to be an opera singer and her place of residence.

"Perhaps we have found ourselves in this uncomfortable situation because we have an inadequate knowledge of one another," he threw out more or less at random, following upon that thought. "Rather than kissing one another madly, it might make it easier for us to work together if we established a more . . . regular conversational footing."

Maggie surprised him with a snort, her dark eyes narrowing with amusement in a catlike way that did nothing at all to help him achieve the proper disinterest that he was striving for. "I may be young, sir, but I'd bet my last yennep I've seen more of life than you, and I can tell you that there isn't anything much more regular than a man and a woman 'kissing one another madly,' as you call it."

"You are supposed to be learning to be a lady," Charles made himself say sharply, ignoring the urge to do exactly that. "Therefore, you must learn to do what is normal for a lady."

The wicked light in Maggie's eyes flared again, but she just pressed her lips together around whatever response she seemed half-bursting to make.

"I think that it would help if I knew a little more about you. And for the last time, button up your dress," he added, trying to keep the frustration out of his voice.

This time, the girl obeyed, though with agonizing deliberation.

Charles attempted to look disapproving, as if he were not following each movement of her fingers with acute attention. "We will make this an exercise in small talk. Now, I will begin by asking you a polite question about your background, to which you will give a polite answer. Understood?"

The girl's fingers paused in their work. "Is that supposed to be a polite question?"

Charles frowned, uncertain whether she was being facetious. He decided to ignore the question. "So, Miss King, how do you find London?"

She gave him a look as if he'd grown a second head and fastened the button. "It's the only place I ever been."

"I have ever been," Charles corrected.

If she were annoyed by his correction, she didn't show it. "Have ever been. I ain't—haven't anything to compare it to."

Charles nodded, hoping that he appeared the collected instructor. Only four buttons left, and then her delicate pink throat would be hidden behind her collar again, and he would be safe. "You were born here, then?"

"On King Street, in the Holy Land," she said, divulging the information with patent reluctance.

"That's quite the coincidence," he remarked. She treated him with the stare again, and he made a mental note to teach her to stop that.

"What is?" she demanded ungraciously. "Sir."

"That your name is Margaret King and you were born on King Street."

Maggie laughed. "It wasn't no—any coincidence. I was named after the street."

"How could your surname come from a street?"

Maggie finished fastening the last button. "My mum died when I was a babe. I don't remember much about her. My brother Bill kept me for a few years, and he told me that her Christian name was Siobhan, but if she had a family name, I never knowed it."

"Knew it," Charles said reflexively.

"Knew it. So anyhow, there was already Big Maggie and Little Maggie and Young Maggie when I came along, so people called me Maggie of King Street, or Maggie King. It works as well as any other name."

"I suppose it does," Charles said, bemused by the idea. "Your brother was the young man in the clerkish day suit?" That wasn't possible—that boy must be younger than Maggie, and his pristine accent made such a close relation improbable. But Charles found that he wanted to exploit her willingness to divulge information to learn more about her.

Maggie wrinkled her nose. "No, that's Harry."

"Another brother?" Charles hazarded.

"He's a poor little orphant child, like me." Maggie's tone was steeped in sarcasm. "Aren't we just so sad? Don't we make you want to cry?"

"Not particularly," Charles said evenly.

Maggie gave him a look as if she were reassessing him, and after a moment, she smiled. "Good on you. I always hated the charity ladies with their sermons and their pity. Talk like that never did anybody good. Anyhow, Harry's da was a chemist, but he got sick, and between doctor's bills and not being able to work, Harry and his mum had nothing left when the old man finally kicked the bucket. His mum tried her hand at warious—various—things, but she was allus sick, so it didn't take her long to die, too."

"Is he your neighbor, then?" Charles found himself asking, his curiosity of her past not without a morbid tinge. He sat down next to her, and she turned to face him with a shrug.

"Oh, no, he lives with us. See, I'm allus running into people down on their luck," she said. "And when you can do somebody a good turn, well, you do. And they won't forget you if you need something someday. Harry was a nice bloke, didn't deserve what had happened to him, so I got a man I knows to talk to a law stationer he knows and set Harry up as a law writer, since his lame leg and nobby childhood makes him useless for any kind of labor. Harry wasn't making enough on his own for a furnished room, not if he wanted to eat, too, so I suggested that he flop with us. And after a while, he became one of us."

"Us?" Charles asked. He'd assumed that the girl named Nan and the two little ones belonged in the flat—the others he had thought were just visitors, but now he wasn't sure.

Maggie's look turned to surprise. "Why, you met most of them. Giles was the only one not in."

Charles did a mental tally. The three at the table, the two in the cot, Maggie, Nan, and the unknown Giles . . . "That's eight people!"

He must have had a note of reproach in his voice, for she gave him a defensive look. "We got three rooms, you know. Frankie, Giles, and Harry sleep in the parlor, Moll and Jo have the cot in the kitchen near the stove, and Nan, Sally, and me have the bedroom. We get along all right. There are some who would be grateful to have a whole room for a family as large as ours."

"I see," Charles said.

"Harry's a good lad," she continued. "He taught me and Sally how to talk better, and Giles, too. And he taught Moll and Giles how to read and write."

"Can you read?" Charles lifted his eyebrows in surprise.

She smiled as if at a private joke. "Yeah. I got a right neat hand, too. I don't have much of a call to practice, but I read them stories out of the papers to the chavies when Harry has copy work to do."

"I see," Charles repeated. It was the only response that he could think of that she would not reject for its condescension out of hand. How many parlors had he sat in, and with how many women had he talked? This conversation was bizarre in comparison, too tawdry and, at some level, too real for such surroundings.

He cleared his throat and stood, smoothing his hair and straightening his clothes. "I think it is time to see the rest of the house."

"Of course," she said, a flash of arid amusement crossing her face before it was replaced by blandness again. "Why not?"

Charles stalked out of the room with the unaccountable feeling that she was laughing at him for his retreat. He ascended the stairs, stopping at the half landing for her to catch up with him.

"The water closet," he said coolly, swinging open the door, and Maggie looked inside, eyes wide. He hesitated. "I don't suppose you know how it works."

Her awe was broken in a flash of withering contempt. "Of course I do." She brushed past him, and his body responded to her proximity, sending orders to his brain that he decided to ignore. Maggie examined the fixtures with the same care she had taken with the rooms downstairs.

"A bath, too! With hot water from the stove's boiler?" She said it as if it were too good to be true.

"Certainly," Charles replied.

She nodded, looking thoughtful, and stepped out onto the half landing again. "The chavies and I might get along all right, but 'all right' isn't very well at all, you know," she said in a rush, as if relieved to have someone to finally confess it to.

How should he respond to that? Charles made an inquisitive noise, which he hoped expressed both reassurance and encouragement.

She threw a look at him over her shoulder as she started up the stairs again. "I'm not looking above my place. No one's ever said that I look above my place. But I can't help but think, sometimes . . . Moll and Giles need a regular school so that they can learn their sums and how to read and write well enough to not get gammoned by blokes what has more learning—Jo, too, for all that he's still a babby. And Harry wasn't born to this life. He was meant to be a regular gent, and he should be a real clerk, maybe even studying to be a solicitor instead of just making copies for them."

The second floor was originally meant to contain three bedrooms, but since this had never been a house for children or guests, one served as a study and the other the dressing room to the main bedroom. Maggie glanced in at the study, then stepped inside the bedroom and stopped.

Charles followed. Mrs. Pershing had worked fast. The merry gaslights revealed a room perfectly prepared to receive them, with a small fire burning in the grate, every gaudy ornament restored to its place, and Maggie's small, pathetic bundle of possessions on the center of the pink-draped bed. The legacy of his father's last mistress was painfully imprinted upon everything in the blowsy boudoir, from the hundreds of ugly little china figurines to the layers of doilies and ball-trimmed cloths on every surface. Charles could almost imagine that he still heard Frances bustling around in the dressing room, and he suppressed a shudder. He'd not had an attachment since his father's death that he'd cared to place among the old baron's ghosts.

"It is very . . . distinguished," Maggie said, a hint of doubt in her voice.

"It is tawdry," Charles said crisply. "The last occupant had poor taste." And the eyes of a siren, the body of a goddess, and the morals of an alley cat.

Maggie shrugged as she circled the room, examining everything. "It is your house."

Charles couldn't help but smile at her pointed riposte. "That it is." The memories in that room combined with his proximity to Maggie were making him deucedly eager to escape. And why not? he thought suddenly. He didn't owe her anything.

"Here's the bell," he said, nodding to the rope that hung down beside the bed. "Mrs. Pershing is probably making your supper by now." And if she'd passed the parlor on the way down, how much had she heard? How much had she guessed? "You may ring if you need her for anything."

"I suppose you're leaving, then." Maggie stopped and turned to face him. It struck him again how small she was, her head not even coming to his shoulder, and how slight. Why was it, then, that she seemed anything but frail?

"Yes. And you should call me 'sir,'" he added.

"Yes, sir," she said, and he did not miss the touch of sarcasm in her tone.

"Good night, Miss King," he said coldly.

"Good night," she replied. "Sir. Would you like to kiss me again before you leave?"

Was she serious? Her tone was facetious, but her eyes were shadowed with intensity. Dammit, he wanted to, but if he did, he was not going to stop, not this time, no matter how much he regretted it in a day or two. He gave her his most quelling look even as reaction shot through his body from groin to gut. "The next time you ask me that, you had better be very, very sure that you mean it. And want everything else that will follow. Because I promise you, it will."

With that, he turned on his heel and walked out.

Maggie lifted a hand to her mouth, staring at the doorway the baron had just left. Her lips still felt swollen with his kisses. She wasn't sure how she felt about the discovery that the baron was not expecting any more from her than he had explicitly requested. Relieved, certainly, but also . . . afraid. Uncertain. And, strangely, disappointed.

She knew, at least in theory, how a relationship of the carnal kind was supposed to go between a man like that and a woman like her, whatever extraneous conditions there may be. But without such conditions, she was at a loss. What was to bind him to his half of the bargain? How would she keep him from getting bored with his plan and simply dumping her out onto the street again?

An inadequate knowledge of one another, he had said. But when they began to talk, he was the one asking all the questions, and she had given all the answers. She knew nothing more about him than she had ten minutes after they had met. Except that his kisses made her feel dizzy and empty and suffused at the same time.

There was a rap on the door frame, and Mrs. Pershing's prim head appeared around the corner. "I brought up a tray for your supper. And this young man knocked—at the area door." Those words were laced with disapproval. "He said he knew you."

She stepped inside, and Giles came strolling after, looking like a tattered little prince and bearing an enormous sheaf of flowers.

"Cor, Maggie!" he said, his face shining with approval. "Just take a butcher's at this ken! You got yourself a posh toff now."

Mrs. Pershing's expression was one of studied indifference, but Maggie knew she was listening avidly. Maggie cast about and settled on a small, round table that was slightly less cluttered than the rest. "Here," she said, clearing it hurriedly and piling the gewgaws into a chair. "You can put the tray here. Thank you."

If Mrs. Pershing were disappointed at the dismissal, she gave no sign. She left, shutting the door behind her.

"How did you find me?" Maggie demanded of the child as soon as the housekeeper was gone.

"I was told," Giles said unhelpfully. He extended the flowers. "For you, mum, wif compliments."

Maggie stared at the bouquet with a sick feeling in the

pit of her stomach. She could think of no one who would send her such a tribute except—"Danny."

"I reckon so, too," the child agreed. When she made no move to take the flowers, he set them next to the dinner tray.

"You mustn't call me 'mum' in front of Mrs. Pershing," Maggie said, even as her mind worked at what Danny's present could mean. "It will confuse her."

Giles grinned. "Right-o, mum."

"Who gave you them flowers?" she asked, trying a different tack. Giles tended to answer exactly the question put to him and no more.

"One of the delivery men what works for Parks, the flower wholesaler." He hovered over the tray, eyeing it hungrily. "I say, Maggie, mightn't I 'ave just a little taste of this 'ere grub?"

"Of course," Maggie said, even though she knew that he would eat most of it. Without waiting for further encouragement, he began to tuck in. He'd been a tiny thing when he'd found Maggie, hardly taller than her waist, but in two years, he had shot past most of his peers and showed no signs of slowing. His wrists stuck out two inches beyond his coat sleeves, and Maggie had forced him to buy that one, a replacement for one that had been even more badly outgrown, just that summer.

"And this flower man, he knew where to find you?" Maggie asked as Giles stuffed another bite of crown roast into his mouth.

The boy swallowed hurriedly. "No," he said with every evidence of pride. "I 'ardly knows where I'll be meself two hours ahead. I fink 'e was looking for Nan, as 'e was going down one of 'er streets, but she wasn't there yet. 'E found me, though, and 'e knows I know you, so 'e gave them flowers over wif a whole tanner, as I was too blooming stupid to know where to find you till I been paid."

"And what did he tell you?" Maggie asked. Knowing the boy's talents of confabulation, she added, "I want his exact words, now."

"Well, I don't rightly remember 'is exact words, but 'e told me where to find you and to tell you 'for you, wif compliments.' "

"Danny knew where I was." Maggie's stomach lurched.

Giles shrugged, looking annoyed at her disinterest in his own role in the flower delivery. "I suppose 'e did. 'E must 'ave, if 'e was the one who told Parks' man what to tell me."

But how could that be possible? Any number of people had seen Maggie get onto the baron's carriage both at Covent Garden and in St. Giles, but how would anyone have known who the baron was and that he kept this house? Unless, of course, the carriage had been followed. They hadn't traveled that quickly, after all—a good jogger could have kept up. The back of Maggie's neck prickled. She of all people knew that someone couldn't really tell when he was being watched, and yet at that moment . . .

She stepped up to the window and twitched back the curtains. Here, the gas lamps were close together, their tall, slender forms twined about with ropes of dark brown fog. The commercial men were just coming home from their work in the City, and two hansoms and half a dozen hat-and-coat-clad men were in view. But Maggie's attention was drawn by a small, dirty figure at the corner of the street, clad in an outsized coat that nearly reached the ground, a broom bristling over its shoulder.

The crossing sweep. Was he Danny's? These days,

who could afford not to be? The child's head turned toward her, and for a moment, Maggie might have sworn that he treated the baron's house to a long, hard look. Then he turned away again, and the moment was broken.

"Steer clear of Danny, you hear, Giles?" Maggie said firmly, stepping back and letting the curtain fall.

"Yeah, mum," he said indifferently. He surely knew as well as she did that if Danny wanted you, there was no place in London for someone like them to steer to. She had hoped that she'd be safe in the baron's house, but now she feared she'd been wrong. The room seemed suddenly more grotesque than gaudy, the gas jets dimmer, the walls crowding her. Maggie longed for the familiarity of Church Lane, where she knew what sounds meant danger, where she could read the traffic in the street like an old sailor felt the weather in his bones. But that familiarity was merely an illusion of safety. The best thing now, for everyone, was for her to stay far away from the chavies, so that if Danny did get her, at least they would still be safe.

On that thought, she turned back to Giles. "You should be getting back home."

Giles mopped up the last smears of gravy with the last fragment of a dinner roll and stuffed it in his mouth with a smack of relish. "Yeah, mum," he repeated around the food in his mouth. "There's supposed to be a new gaff in St. Giles, and I'd better scarper if I'm gonna make it in time to get a butcher's." He patted his stomach in satisfaction and strolled out the door.

Maggie only wished she could share his nonchalance. She stared at the empty plate he had left behind without the least pang of hunger, trying to guess what exactly Danny could want from her—if not everything. Whatever he wanted, it would have more to do with the life she had

left on the bridge that night four years ago than anything
she had been since then, and that time of brazen thievery
and desperation was a part of her past she never wanted
to relive.

Slowly, Maggie went to where her bundle lay upon the
bed and unwrapped it. Last year's dress, her two spare
shifts and pairs of stockings, and the three petticoats she
wasn't currently wearing went into a giant wardrobe in
the dressing room—all the clothes she owned save Little
Peg's costume did not even fill a single shelf. Her old tor-
toise shell comb, its matching brush, and her extra hair-
pins and ribbons went on the dressing table, along with
the pot-metal necklace an admirer of Little Peg had once
sent, and then there was nothing left except the pistol,
glinting sullenly in the center of her spare shawl.

Maggie picked it up. It weighed what a gun should
weigh, heavy and inert, its mother-of-pearl handle cold in
her hand. She started to put it in the drawer of the secretary in the bedroom, changed her mind, and shoved it between the feather bed and the horsehair mattress beneath,
putting it just under the edge so that she could get to it in
a hurry. She should sell it, she should have sold it long
ago, but since the night she'd shot Johnny, she hadn't
been able to let it go. What the revolver was to her, she
didn't know. Her freedom, her guilt, her old life and new
all wrapped up into a single lump of metal—yes, all that,
and also a reminder of the fragility of her independence
and things left undone.

Things she feared that she would have to do, if she was
ever to be free again.

Shoving that thought aside, she stripped down to her
shift. She could smell the baron on her clothes, and when
she pulled off her shift, she could smell him on her body,
too, a rich and spicy muskiness that made her wish, with

a wild and keening need, that he had not left her to face the night alone. Surely his arms were strong enough to hold against Danny. But she must not forget that the baron was a danger in himself—a man used to getting his way, to being obeyed. In his arms, she might be safe from the arch rogue, but she wasn't sure that she could remain herself, intact, and not be shaped by the sheer autocratic force of his personality into what he expected her to be. There was a smear of blood on the inside of her thigh, and Maggie stared at it for a moment before spitting on the edge of a bed sheet and scrubbing it off.

There were no pegs here on the wall as there were in her bedroom back in the flat, but she had the vague idea that she shouldn't fold up those clothes with her clean things, so she draped them over the footboard before pulling on a fresh shift. Then she turned off the gaslights, pulled back the covers, lay down, and tried to sleep, feeling very, very alone.

Chapter Five

As the coach rattled west, the fog lost its thick, filthy taint, drifting across the road in opalescent eddies. Charles watched as they passed an inn with horses standing patiently in darkness in the oil-lit yard, waiting for the next coach to come in.

How different it was here from Chelsea's oppressive sameness, Charles thought as the great houses slid by his window, half hidden from common eyes by walls and gates and hedges. How very, very different from St. Giles' maze of dark alleys and filthy courts. Here, high society had found a temporary refuge from the brown fogs and bourgeoisie that increasingly choked the old haunts of the nobility in Mayfair and Piccadilly. Here, houses were not crammed one against the next, and impatient fops did not have to wait for their horses to be brought around from the nearest livery stable, for each mansion had its own miniature estate so that the rich might enjoy the benefits of the London Season without suffering from any of its inconveniences.

And he was going to take a girl from the grimiest part of that grimy city and bring her . . . here? Maggie's face rose in his mind, cunning, wary, her expression alive with intelligence and a precocious knowledge of the evils of the world, and he tried to imagine such a girl with such a face *here*.

Not as precocious as you thought, a part of him whispered, the worrying part of himself where all his doubts lurked in shadow. He scowled at a crenellated manor, meant to look centuries old but so new the mortar had scarcely dried. Maggie had been innocent, at least technically. But she'd done things no innocent woman had any right doing.

And he'd done things to an innocent woman no gentleman had any right doing. . . .

He shuttled that thought from his mind, and to replace it came the memory of her, in his arms, her small body drawn with such intensity that he feared it might break, her skin smelling of lye soap and of the delicious, raw smell that was woman . . . that was Maggie.

Damn. He shifted uncomfortably, willing his erection away. He'd deal with that later, alone. He didn't want any complications. He just wanted to win a bet.

He frowned at an Indian pleasure palace that loomed, startlingly, out of the fog, its onion-domes shining in the diffuse moonlight. That mansion marked the edge of Edgington land—his land. In the past century and a half, his family had turned the property from farming cattle to farming nobles. It was his, irrevocably entailed, but each of the houses, rented for five years or ten or ninety-nine, had been built on credit, and while the income from the leases was quickly squandered, the barony's total liability had reached a staggering sum. The only option now was to hurl himself forward in a frenzy of new building, using new income to pay old debts and retrenching his expenditures to a manageable level without ever showing a crack to the watching world. For the first time in several generations, the fabulous income of the Edgington estate exceeded its fabulous expenditures. In a very real way, Charles had rebuilt the wreckage of his family's fortune brick by brick. He did not need entanglements now, no drains on his funds or his energy. He needed clarity, probity, decisiveness. And if he could find those, he hoped that somehow he could recover himself, for he had the terrible dread that he had dropped his selfhood sometime between the day he left the nursery and the moment of his inheritance, and he had no idea how one went about finding oneself and picking it up again.

As Charles finished that thought, the gates of Edgington House itself reared up. It alone sat isolated, perched on a remnant of its ancient park, the houses and play places of the wealthy spreading out like a gaudy skirt around it. It was not really Edgington proper—that was out in Lancashire—but the Edgington family had long looked more to London's glittering dissolution than to the more wholesome pleasures of the countryside, so that this manor house had long since eclipsed the actual family seat.

The gates creaked open with the gatehouse keeper's arrival, and the coach rattled over the bridge that crossed the stream at the end of the drive and passed between the yews of the long double allee, dirt crunching under its wheels. The manor hunched upon the crest of the hill, its wings closing around the paved courtyard at its center. Its limestone facade pulsated with the shifting colors of the fog, uncompromisingly solid in its Baroque grandeur. Mottled by verdigris that had trickled down from the copper mansard roofs, it was both ethereal in its mother-of-pearl marble and brute in its cold, blunt lines.

Too old, his mother called it, sniffing at the ancient paintings and tapestries that still adorned the walls. Too cold, and it certainly was that. Even in the height of summer, when all of London sweltered and the Thames crawled back from its banks to expose long flats of stinking mud, fires burned on the hearths at the Edgington House, as the stone radiated the chill of centuries into the high rooms.

The horses' hooves clattered on the cobbles of the courtyard, and the coach pulled to a stop in front of the house, where the double doors stood closed at the top of the sweeping stairs like an old man's tight lips. Charles pushed open the carriage door and leapt lightly to the ground.

Impatient, he heard his mother complain in silence of his mind. *Undignified*. His mother seemed not to care particularly what sins her offspring committed as long as they were committed with dignity.

Charles began to mount the stairs to the entrance of the house, but before he was halfway up, the doors burst open, and his mother appeared, followed by her two companions in their eternal black bombazine and a flutter of maids as a pair of footmen attempted, without much success, to act as if they had been the ones to open the door so precipitously.

"Charles!" she cried, sailing down the steps toward him.

"Mother," he acknowledged. He regarded the woman coolly. Once, she had been *dear Mamma*, her flutterings kind if absentminded, her arms always ready to envelop her children in a perfumed embrace, her ear ready to listen to infant woes and alleviate them with the proper mixture of sympathy, lightheartedness, and sweets. But then he had gone off to school at Rugby, and every year when he had come home for holiday, she had seemed a little changed, her laughter turning slowly to complaints, her embraces accompanied more and more often with some small nag or piece of advice, her little presents turned to bribes in hopes that he would "remember his dear mother, who loves him so very much." And now, when he looked down at this birdlike, twittering woman, jet beads clattering about her thin neck, he realized that, though he loved her, he had stopped liking her a long time ago.

"Charles, where have you been? I have had tea held for you for ages, just ages, and now it is nearly supper time!" Lady Edgington said. She did not snap. She worried. She fussed.

Charles ignored the temptation to simply brush by her and offered his arm instead. She stared at him for a moment and then took it, her momentum broken, and Charles mounted the stairs with frigid dignity as she stepped helplessly at his side.

"I do not take dinner and tea with you every day, madam," he said reasonably as they passed through the doors. "You have no reason to expect me. Even when I am at home"—he emphasized the *when*—"I often take my meals alone."

"But I want to know where you are," she protested. "You did not tell Robbins that you would not be in, nor even Kendall. I worry, you know. I was afraid something dreadful might have happened. If you would only tell me what your plans are, then your food would never be cold. And I wouldn't worry so. But I think it would be better if you took your meals here. It's better for the digestion, I think. Eating here and there, in this haphazard way—it just isn't proper. Or it shouldn't be."

Charles halted as his mother's litany went on. They were now in the center of the frigid gilt-and-white grandeur of the entry hall, his mother's entourage spread out like a fan around them. High above, an abundant Europa smirked down at them, her voluptuous legs clasping the bull as he charged into the waves.

Charles dropped his mother's arm so he could strip off his outerwear, handing them to the nearest footman as her complaints bubbled in his ears, wearing at his patience until there was nothing left. He stepped forward, toward her, cutting off her chatter midsentence and leaning down to her ear before she could back away.

"I am not my father," he whispered, so softly that no one else could hear. He owed her that much. "You have no reason to worry about me, for your marriage bed is not being defiled in *my* absence."

She jerked away with a little shriek, her face going as pale as marble under the two spots of rouge on her cheeks. Charles almost regretted telling her that— almost. But he had suffered at the table too many nights as a boy, his stomach clenching on nothing as the soup cooked away and the roast went dry and his mother fussed and flitted about the dining room, waiting for a husband who came far too late, if at all.

"How dare you say that?" she gasped out, and yet she was neither outraged nor horrified. Her retort was a pathetic appeal to the pretence of propriety—only the pretence, though, for forms were all that mattered. "How dare you talk to your mother that way?"

Charles sighed, feeling suddenly tired. His words had made no difference. Nothing he said ever did. "I will eat in my study tonight. Have your tea, madam. Or your supper, as it is so late. And do not wait for me again." He raised a sardonic eyebrow. "I am sure that Millie didn't."

Lady Edgington said nothing, her failure to contradict him its own confirmation, and so after a moment, Charles turned his back and mounted the stairs, his steps echoing in the silence as his mother watched him from below with bright, dry eyes.

He walked down the East Gallery, passing his sister's door and continuing to the suite at the very end of the wing that he had taken when his father died. He'd had no wish to evict his mother from her rooms, nor had he particularly desired to rest his head upon his father's pillow, and so he had relocated to a suite of four rooms that had originally been constructed for another Lord Edgington, which, not incidentally, contained its own, private staircase down to the library and up to the second floor above.

He opened the door to his study and was met by the banked red glow of the coals in the grate and the pale fire of the gas jet, blanched into pastels by the stark walls. Tudor and Baroque clashed strangely in the room, the high wainscoting and coffered ceiling decorated in gilt-touched white, a seventeenth-century interpretation of an earlier age. The heavy furniture was made of pale maples, rippling with birdseyes and tiger stripes, which, in this age of mahogany, gave the room an insubstantial cast.

"There you are!"

Charles paused at the unexpected voice, then shut the door with a firm click behind him. "For a given value of *there*, that is where I always am."

Millie stood from the sea-green embrace of a wing-back chair and turned to face him. "You have been gone all day. You must have begun your plan to try to win the bet," she said, narrowing her eyes at him. "I know it."

"You presume a great deal," he said curtly. He had no desire to deal with his sister now, not her curl tossing, not her little pouts, and not her wheedling ways. He wanted to have a finger of brandy—all right, perhaps three—and think of a very different woman in highly un-sisterly terms. He crossed to the fireplace and gave the bell rope a sharp tug. His man Kendall would know that such a summons at such an hour meant that he wanted his dinner.

"Oh, come now," Millie said smugly. "I'm not an idiot. Two days ago, you bully me into making that silly bet, and then today, you're late, and I wrote Sir Nathaniel's sister, Lady Victoria, and Leticia Mortimer, and none of them knew where you were."

"You should join Scotland Yard," Charles said, going to the spirits cupboard as he loosened his necktie. "I am sure they would hire you as a lady detective on the spot."

"Who is she?" Millie demanded, ignoring his gibe. "I want to know!"

"Even assuming I had set to work on our little wager—and you flatter yourself if you think I waste much time upon thinking about it—why on earth would I tell you?" Charles demanded, rising, inevitably, to his sister's bait.

"It's not me you have to fool," she said primly. "You must fool everyone."

Charles poured himself a generous splash of spirits. He lifted it inquiringly at his sister, who wrinkled her nose at him, recognizing the tease for what it was. "But you, my dear sister, are a significant subset of everyone, and in particular, you are the subset of everyone most likely to spread such information to anyone at all."

Millie scowled at him. "I am going to find out who it is. I've asked Lord Gifford . . . that is, I asked his sister to tell me everything. He's kind to me. More kind to me than you are."

Charles sighed, flopping into the wing chair Millie had vacated. "For God's sake, Millie, you're not in the nursery any longer. You can't go about writing letters to any man you please. Christopher Radcliffe fancies you well enough, God knows why, but if he finds out just how indiscreet you are, I doubt that will count for much. Unless you want to die an embarrassing maiden aunt, do grow up a little."

Millie's face stiffened, and for a moment, Charles was afraid that she was going to try crying. If she did that, he would throw her out, bodily if necessary. Instead, she gave a sad little exhalation and sat upon the ottoman at his feet. "I used to think you were the best brother in the world," she said plaintively. "You'd give me rides on your pony and smuggle me sweets. But when you came back from Rugby, you were so quiet and dark that you scared me a little, and now . . . why, I can't even buy new dresses anymore!"

"You have already had five new dresses this year, Millie," Charles said wearily.

"But Papa never restricted me so cruelly, and if I thought you had meant it when you said that I have to live within grandmamma's bequest, I wouldn't have had them all made this winter. Now I must wear last year's rags all summer and autumn long!" She paused for effect, but Charles merely took a long, slow drink of his brandy, savoring the burn down his throat. "What happened, Chas?" she asked softly, using the nickname he hadn't heard in ten years and more. "Why don't we have fun like we used to?"

"I grew up," Charles said shortly. "As should you. The world does not hand me ponies and sweets anymore."

Millie just stared at him in blank incomprehension. He took another drink as a knock came at the door.

"Come in, Kendall," he called out. The door opened,

revealing his valet. "Good night, Millie," he told his sister firmly as the man entered.

She stood stiffly, a frozen expression on her face, and drifted out the door.

And so does the tyrant brutalize his family, Charles thought dryly.

He examined the tray that Kendall sat upon the table next to his chair. "Roast duck in apricot sauce," he remarked. "Why, the chef has grown quite daring these days." And with a show of heartiness so complete that he nearly fooled himself, he dug in. But even as he ate, his mind's eye was filled with the image of a small woman on a stage, singing against all the tyranny in the world.

Maggie's morning began at dawn when Mrs. Pershing drew back the curtains and a startlingly unseasonable flood of light spilled into the room. Maggie struggled upright among the many blankets, her buttocks sinking even more deeply into the thick featherbed. She scrubbed her eyes. She had not slept well. The mattress was too soft, the sheets too smooth, the entire bed too large and empty for one person to sleep upon it alone, for it was fully twice the size of the iron bedstead she shared with Sally and Nan. The silence of the neighborhood was strange, too, and oppressive, for once the church bells struck ten, the street had fallen into a noiseless slumber except for the occasional nightsoil man's wagon and the slow, deliberate swagger of the bobby on his beat.

After midnight had arrived, Maggie had risen to open the curtains just enough to see the street corner where the sweep still lurked even though no one had used his crossing for hours. The bobby stopped next to him once and spoke to him: After that, the boy slipped away a minute before the officer was due around the corner again and reappeared only after he had gone.

Good to know, Maggie had decided after seeing this cycle repeat three times over the next hour. Then, the strain of the day giving way to exhaustion, she lay down on the too-large, too-soft bed again and stared for a long time at the pink silk of the hangings above her before finally drifting off to sleep.

"Good morning, Miss King," Mrs. Pershing said, tying the draperies back with brisk efficiency.

"Good morning," Maggie muttered. She eyed the blue sky, still pale with dawn. No one could be expected to buy pease soup before ten o'clock, and since Little Peg's performances usually lasted late into the night, Maggie rarely saw much of the mornings between dawn and when she woke at noon to take over the barrow until evening. She decided that she had not missed them. "What time is it?"

"Going on nine o' clock, madam," the housekeeper said amiably. "I let you sleep until Mme. Rochelle's girl arrived. I brought you breakfast, but you'll need to eat up quickly now." She nodded at the tray upon a little table. "Don't bother to dress; I'll just have her sent up here in a few minutes."

And thus began the most dizzying day of Maggie's life.

She was measured and examined, first by a tall, pale shop girl and then by the dressmaker Mme. Rochelle herself, who stopped in briefly and assured Maggie that she would personally arrange every detail of Maggie's wardrobe, from her millinery down to her shoes. Maggie could still smell the baron on her skin, and she was half afraid the shop girl might notice it, too, but if she did, she gave no sign of it.

When they left, Maggie indulged in the novel luxury of taking a bath, filling it with water so hot it was nearly scalding and sinking in up to her breasts. It was a strange sensation, to half float in the broad tubful of kettle-hot water, and oddly soothing despite its unnaturalness. There was an entire selection of soft, scented French-milled soaps to choose from, and she experimented freely until she found a combination of two that she liked best. They slid across her skin almost like a caress—there was no need to shave flakes of them into a pan of boiling water to dissolve them first, and the suds did not bite at her skin or even sting when they touched a scratch on the back of her hand.

Mrs. Pershing knocked on the door all too soon, announcing that her chaperone had arrived. Chaperone? Curious, Maggie struggled into her own shift, corset, and petticoats, pulling on a readymade dress that Mme. Rochelle had left as a stopgap measure of respectability. With the linsey-woolsey skirt dragging at her ankles, she went down to the parlor to receive her new arrival.

Maggie was glad to find that the sheets had been removed from that room, quite transforming it from the night before. Yet still a ghost of the baron still seemed to linger there even as the young woman waiting within stood from a stiff side chair and introduced herself. *Chaperone,* as it turned out, was a politely fictional appellation for her governess and etiquette instructor.

"I understand that you are to be introduced into society from a less than polished background," Miss West said, frankly and yet gently as she extended her hand. She was a smart young woman, and Maggie's experienced eye added up the value of her clothing and came to a respectable but not excessive total.

Maggie shook her hand. "That's true enough," she said cautiously.

"Have no fear, Miss King, for my agency has voluminous experience in transforming the daughters and wives of those who have been suddenly thrust into higher circles." Without further ado, Miss West began to unpack her valise and outline their hurried course of study. Maggie was to learn deportment and dancing, read a smattering of literature and memorize a touch of French, acquire a veneer of knowledge about geography and history and politics, and learn some arithmetic that went beyond the basic figuring Maggie already understood. They would begin strictly in private, but as her abilities grew, Miss West would take her into public under her watchful eye.

"But when am I going to sing?" Maggie asked. "I am to have voice lessons, as well."

"Ah, yes," Miss West said, consulting a schedule in her lap. "I arrive at nine sharp. From eleven to one every day, I take my luncheon while you take voice." She smiled at that quip. "You are to take your luncheon immediately afterward, during geography and mathematics. I leave at seven in the evening, after your supper, so that you may study your lessons for the morrow."

"I see," Maggie said, feeling a little overwhelmed.

Mrs. Pershing stepped into the parlor again. "Mrs. Arabella Ladd is here for your voice lessons."

"I will just watch," Miss West said. "To observe your deportment."

Maggie had heard of Mrs. Ladd. Everyone associated with the London opera world had. Arabella Newcombe had been hailed as the next Jenny Lind until her voice gave out only five years into her career. She had married and used her expertise to found a voice school, the most well regarded in England. Maggie felt a little awe as the redoubtable woman sailed into the room, amazed that Lord Edgington had contracted with her and even more amazed that he had managed to do it literally overnight.

Mrs. Ladd wasted no time but immediately sent Maggie through a series of exercises, accompanying her on the piano that sat in the bow window at one end of the room. She efficiently identified a good half dozen weaknesses in Maggie's voice and declared that they would start with the basics. For two hours, Maggie practiced breathing properly as she sang, and by the end of the time, her stomach muscles ached with fatigue, her back was stiff, and her feet were numb.

Luncheon came then, and Miss West engaged Maggie in conversation, carefully guiding and correcting her mistakes and indelicacies while giving her instructions on various facets of etiquette. The rules seemed to swarm in Maggie's mind, as nonsensical as the buzzing of bees, but she tried as hard as she could to remember them all and to keep them straight. Her body felt hammered out into a thin, brittle sheet by the time supper arrived. By then, she could hardly keep her eye off the clock, she was waiting with such anticipation for seven o'clock to arrive.

It was still ten minutes 'til when Maggie looked up at a sound in the doorway, expecting Mrs. Pershing to enter, and caught her breath at the unexpected sight of Lord Edgington. She stifled the visceral reaction that fluttered through her, leaving her feeling slightly unbalanced. Memories from the night before flooded her: his mouth over hers, the heat of his hands against her breasts, his body—

She jerked to her feet. "Lord Edgington," she croaked, "how nice of you to visit."

He cocked an eyebrow at Miss West. "Your agency told me you were good."

"Your lordship, I am the best," she said complacently. "But Miss King forgot that we do not rise for gentlemen."

Flushing with irritation and embarrassment, Maggie sat.

"Like a lady," Miss West added primly, and Maggie straightened and pulled her shoulders back until they protested as her cheeks flamed even redder.

"Please, do sit," she managed in her most aristocratic tones as a private corner of her seethed. What a blooming load of rubbish it all was, this posturing and preening, calculated to make a grown woman look like a fool. But she knew it was important, necessary, even, and so she tamped down on that part of herself and smiled even though it felt like it was going to crack her face.

The baron smiled back and took a chair across from hers, but the pleasantly courteous expression did not reach his eyes, which flared with an intensity she was sure he did not intend as they bore into her own.

He hasn't forgot either, Maggie thought. *He feels something, too.* A small thrill passed through her, excitement and uncertainty combined.

"Did Mme. Rochelle come today?" the baron asked, his tone indifferent.

"Yes, sir," Maggie said with her best attempt at diffidence. "The first of my clothes will arrive tomorrow, says her."

"She says," Miss West corrected composedly.

"She says," Maggie echoed, crushing the urge to squirm in her chair. "She's making up more than a dozen dresses."

The baron nodded shortly. "I know. You must have a

full wardrobe to play this role, I fear. The cost is considerable." He frowned at the dress she was now wearing. "Is that from Mme. Rochelle?"

"Yes," Maggie replied.

His frown deepened. "Stand up so that I can see it better."

She obeyed, turning slowly at his impatient motion.

"Quite unacceptable," he pronounced, glaring at the gray linsey-woolsey as if it were something offensive.

"I think she just gave it to me so that I'd have something else to wear while the first dresses are being made up," Maggie ventured.

"Once they arrive, you are never to wear this dress again," the baron ordered. "Do you understand? Have it sent back to her. I won't pay for such a rag."

Maggie gaped for a moment. "Yes, sir," she managed.

The baron made a dismissive gesture, and she sat. The room fell into silence. Maggie found herself gazing at the point where his throat disappeared under the collar of his shirt. Miss West coughed pointedly after a moment, and Maggie obediently began to talk. "I will be interviewing servants tomorrow, sir—a cook, a housemaid, and a lady's maid."

"Good," the baron said. He seemed to be trying to look at his ease, but Maggie was skilled at recognizing the small signs of tension in a man. Four years ago, they'd warned her when Johnny was in the mood to send a punch or a kick flying at an unwary chavy. In Lord Edgington, there was no threat of impending violence, and yet the tension was no less real for that, and no less frightening in its way.

Maggie shifted slightly. "Since you want our arrangement to be secret, I thought of getting two girls I know. You can trust Nan and Sally to keep their traps shut."

"To keep a confidence," Miss West corrected with a hint of disapproval.

"That, too," Maggie said, making a face.

"Good," the baron repeated.

"But Sally would lose her position if she stopped going to her regular houses," Maggie continued doggedly, "and Nan would lose her streets to some other coster."

"I see," Lord Edgington said.

Silence fell again. Was he trying to make this difficult for her? "I am learning how to eat like a lady," Maggie provided tentatively, in the hope that he would carry some of the weight of the conversation for a while.

"Good," the baron said, yet again.

Her patience reached its breaking point. "Mme. Rochelle ordered me five pairs of pantaloons. I've never owned pantaloons before, but she says all the ladies wear them under their crinolines. Do you like pantaloons?"

Miss West's eyes widened, and Lord Edgington cleared his throat. "Miss West, if you will excuse us for a moment?"

"Certainly," the woman said as she rose hurriedly. She left, shutting the door behind her with care.

The baron looked at her steadily for a moment. Maggie glared back, her chin up.

"You were making it hard for me on purpose," she accused.

He raised an eyebrow. "Pantaloons?"

"At least it made you say something other than 'good,'" Maggie said defensively.

"What would you have me say?" Lord Edgington demanded, running a hand irritably through his dark gold hair, his first unstudied reaction since he had arrived.

"I don't know, sir!" Maggie snapped. "Something.

Anything. Just don't sit there and stare at me as if I were a steak dinner and act as if I am supposed to pretend that everything is ordinary."

A surprised bark of laughter escaped him. "A steak dinner?"

Maggie scowled. "You know what I mean, sir."

He seemed to relax into his chair, some of the strain leaving him even as his eyes heated with amusement and a kind of intimate analysis. "A steak dinner. And here I was, convinced that I was betraying nothing at all and even more certain that if I did betray some small sign of the very improper thoughts that have hounded me since I left you last night . . . well, that they would be at least more carnal and less culinary."

Maggie bit her lip as her body tightened instinctively, anticipatorily at his words. "Hounded you, sir?"

The baron shook his head. "I should not have admitted it. I did not intend to admit it."

"I have been hounded, too." She shrugged, helpless. "I keep thinking of what happened, how it might have ended if you had not . . . left."

"I am sorry for my unusual lapse in self-control," he said, his face closing.

"That's not what I meant." Maggie stood, agitated, and he rose, too—automatically in the presence of a lady, she thought with an edge of the absurd. "What I meant was—I mean that, that I took a bath this morning," she said, all in a rush, "in the fancy tub you have. But I swear I can still smell you on my body, on my clothes. It's half driven me to bedlam, all day long. Sometimes I want to scrub and scrub my skin away, and others . . ."

He no longer looked at ease, not at all. Standing

across from her, his entire body seemed strung tight, as if it were about to break. "And others?" he prompted.

"And others, I wish that you hadn't stopped, that you hadn't left, that you had stayed, and that all night long . . ." Her voice died in her throat.

The baron made an abortive noise of protest. "You shouldn't say such things." His voice was suddenly rough, abrupt. "I am not a man of stone."

"Then you feel it just as much as I do," Maggie said, feeling an obscure sense of satisfaction. "I wasn't completely sure that was what you meant with your 'hounding'—"

"You don't know what you are talking about," the baron interrupted. He strode past her to the bow window, where he stared out onto the street with his back facing her squarely. "You're—you're an innocent."

"Not no more, I'm not," Maggie said quietly.

"Well, you should be an innocent," the man returned. Inanely, he added, "You're not even the kind of woman I prefer."

"Ain't I?" Maggie asked, narrowing her eyes. She crossed the room to stand directly behind him. "Kiss me, then. Kiss me and then tell me you don't *prefer* me."

He turned, and Maggie caught her breath at the intensity in his golden eyes.

"I warned you not to say that again unless you really meant it," he said.

"I mean it." The words came out at a whisper.

His arms were around her before she could react, pulling her hard against him. Her body jolted with the contact, setting her head to spinning wildly. His mouth came down immediately, roughly, smothering her gasp with its heat. There was nothing exploratory or teasing about this—nothing polished or refined. It was raw and powerful, and the urgings of his mouth sent an answering roar of need blazing through her.

He released her as quickly as he had siezed her, and her senses reeled as she fought to keep her balance.

"Was that a mistake?" he demanded. His words were even, his face impassive, but his eyes now glittered darkly and his breath came faster.

"I—I don't think so," Maggie managed, swallowing.

"I don't want a mistress," the baron said bluntly.

Maggie's heart jerked inside her chest. A mistress? She looked around the gleaming parlor, imagining that it would be hers, not for the space of a few months but maybe a year, two years, maybe even three. . . . "I do not want to be your mistress," she lied. She could tie him to her, could make him want to never give her up. The idea was both heady and frightening, to imagine him having such desire for her. He was one to want to control her every move, her clothing and actions and entertainments. But even so, he was safer than Danny. He had to be. He must bed her again, as soon as possible. And if their union bore unwanted fruit, she must make him swear, upon his honor, to support it and hope that his honor was enough.

Then she might be free, free of Danny forever, for he could never reach her here.

She took a deep breath. "I want you to make love to me."

Emotions flickered so fast across the baron's face that Maggie could scarcely read them—surprise, cynicism, regret, pleasure, and, most of all, hunger. He opened his mouth to speak—

—and the door burst open so hard that it slammed against the wall. Maggie whirled, tensing automatically.

Giles stood in the doorway, his eyes wide and white in his dirty face.

"It's Nan, mum!" he said. "She's been beat up bad. And the barrow's all smashed!"

"Danny," Maggie whispered, her stomach lurching. "No!" She was running before she had consciously told her feet to move. Giles scampered in front of her, and heavier feet on the stairs told her that the baron was following. She dashed past a bewildered Miss West, who stood in the front hall, and charged out the front door. The street was empty except for the baron's large black carriage and the crossing sweep at the corner.

"Take my carriage."

Maggie turned to see the baron standing a mere foot behind her. "Why?" she blurted.

He treated her with a kind of humorless smile. "Because it is faster."

"I mean, why are you helping me?"

"You will go and see her, whether I help or not, correct?" he said.

"Of course."

"Mme. Rochelle is making up more than a hundred pounds worth of dresses that fit only you even as we speak. I am protecting my investment. Take my carriage. I am coming, too." He spoke calmly, as if to quash disagreement before it was voiced.

But Maggie needed no further invitation. She grabbed the door handle and swung it open, scrambling inside. Giles ducked in behind her, followed by Lord Edgington.

"Where are we going?" he asked, pausing in the doorway.

Maggie looked at Giles.

"To Old Bess' place," the boy said. "Frankie's gone

missing again, but Sally got scared and made everybody else leave the flat."

Maggie rattled off directions, which the baron relayed to his driver. He shut the door and sat, and Maggie found herself next to him, with Giles facing them both.

"Where are we going?" the baron repeated.

Maggie smiled grimly in the darkness. He'd find out soon enough, she supposed. "I think toffs like you would call it—a house of ill repute."

Chapter Six

A brothel. Charles' life seemed to suddenly have acquired the strange property of canting to one side, slipping into absurdity. Two days ago, he had not known this girl, and now he had put his carriage at her disposal to visit a drunken slattern who had taken refuge in a brothel from some criminal sort of fellow.

Charles shook his head and asked the natural question. "Who is Danny?"

Maggie jerked her head around to look at him squarely, and he had the impression that she wasn't pleased that he knew the name. "Nobody," she muttered.

"He's obviously someone if he's beating up poor girls in the street," Charles countered, raising a skeptical brow.

"I don't know that it was him, sir," Maggie said uncomfortably. Charles didn't think she believed what she was saying. She made a face. "Maybe it was a thief. Or maybe she owed somebody a few shillings and missed the interest payments one too many times."

The child sat across from them, watching the exchange with sharp eyes. Was he the unknown Giles, the one occupant of the flat Charles had yet to meet? Charles slipped his hand into his pocket, found a shilling, and flipped it to the boy. "Who is Danny, Giles?" he asked.

The child rubbed the shilling on his sleeve, then made it disappear among his rags. "Everybody knows Danny O'Sullivan! 'E's the biggest arch rogue in London—owns 'alf the gangs direct, and another third pay 'im their dues."

Maggie's jaw tightened at this explanation, but she just said, "There are a lot of Dannys in London."

"Why would he want to hurt Nan?" Charles asked the child, ignoring her.

Giles' eyes met Maggie's a moment before he answered. "I dunno, guv," he said. " 'E's never messed wif 'er afore."

Whatever the child knew, he wasn't telling. And why should Charles care? He was just protecting his investment, as he had told Maggie. He'd escort her to see her friend and then escort her right back the Chelsea, all safe and sound, and no one would be the worse for it.

Resolutely, he turned his mind away from idle speculations in matters that did not concern him, and it devolved, inevitably, upon the scene that the ragged child had interrupted in the parlor.

He had been ready to make love to her—to Maggie King, the little dance hall singer street waif. No, not a waif. It was her utter contrast to all waifishness that was so compelling about her. Despite her size, there was nothing that was delicate about her, nothing artificial. She was blunt, brazen, almost raw. She did not have the calculated vulgarity, attempted coyness, or rigid shyness of the few street-class women he'd ever attempted to converse with before—on the contrary, she seemed to be more herself than anyone he'd ever met.

He surveyed her covertly as she stared rigidly out of

the window, her entire body radiating impatient concern. That force of personality—that must be why he'd fallen asleep thinking about her, woken up thinking about her, drifted through his day with her preying at the corners of his mind. She was simply so different from anything in his experience. She was like a novel wine—upon experiencing her for the first time, his interest was strongly piqued, so he would get drunk on her once or twice, and after he'd had a surfeit, he would feel nothing stronger than an urge to sample her every so often, to remind himself of how interesting she had once been to his jaded palate. As she said herself, she wasn't an innocent any longer, and he had made it perfectly clear what she could expect from him if she continued to pursue him . . .

Their arrival at their destination interrupted those thoughts. Charles opened the carriage door and stepped onto the pavement. It was a good address as far as brothels went, just around the corner from the Haymarket and several expensive restaurants, a vicinity familiar to every young gentleman of Charles' slightly fast set. The white façade was freshly painted, marked by only the street numbers discreetly affixed above the door and two flaring gas lights. Maggie scrambled out behind him, taking a quick glance up and down the street before fixing her gaze uncharacteristically on her own feet and hurrying to the door and inside. Giles stepped out, too, but he made no move to enter the establishment, instead slouching against the nearest wall in a manner that announced that he intended to loiter there until Maggie's return. The crowds of people on the pavement took no notice of him. Though dusk was more than an hour gone, the streets here were thronged with professional men, well-dressed bucks, and young girls in expensive dresses, with painted lips and darkened eyes—the usual evening complement of thrill seekers and prostitutes that swarmed over the Haymarket and Regent Street. Charles didn't recognize anyone at first glance, but if he stayed on the street, it was only a matter of time before he was spotted.

Charles moved to follow Maggie inside, and he had his hand on the doorknob when a very small boy scampered up to him.

"Want me to find you a lively one, guv'nor?" he chirped, leering meaningfully as he doffed a filthy little hat.

"No," Charles said firmly. "I brought my own entertainment."

Pulling a face, the boy dashed between two whores, who stood arm-in-arm with an old woman minder frowning at them from across the street.

Leaving Giles leaning against the wall, Charles stepped into the establishment's front hall, where he was confronted by the sight of Maggie facing a small girl of no more than eleven while two enormous men lounged on chairs at the foot of the stairs. Was it one of those establishments, then? His disgust must have shown on his face, for when Maggie glanced behind and saw him standing there, she murmured, "That's Nell, Old Bess' youngest."

The proprietor's child, then, Charles guessed. He relaxed.

"Sweet Sally's in the second garret room on the right," the child reported. "'Er friend should 'ave gotten a room 'ere instead of trying it on in the streets. We make the johns behave." She nodded to two huge men behind her.

"Fanks, Nell," Maggie said, her cockney accent suddenly thick.

Upon that information, Charles stepped past her and began to mount the stairs. The sooner they found Nan, the sooner they could leave.

"You don't need to come up," Maggie said quickly as she started after him. "I'll be fine. Nan won't want to see you."

"I told you. I am protecting my investment," Charles said. He wasn't sure why he was being so stubborn, but something in Maggie's manner needled him. Independence was all very well, but hers went so far as a kind of hidden contempt.

"You can protect it just as good downstairs," she retorted.

Charles shrugged, giving her no answer, and she huffed slightly but made no further protest.

At the first-floor landing, they were met by the sight of a well-lit, scarlet-carpeted corridor running down the length of the building, and from the doors that lined it filtered giggles, moans, and the occasional cry. Charles would have scarcely noticed the sounds of copulation if it weren't for his unorthodox company. He glanced back at Maggie over his shoulder, to see how she was reacting. She simply cocked her head sideways, as if to say, *What did you expect?*

No, she certainly was no innocent.

They continued to the second floor, and Maggie slipped ahead of him to the half-hidden servants' stairs that led to the attic. It was small and dark, and it opened onto a narrow hallway with bare floorboards illuminated by only one small gaslight. Charles pushed past Maggie and tried the knob to the second door on the right. It opened at his touch.

The tiny room was even more crowded than the kitchen of Maggie's flat had been. Harry the law writer hovered near the door, and the two children who had been in the cot in the flat now huddled at one end of the narrow bed while the scarred Sally knelt in the middle, hold-

ing the curled-up and sobbing form of another girl. Nan.
Her hair was even more wild and tangled than before, her
face mottled with emerging bruises and her tears. The
sight of her battered face made Charles' guts tighten—
despite what Giles had said when he arrived at the
Chelsea town house, Charles had not quite made the attack real in his mind. That kind of thing didn't happen to
people he associated with. They could walk through the
darkest alleys unscathed.

"Anyfing broken?" Maggie demanded, pushing past
Charles and Harry to the crying girl's side.

Nan shook her head but began sobbing even harder.
Sally stared at Charles with a hard expression.

"What's 'e doing 'ere?" she said softly to Maggie.

"He's no trouble," Maggie replied shortly.

"I can't be 'aving another one, Maggie!" Nan burst
out, interrupting the incipient argument. "I just can't!"
Then she let out a wail that dissolved into more tears. The
little girl at the end of the bed began to cry, too, even as
she patted and bounced the infant in her arms in a vain attempt to comfort him. Sally's face spasmed, and she held
Nan tighter, sending Harry a mutely pleading look.

Obediently, Harry took Maggie's elbow, pulling her
toward the doorway. With a sideways look at Charles, he
lowered his voice and said, "Three bruisers pulled her
into the alley that runs behind The Gilly Flower. They
grabbed her so fast that no one saw. They shattered the
barrow, beat her bloody, then raped her. They said Danny
sent them."

Maggie's hand tightened visibly on the boy's arm, and
despite Charles' own reaction to the youth's words, part
of him could not help but wish that it was him that
Maggie was holding on to, not a stripling in a shiny suit.

"Sally doesn't want anyone to go back to the flat,"

Harry continued tensely. "But I have to. The law stationer will stop sending me work if I disappear, even for a few days. I am young. I can't afford to be unreliable, too."

Maggie's face was pasty in the lamplight. She nodded slowly. "Shove a chair under the doorknob when you're home. And be careful. And tell Giles that if he goes back, I'll give him the hiding of his life."

"I will, mum," he said, and with a grave squeeze of her hand, he slipped out of the room.

"We should stay 'ere," Sally said, holding Nan against her thin chest.

Maggie nodded. "Yes. I've got a kind of idea. I'll send Giles to you when I figure it all out."

Sally laughed hollowly. "I 'ope it works better than your plan to steer clear of Danny."

Maggie looked like she wanted to say something and then compressed her lips hard. "I'm going to go and see him."

Sally's expression turned to horror, and even Nan looked up. "You can't!"

"I have to," Maggie said curtly. "You think I like it? This was a sodding warning, don't you see?" She made a frustrated gesture. "If I don't go now, tomorrow one of you is going to turn up dead—or not at all! And all because of me, right?" Her control slipped. "This is all my fault. You think I'm so bloody good and nice to keep you all around me, but do you know what? I'm not. I'm just putting you in Danny's way. You should all just—go away. Go far, far away . . ." She trailed off, and for a moment, Charles thought she was perilously close to tears.

But she swallowed hard, crossed over to Nan's side, and kissed her on the forehead. "Don't worry, chavy," she said, so softly that Charles could scarcely hear it. "I'll get 'im for you. One way or another, I'll get 'im."

Then she stood, and with a stony face, she walked out.

Charles caught up with her on the pavement. Maggie turned away from a quick exchange with Giles and then started walking up the gaslit street, away from the carriage, avoiding Charles' eyes. Charles closed the distance between them in three strides and took her elbow.

"What's going on here?" he demanded.

She shook loose, casting a furtive look at the nearest clump of whores who formed a gaggle next to a brilliant illuminated shop façade.

"Not here," she muttered. She began to walk more quickly, turning onto the Haymarket and heading south.

Charles followed, reining in his temper. He was not used to being treated like that and even less used to tolerating it. She showed no sign of slowing, and he was about to grab her arm again when she ducked into an alley and stopped with her back against the wall. "Too many people here know me," she explained.

"What is going on here?" Charles demanded again, planting himself squarely in front of her, bracing his hands on either side of her head so that she could not shake him off again. He felt as if he had stepped into a bizarre new world, one where nothing that he knew mattered or made sense. "Who is this Danny, really? And why does he have anything to do with you?"

Maggie's body was so tense that her small frame seemed insufficient to contain the intensity of her emotion, her expression hard in the light from the lamp on the corner. "You saw what's going on, sir. Nan's been worked over real good. Giles told you clear enough who Danny is. Danny hasn't got nothing to do with me, and I want to keep it that way."

Charles stared down at her, unconvinced. "Then why did he have that girl raped?"

Maggie lifted her chin. "Because even though I want to stay clear of Danny, he doesn't want to stay clear of me, right? He's been sending messages that he wants to talk to me, but talking to Danny is dangerous." Her voice turned bitter. "I guess he wanted to tell me that not talking is even more dangerous."

Charles had the unpleasant sensation that he had stumbled into the middle of something nasty that he didn't understand and could not control. "Why does he want to talk to you?"

"'Cause I'm a respectable-type person who has helped a lot of people over the years." She almost sneered the words. "And I once saved his life. I guess he has a queer way of saying thank you."

Strangely enough, Charles found the second claim more believable than the first. Saved his life? How? When? Instead, he asked, "You've been avoiding this, this arch rogue for—how long?"

"Two and a half weeks," she said, her tone slightly resentful.

"So after avoiding him for two and a half weeks, now you're just going to stroll up to him and tell him that you changed your mind and want to talk to him, after all," Charles said skeptically. "And he's going to say his piece and then let you stroll away again. Is that what you expect?"

"Yeah, something like that," she said, but her eyes shifted away from his.

Charles stared at her for a long moment. He hadn't bargained for this. All he wanted was a few months of her studious attention with no interruptions and no complications, certainly not any that involved a violent criminal. He didn't owe this girl anything. He should just turn and walk away right now, tell her the deal was off—he hadn't agreed to get involved with arch rogues and extortionists. This girl was nothing more to him than a part of a wager. He could easily get someone else, someone more suitable. He had been too ambitious, choosing a woman from too low to raise so high in a space of weeks. He should find a shopkeeper's daughter, perhaps, or a butcher's.

But even as these thoughts circled through Charles' head, he could not quite make himself believe them. He kept seeing Maggie comforting Nan with such self-possessed fierceness, kept remembering the taste of her mouth and the heat of her body, kept wondering what more there was to this angry woman who seemed, in her way, as old as London itself and yet as young and as fragile as a blossom pushing between paving stones, so easily crushed with a careless or spiteful boot heel. Just as fascinating, she seemed to realize her own fragility . . . but what could she do about it? Charles wondered suddenly, his mind rocking a little as he tried to fit his perspective to hers. It was not she who had chosen the place for the seed to fall. She could either struggle as she could or simply give up and wait for a premature death to claim her, and she was not the type to surrender easily—quite the reverse, she was one to not only fight for survival but to try to spread her scanty leaves to protect other seedlings who were no more tender than she.

"You would trade yourself away if it would save that girl Nan, wouldn't you?" Charles asked upon that thought.

The question seemed to take her by surprise, and all the hard lines flowed from her face at once, leaving it startlingly delicate and vulnerable. She blinked and said, as if it explained everything, "She's one of my chavies."

"Chavies?"

"Children." Her hands tightened convulsively round a

fistful of her skirts. "They're my family. I look after them."

"Your children," Charles repeated in disbelief. "That tall redheaded chap—"

"Frankie," Maggie supplied.

"You call him your *child*?"

"Oh, you know I don't mean it like that," she said with some asperity. "Not like I'm his real mum or nothing like that. But, yeah, he's one of my chavies, and I look after him as much as he lets me these days. They're all I've got, don't you know? It's like"—she seemed to be suddenly inspired—"it's like my honor. You nobs, you've got honor all over the place, but for someone like me, well, my honor's really small, in things like looking out for people you care about and making sure they get treated fair. But just because my honor's small doesn't make it any less important."

The words cut Charles like a lash. *She doesn't know. She couldn't know*, he thought rationally. And yet the truth bit into him: this little street rat of a woman knew more of honor than he did. *Here's your baser stuff, Millie*, he thought bitterly. *We could only hope to equal it.* "Let me get the carriage," he said. There was no decision to make anymore. "I will come with you to talk to this Danny person, and then I will drive you back to Chelsea. It will be over in half an hour."

She shook her head. "He's a scurf, sir, through and through. You don't understand people like that. If you come with me, he'll have you at the slit-and-splash so fast—"

"I'm a peer of the realm," Charles objected.

Maggie looked exasperated. "And a fat lot of good it'll do you on the bottom of the Thames. There'll be an inquest and some poor bloke what Danny doesn't like will be caught and taught the hemp jig, and you'll still be dead and Danny'll still be strolling along as free as a bird."

"What will happen to you if you go alone?" Charles did not fail to notice her lack of attention to that scenario.

"I'll be fine," she said unconvincingly. "I know Danny. He owes me. I'll be fine."

"Why won't he throw you in the Thames instead?" Charles demanded.

"Because he wants sommat out of me, or he wouldn't want to talk," Maggie said. She pushed off the wall, but Charles didn't move, so she fetched up against his chest. His body reacted automatically, tightening in anticipation. She was so small, so lost, so warm and in such need for a man to take her and protect her . . .

"You are very kind, sir," she said quietly, leaning into him. Her eyes were soft and haunted, as if she, too, felt the desire between them. "Very kind."

Then she tiptoed, reached up and, regardless of the people who were passing the entrance to the alleyway, pulled his mouth down to hers.

Her lips were small and hot against his, firm and insistent. He kissed her back automatically, holding her against him as his body sent a heady response jolting into his groin. After a long moment, she stepped away from him, out of the circle of his arms, and gave him a half-regretful, half-wry look as she stood there, surveying him.

"But I can't let you make this mistake," she said. And while his lust-clouded mind was still trying to connect those words to what she had said before, she turned and sprinted down the alley away from him.

For half a second, he just stared in incomprehension. Then it hit him—she had kissed him just to distract him into letting her go—so she could run away to see that criminal Danny and then . . . then what? Would she come back to him then, even if she could? Or was that his last taste of her lips, touch of her body . . .

"Damn it," he snarled, and he ran after her, his boots pounding against the pavement. His longer strides ate up the distance between them, but she ducked nimbly around the corner, and he skidded more clumsily after, his greater bulk unable to sling around the turn as easily as she had. By the time he had recovered his speed, she had regained all her lost ground. She seemed to have predicted this weakness, for she dodged and jigged through the dark alleys, weaving between buildings, sliding into back gardens and scrambling over walls and hopping over piles of refuse that seemed to reach out to tangle his feet. He followed clumsily, his muscle no match for her litheness, and even as he heaved himself over yet another brick wall—to the astonishment of the family gathered in the back garden—he wondered how many times she had run like this from how many men, and what would have happened if once, just once she had been too slow.

He burst around a corner and caught a flash of a skirt disappearing into a side street, but when he made it to the corner, she was gone without a trace. He trotted up to the next intersection and looked around. Nothing. And, he realized slowly as his breathing returned to normal, he had no idea where he was.

" 'Scuse me, gov," came a small voice behind him. He turned to see Giles standing there, smiling expectantly, his teeth unnaturally bright in the darkness. "Maggie told me to follow you in case sommat like this 'appened. Cor, you didn't 'alf suck 'er face off, did you?" His tone was frankly admiring, and it made Charles flush with irritation to discover that Maggie's kiss had had an audience. "Anyways, you want to get back to that bawdy house?"

"I want to get to where Miss King is going," he

growled, even more irritated to realize that Giles' presence meant that Maggie had not only tricked him but had anticipated doing so. Well, he might not be as well versed in trickery, but he had other ways of making things go his way.

"Can't do that," the boy said primly, starting back the way they had come. "I got orders."

"I'll give you another shilling," Charles offered.

The boy shot him a scathing look. "I can't disobey the closest thing to a mum I ever knowed for a bob."

Charles picked up on the implication. "For a pound?"

"Now you're talkin'!" The boy beamed. "Let's get you back to your carriage, and then I'll tell you the way, but you 'ave to promise on your word as a nob that you'll wait for 'er outside and not charge in arfter 'er. She'd be bloomin' furious if she went to all that trouble to save your skin and you went and got yourself kilt, anyhow."

"Fine," Charles said curtly. "I promise." He followed the child, hoping that he wasn't making the biggest mistake of his life.

Confident that Lord Edgington had been lost in the tangle of alleys at least half a mile back, Maggie slowed to a walk as she reached the Seven Dials, moving unnoticed among the costers, street artisans, and laborers. She was good at being overlooked, one small, thin, insignificant figure among so many. Her new linsey-woolsy dress was too fine for this part of town, but its drab gray color and obviously bad fit countered the good construction, and the street lamps were too far apart here to afford anyone a close inspection despite the clarity of the night.

The sweat dried on her body, chilling her, and she tried to ignore it as she had during those long years when she'd owned no clothing but a thin cotton dress and three petticoats. Weak. She had grown weak with her soft life, vulnerable now when she could afford weakness the least. She wished she had remembered the gun.

She moved through the streets toward a particular corner of a particular back court that she had never wanted to see again. She well knew where the old flash ken was—Danny was the fifth or sixth scurf to base his center of operations from there that Maggie knew of, and there had surely been many more before—but Maggie hadn't been there since she had left her old life behind.

There it was—a corner that didn't look like a corner so much as a hole left where two houses didn't quite touch. She slid between, and the tiny alley opened up immediately into a dark court, surrounded by a ragged circumference of houses that may have once been painted but were now encrusted in a uniform layer of soot. Everywhere men and women—Danny's men and women—lounged in the doorways and on the stoops or leaned out of lower windows to speak to others gathered below.

Lamplight filtered into the court through broken-out windows, doing more to darken the shadows than to illuminate her path. In the farthest corner, one building alone bore a sign, its faded, peeling paint so far gone that it might have once said anything. But no one in the Seven Dials needed a sign to know what that beer shop was: Danny's ken, The King's Men. Maggie walked toward it. There was no turning back, now.

The night was clear, unseasonably clear, and Maggie missed the fog that might have concealed her movements. As it was, dozens of eyes fell on her as she crossed—dozens that were seen, and probably even more that were not.

Judies slouched in the doorways of the houses, staring at her with incurious hostility while others tried their wiles on the dirty, battered men who gathered in clumps around the court. A few were pretty but most were not, the kind of worn-out, used-up women who had walked the Haymarket in their youth but were now too old and tired to attract the flush young bucks and stolid bankers of the better whoring districts and too improvident or unlucky to have earned enough to establish themselves as madams of their own brothels.

"Don't you come lookin' for a trick here," one woman snarled from a filthy stoop. "We're full up."

Maggie hunched her shoulders, not pausing as she replied. "I got business wif Danny."

"O-ho! And who might you be, eh?" the woman demanded, showing a row of blackened and missing teeth as she made a grimace of false mirth.

"Maggie of King Street," Maggie said, pitching her voice to carry over the other conversations going on the court. The more people who knew that she'd gone in to see Danny, the better, even if they did belong to him.

The woman's smile disappeared, and other heads turned as pale faces, male and female, appeared in windows around the court. The whispers spread out like ripples in a pond. "Danny's got Maggie o' King Street?" "Maggie King's joining 'im!" "Maggie King's back in the game!"

Maggie ignored them, feeling a grim kind of satisfaction at her notoriety. *Maggie King, the unnaturally talented girl-thief, left one evening with Johnny and a gun, and only Maggie came back. Then, instead of taking over his game, as was her right, she took her friends and left, leaving the territory to the upstart scurf Danny...* Maggie had made Danny—of such things street legends were made.

Maggie reached the entrance to the beer shop and

paused with her hand on the knob. A burst of laughter came through the thick oak door. Too late to turn back now. She steeled herself, turned the knob, and pushed.

It was scarcely brighter inside the pub than in the court. A sullen fire glowed on the hearth, and smoke formed dirty eddies near the ceiling. A couple of men glanced up at her entrance, and a women, who was sitting across the laps of two men, gave her a warning glare. Maggie ignored all three and stepped forward.

A heavy hand closed over her shoulder, and she froze. *Behind the door,* she thought. A man had been standing behind the door.

"Maggie of King Street," a deep voice rumbled softly, slightly slurred with drink.

"Yeah," Maggie said, even though it hadn't been a question.

"Danny's been expecting you."

"I know," Maggie said, her voice calm, clear.

"Come wif me." The hand on her shoulder began to push her forward. She didn't bother to resist. They crossed the common room, earning only a few more dis-interested glances, and the man steered her toward the stairs. At the first step, Maggie braced herself suddenly, digging in her heels, her unexpected resistance making the man behind her stop for a moment.

"I can go up on me own two feet," she said. It was a challenge, but it was a small one. A safe one, or so she gambled. She'd learned long ago that if she acted like she had a choice, sometimes other people would act as if she did, too, which was almost as good as being given one in the first place. One choice could quickly become two, and then three. . . .

For a moment, the hand on her shoulder tightened.

Then, as if thinking better of it, the man grunted and let her go.

Maggie climbed the stairs.

At the first-floor landing, the man took her shoulder again and pushed her into the corridor. He stopped, and before she could react, he ran his hands quickly over her body, skimming over her arms, her back, her buttocks, her legs. He spun her around to face him.

"Oi there, you bloody bastard," she snarled, jerking away and slapping his hand hard. He yanked her forward, ignoring the slap and repeating the procedure with efficient impassiveness on her front.

"Mr. O'Sullivan don't want no surprises," the bruiser said stoically.

"I ain't got no barker nor no skiv under my dress, if that's what you're finkin'," Maggie snapped, jerking away as soon as he loosened his hold. She was glad she had forgotten the gun, now.

The man grunted and nodded to the nearest door. "Mr. O'Sullivan's waiting for you."

Maggie shot him a last look of contempt and stepped forward, her heart beating fast. Her hand closed around the door handle. Once she opened the door, she was Danny's.

Hell. Why was she fooling herself? Opening that door made no difference—she had been Danny's since the instant he had sent the bruisers against Nan. She pushed the door open and stepped inside.

Light. From every surface and from every wall, light washed over her. Maggie blinked in the sudden brilliance, half blinded. Gas jets flared around the perimeter of the room, and a cluster of Argand lamps burned with pale flames on the single table in its center. *Gas laid on?* she thought in disbelief. *In the Holy Land?* Just how much money did Danny have, anyhow? Her watering eyes began to focus on the figure that stood between the glare of light on the table and a pair of heavy-draped windows along the back wall. His single blue eye twinkled as it always did, his sleek blond hair shining with macassar oil and his luxuriant moustache waxed to a vain perfection. Danny.

If she rushed him now . . . she would slam into him, her small weight doing nothing more than rocking him back on his heels and infuriating him—or, worse, amusing him.

She stood her ground.

"Maggie, me dear colleen!" Danny said, opening his arms expansively, as if to embrace her.

"Danny," she said shortly, not moving. "Whatever problems you got, you got them wif me. Leave me friends be."

"Ah, Maggie-mine," he said with a display of regret, dropping his arms to his sides again, "I don't want to be having no problems wi' you."

Maggie stared at him stonily. The broad Irish accent rolled easily off his tongue—too easily, for Maggie had never met a true Irishman who applied blarney and shamrock so liberally to his speech, nor who forgot with such frequency that he was Irish at all. Who was Danny, really? she wondered, not for the first time. And what had he been before he had appeared in London six years ago, with his mysterious eye patch and more mysterious deep purse?

"I just want to be friends wi' you," Danny continued. "I don't understand why you have to make it so difficult now. I asked and I asked for you to come and talk to me, but you just wouldn't listen." Danny cocked his head, projecting an image of helplessness that made Maggie's stomach turn. "What was I supposed to do? I had to send you a message you'd pay a bit o' attention to."

"I'm listening now, Danny," Maggie said. "But if you touch one of me friends again, I'll go deaf—permanently."

Danny, laughing as if she'd just delivered a ripe joke, collapsed into the single chair behind the table. "Maggie, me colleen, you make me remember why I like you so much."

Maggie simply snorted.

"All I wanted is to talk wi' you," Danny said, this time with a plaintive note in his voice. "To be sure. I told you I'd let you know when me debt to you was filled. And it was up two weeks ago."

"I ain't in the life no more," Maggie said flatly. "I ain't kept up me skills."

"I know it. It's a waste now, I tell you, a waste." He shook his head sadly. "But you'll learn again soon enough."

"I'm out of the life for good," Maggie stressed, even as she knew it was hopeless.

Danny leaned forward. "You forget, Maggie. You're from the Holy Land, and the Holy Land is mine. That means that you do be mine until I tell you that you aren't. And I say you're back in the life. I know where you're living down in Chelsea, Maggie. I know what room you sleep in. I know that your friends are staying with that old bawd Bess Shipton, and I know that her house is going to get terrible dangerous for them if you won't be doing what I say."

Maggie stared at him, numbness creeping up from her belly. He had called her bluff. There was nothing she could do. Still, she lifted her chin. "What do you want from me?"

"Now? Nothing." He smiled, and his white teeth gleamed under his waxed mustachios. "You're exactly where I want you. Be a good little student for our good baron. When I want something else from you, I'll send a message you can't miss, to be sure."

"Don't you touch them, Danny," Maggie said, her throat thick.

"Be a good girl now, Maggie," Danny said, smiling, "and I won't be tempted."

He rapped his knuckles against the tabletop once, sharply, and the bruiser opened the door. She had been dismissed. Maggie squeezed past the hulking man, hardly seeing him. The hallway seemed almost pitch black after the glare of the room, but Maggie stumbled through the darkness to the stairs and groped her way down. By the time she reached the pub, her eyes had adjusted enough that she trusted her vision. She crossed the room, pushed open the door to the court, and started to run.

Run, run, run away. Her feet beat a desperate counterpoint to her thoughts. She had to get free. Southampton, Leeds, bloody hell, America or Australia—she had to get out of London and far away, where Danny could never find her, could never touch her. But Nan would never come, and neither would Frankie or Giles, and Danny would kill them for her flight, she knew he would. She was trapped like a fly in a bottle. Her breath sobbed in her lungs, harsh and loud. She ignored it and plunged between the buildings, bursting out onto the lane—

—and was nearly jerked off her feet as a hand closed hard around her upper arm.

Chapter Seven

The rebound slammed her against a hard chest, and she swung wildly at her assailant's nose—the blow too weak to break it, her experience warned, but she could not put her shoulder into it, crushed against him as she was.

"Maggie."

The cultured voice rolled the name into an aristocratic drawl, startling her into pulling the punch. Her hesitation cost her, for he captured her wrist in his free hand. The face looming above her registered—the firm chin, not jutting but well shaped, the hard mouth, the wide forehead and brandy-colored eyes.

"Lord Edgington," she blurted. "Why are you 'ere? You—you can't be 'ere. It's not safe."

His grip did not loosen, and he started to pull her after him—toward his black carriage that waited a mere dozen feet away. How could she have missed it? A chill went through her. She had been blind in her fear, blind and stupid, and in these streets, people often got the chance to be stupid only once.

"If it is dangerous for me, it must be doubly so for you. Get in." His voice was like ice, and Maggie suppressed a shiver. She had tricked him—betrayed him. She had thought he would wash his hands of her after that, and she would get along as she always had, by whatever means necessary, as his protection had proved more scant that she would have dreamed. Never had she thought that he would follow her, not into the Seven Dials. Why had he come? Out of anger, to exact a price for her treachery? He flung open the door to the carriage and shoved her inside. She barely caught her balance in time not to be knocked onto the bench.

"Drive," Charles snapped as he stepped into the coach, controlling his anger with a frigid resolve. Stephens obeyed, and it lurched into motion even as he braced against a strap and snapped the door closed with his free hand. Unprepared, Maggie was jolted off her feet, landing unceremoniously against the squabs.

Charles sat across from her, moving slowly, with deliberation, even as his ire formed a roiling mass in his belly. In the light of the coach lamps that burned outside the windows, Charles watched the girl look around. He already knew there was nothing to see but the carriage and Charles himself.

"Giles," Maggie said.

"I sent him on his way," Charles informed her crisply. "He was quite loyal to you. He held out for a pound and made me promise, upon my word, to not try to go in after you."

"You honored your word to Giles?" Her voice stopped just short of scoffing. Despite the brazenness of her words, she had wedged herself into the farthest corner of the carriage, away from him.

You have reason to fear me after what you did, he thought brutally. But aloud, he said, "Of course not. You came out just as I was planning to go in."

"But why?" Her bewilderment was palpable.

"Because you ran away, damn you," he snapped back. "A man doesn't let a lady—a woman dash into danger alone. Not if he knows about it. He must stop her, or accompany her, or something."

She made a despairing sound, half laugh, half sob. "You are an idiot."

Charles clenched his jaw for a moment before he forced himself to relax enough to reply. "You said that your honor was to protect your—your chavies. Well, this is part of mine." *Or it should be,* he added in the privacy of his own mind. He had been staring at the narrow alley that led to Danny O'Sullivan's court, wondering if he had it in himself to enter, wondering if such an effort was right and proper or if he was just a damned fool about to throw his life away for a beggar and an empty word. Then Maggie had burst out, rendering his internal debate moot but not, unfortunately, ending it. In that moment, he had wanted to shake her, to slap her, to crush her against him, to kiss her. . . . But he had done none of those things, nor even now was he sure which would have been best, if any.

She stared at him for a moment in unblinking incomprehension. "I told you it was too dangerous to come."

"If you hadn't plunged on, I would not have been faced by the possibility of chasing you down alone," Charles returned, keeping his voice flat. "I could have picked up a pair of footmen and sent them with you."

"A pair? How about a few dozen? Then it would have been much better—we'd have had a war instead of a murder. That entire court is full of Danny's men!" She huffed with exasperation and her chin, inevitably, tilted up, the futile stubbornness of the gesture making him want her so much that he ached with it. "I don't have to do everything you say, sir. You do not own me."

"I have bought your time—all your time—for two pounds a week," he reminded her, narrowing his eyes.

At those words, she seemed to collapse in on herself, wrapping her arms around her middle and hugging hard, becoming in appearance what she always was in fact yet worked so hard to hide: small, young, and fragile. "The deal is off. I am leaving England, somehow. I can't stay."

"Because of this Danny," Charles said.

Her eyes flared with some of her old spirit. "Because I suddenly thought, 'Maggie, me girl, I wonder what Australia is like this time o' year!'"

"No," Charles said flatly, making a decision. All his common sense shouted a warning against allying himself with such a woman. But he couldn't give Maggie up to her shadowed past, no matter how sensible it would be. He could not overcome his urge to put himself between her and the world—and if he was going to do that, he'd do it properly.

"What?" Maggie stared at him, disbelief written starkly on her face.

"No," he repeated. "We will go to Scotland Yard—"

She laughed caustically. "The peelers know all about Danny. Do you think they care? They nab pickpockets and independent shoeblacks, not bloody great scurfs who run the half of the city the nobs don't care about!"

"Well, I care now," Charles snapped, stung.

"You are not enough. Sure, you're a bloody important bloke and no doubt, but you're not important enough for the bobbies to die for," Maggie countered.

"You still aren't leaving," Charles insisted. Here, at least, his way was clear; here, there were no questions of foolhardiness, merely expense, and expense was a burden, however heavy, that he was used to. "If we can't go to the police, then we will not go, though I still think that it would be a sound idea to at least make a complaint." He ignored Maggie's incredulous snort. "Whether or not the police can do anything, you are in my employ. If a man is threatening you, then he is threatening me. If I have to post armed footmen at the Chelsea house, I will, but he shall not prevail simply because I refuse to do my duty to shelter someone who should be under my protection."

Maggie's brows drew together for a moment before relaxing in realization. "This is all about your pride, isn't it?" she accused. "I ain't going to die for your pride any more than the bobbies will."

Charles' temper snapped, boiling up his throat to seize control of his tongue. "Just shut up for a minute."

Maggie actually rocked backward slightly at the force of his words. She shrank, coiled with tension, into the corner of the carriage.

"I am trying to do the right thing," he continued, ignoring her reaction. "Don't you think that part of me wants nothing better than to throw you out on your ear, Mme. Rochelle's wardrobe be damned? For once in my life, though, I am trying to do what I ought to—the dutiful thing, the honorable thing. Why do you have to make it so blastedly difficult? And God, even though part of me wants to throw you out, another wants nothing more than to keep you—for reasons that are as dishonorable and selfish as any I've ever had."

Then, with anger and desire and fear blinding his actions, he leaned across the carriage, caught hold of her arm, and yanked her into his lap. His mouth caught hers unprepared, but after an instant, she made a kind of desperate hiccoughing sound and kissed him back as hard as he took her. Her mouth was small, slick, and brutally unyielding, sending a shock of heat lancing straight through him, down into his groin. His fingers were in her hair, tangling in it, locking her head to his as her thighs circled his waist and her body pressed hard against him. The scent of lye was gone, in its place the expensive, flowery soaps Frances had favored, but underneath was still the same carnal smell that was Maggie, and it intoxicated him.

His hands began working jerkily at the buttons down the front of her bodice, almost of their own accord. She braced her hands against his shoulders as he worked.

"I want you," he ground out. "I should protect you because I am a good and honorable man, but I am afraid it is only because I want you for myself, which is insane because I don't even like you, I don't think. How could I? I scarcely even know you. You're a liar and a fighter, a shameless trickster and a woman of astonishing nobility, and I can't fit all of those things into my head at once, much less form any kind of judgment of them. I couldn't get you out of my mind last night, and when you ran, my first thought was that I wouldn't be able to do this again."

The bodice was half open, and he slipped his hand inside her corset. Her skin was hot under his hand, her nipple hardening suddenly against his palm. He rolled it between two fingers, and she cried out, the sound stabbing through him with a carnal joy. He kissed her mouth again, hard and fast as she shuddered against the hand moving across her breasts.

He took her ankle in one hand and followed it up, past the top of her stockings and under her disarrayed skirts. Her skin was smooth and soft, startlingly delicate as he neared the juncture of her thighs; she seemed to be made of bone and fire and sinew and little else.

Her breath came short and fast, the hands on his shoulders tightening to the threshold of pain. His hand encountered a soft nest of curls, and he found her opening, already damp with lust. He slid his other hand down to hold her buttocks firmly against him, and then he plunged a finger in up to the knuckle.

She gasped and rocked against him—she wanted him, wanted him as fully and desperately and insanely as he wanted her.

"Tell me that you will stay," he demanded, exploiting her desire without shame.

"No!" she said, the word torn from her throat.

He pressed a second finger into her. The hot slickness nearly undid him. "Tell me," he rasped.

"No!"

He pushed a third into her. Her hands tightened convulsively, and though she stared at him she did not seem to see him.

"Tell me!"

"No!"

He began moving them inside her, and she rocked with each stroke, making little sobbing sounds of pleasure, but under it, she kept repeating, "No, no, no," in a low and insistent moan.

He wanted her—no, he *needed* her now. He couldn't wait. He pulled free and used his slick hand to jerk open the buttons of his fly and free his swollen member. She would agree—he would make her agree. He was not going to shirk this duty, no matter what muddled reasons he had for accepting it. His erection pressed against her entrance as his hand slid lower still, until it found her second, puckered opening. "Tell me you will stay," he repeated, the words so guttural that they were scarcely recognizable as his own.

"No," she said, her voice half strangled.

He entered her hard, his erection sliding sweetly into her welcoming heat, his other finger pressing in and holding her against the surge of his thrust. She cried out, a startled moan, and he tried to thrust into her again, but he had no leverage with her weight on his lap. He withdrew with a shudder that was echoed in her body, and he twisted her around so that her back was pinned against the squabs while he knelt on the carriage floor in front of her.

"Don't stop!" she pleaded, wrapping her thighs around him, but he couldn't have if he had wanted to. He entered her again, and she arched against the squabs, whimpering even as her hands tugging at his shoulders urged him closer, deeper.

He surged against her, again and again, the heat and need building into a wall of fire that roared in his ears, filling his mind until it almost burst. He felt her climax around him, tightening in a rhythm that drove him over the edge after her, into the heart of the furnace that blasted through him, stealing breath, stealing sense, stealing mind. Then it was over, and she slumped against the cushion under him, gasping, as his own breath rasped fast, filling the carriage with the sound. He slid away from her, straightening his clothes with breathless dignity. She did not move, lying where he left her with her skirts tossed around her hips and her eyes wide in the darkness. He stared down at her spent form.

"You will remain in my Chelsea house." The words were meant to be cool, but they caught hoarsely in his throat.

She shook her head, rocking it against the cushion beneath her, staring fixedly at the ceiling above. "I can't. Danny told me to stay with you."

"I don't understand," Charles said, the temporarily banked fires of his frustration stirring sluggishly to life.

"If he wants me to be there, then it can't be safe," she

said in a tone of deep patience. "He has some sort of plan for me, and it's going to be terrible, so I need to be far away."

Charles frowned. "Why would he want you under my protection? The man is bluffing. He just wants to scare you."

"Well, he's certainly done that." Her voice was quiet, matter-of-fact, and it chilled him in a way no dramatic declaration ever could.

"He is trying to flush you out," he said, making his tone as reasonable and persuasive as he could even though what he really wanted to do was order her to do as he thought best. "Do you really think you'll be safer out there, away from me?" He waved to the carriage window.

Slowly, she shook her head, levering herself into a sitting position. "I don't think I'm safe anywhere."

"If one place is as good as another, then you might as well stay in comfort," Charles pursued. He reached for her automatically, but when he touched her she stiffened a little, and he dropped his hands.

She bit her lip and reached out to rest her hand on his arm in mute apology for her reaction. "I suppose."

"I will send over footmen to keep guard," he repeated, placing his hand over hers. "Stay inside, and you will be safe."

"And the chavies?" She looked at him squarely. "I might be your responsibility, but they're mine."

"You said something about Nan and Sally taking positions as servants at the Chelsea house, didn't you?" Charles asked, warming to the subject as he saw a way to make her agree to his plan.

"But what of Moll and Jo, not to mention Harry, Frankie, and Giles?" Maggie was frowning again.

"Ah . . . my solicitor takes in promising young clerks," Charles said with sudden inspiration. "They study law, stay in a room in his house, and sit at his table. For all Danny would know, your law writer will have simply disappeared, and if Harry is good enough, well, then he shall have a career ahead of himself when this is over."

The expression that dawned on her face came slowly, as if it had little practice being there. It was hope, he realized, so out of place that it was almost unrecognizable. "You would do that?" The words were a kind of holy whisper.

"Why not?" Charles shrugged uncomfortably. "It is no promise, of course—all depends upon the youth. It is a peculiarity of my solicitor that he conducts his business in such a manner, seeking out talent and a pledge of repayment upon success rather than allying himself with fathers who are willing to advance a certain sum in return for an education. He says it gets him more satisfaction and less trouble all around. It is not a system of my invention, and so I deserve no credit for it."

"Yet you will see that Harry gets a trial, something I could never have dreamt of getting for him. Thank you," Maggie said, and for a moment, he thought he saw tears in her eyes before she blinked hard once, and they were gone.

"For little Giles, I'm sure there's a rigorous and obscure boy's school in the country that would take him for his moral and intellectual improvement for a term or two," Charles continued briskly, strangely embarrassed to witness her moment of weakness. It wasn't that he hadn't seen a dozen or more women cry in his time—but none of them had been Maggie, and never had he felt like he was witnessing something so profoundly personal that it was almost indecent. "And for Frankie . . . well, what are Frankie's talents?"

Maggie gave a mangled kind of laugh. "Cheating at cards, mostly."

"I guess he could be a footman," Charles said doubtfully. "Out on one of the estates."

"And Moll and little Jo?" Maggie asked quietly. "They need to stay with Nan. If she were a day cook, she could come home to them, but she will be living in your house . . ."

"Then they must stay, too," Charles said, ignoring a stab of reluctance as he realized that he was inviting a herd of people who might fairly be given the label "undesirables" to share the abode in which he had installed the woman who had become, however unintentionally, his lover.

Maggie pulled away and began to button the front of her bodice slowly, every movement an unconscious titillation. He had to stifle the urge to pull her to him and take her mouth with his again.

"You really mean that, don't you?" she said. "Yet you're still afraid that you aren't honorable."

Charles laughed mirthlessly. "Perhaps I am only doing it to make sure that you will stay and make love with me again."

"I don't believe that," Maggie said stubbornly, shaking her head. "You don't have to send Giles to school to make me stay. All you have to do is keep him safe out of the way somewhere." She paused, and then her tone grew tentative. "Why don't you trust yourself to be good?"

"Because I have known myself for a very long time," Charles said flatly. "No one in society would have even asked that question. The name 'Edgington' would be enough to tell them exactly what I am—what we all have been."

Maggie's fingers paused on the last button at her throat, and her hand fell away. "What is that?" Her voice was soft, as if she feared reproach but was still driven by curiosity.

Charles' mouth twisted in a smile. "Intemperate sybarites. Sensual gluttons. Self-indulgent lechers. You choose your corruption of choice, and at least one of my ancestors will conform to the description."

Maggie shook her head, looking baffled. "But you don't have that kind of reputation with the opera girls. A few of the prima donnas have had brief affaires de coeur, as they call them, with you, but none of them speak badly of you."

Charles snorted. "They have a very simple view of gentlemanly conduct. If they are wooed appropriately and presented with sufficient gifts, they are pleased. They expect no honor, no loyalty, and they harbor no hopes."

"Nor do I," she said, her gaze never wavering from his.

Charles raked his fingers through his hair. "Exactly," he said, his smile wryly bitter. "Do you know how I discovered that my father was unfaithful to my mother? I was six years old, and a groom was leading my fat little pony through Hyde Park when I spotted my father riding in his curricle with a pretty woman at his side. I called to him, and he looked at me with the most curious expression for half a second. I didn't understand it then, but his expression was so strange that I engraved it upon my memory, and when I was older, I recognized what it was—guilt. But it was gone in a heartbeat, and he began laughing and drove right over, taking the greatest delight in introducing me to his special friend, Miss Dorcas Pershing."

"You mean Mrs. Pershing?" Maggie asked, her expression incredulous.

"The one and the same." Charles shrugged. "She was the fourth or fifth occupant of the Chelsea house, and when she fell from his favor, she used his lingering friendliness for her to secure the position of housekeeper, though I only learned that much later."

"Housekeeper to her old lover's new women?" Her disbelief seemed to grow.

Charles settled back against the squabs. "Mrs.—or Miss—Pershing has always been the practical sort. I don't think she ever loved my father, which was safest around him as I think the only being he ever loved was himself." He remembered the long days of that hot summer, the palpable anticipation of seeing the kind and lovely Miss Pershing any time he was brought through Hyde Park. "She bought me ices every time I saw her, you know, and I thought she must be a fairy or an angel. My father gave me toys and little bows and ponies, of course, because the future Lord Edgington should have all those things, but it never occurred to him that I might like ices in the park."

As he spoke, the carriage came to a stop. Charles looked out at the red brick façade of his Chelsea house.

"Well, we are here," Maggie said, her tone suddenly acquiring a strange bright brittleness. "I suppose I will see you later, sometime. Unless . . . unless you plan to come inside?" A hint of hope laced her voice, which sent both desire and a poignant kind of gladness through Charles.

He looked at the crisp black door at the top of the stoop. Gaslight shone through the transom window above and peeped between close-drawn curtains, making the façade look both dreadfully conventional and cozily snug. He allowed himself to imagine for a moment that he would offer her his arm, lead her up to that door and inside, up to the garishly appointed bedroom . . . But his place was not that of a man in a Chelsea terrace house. He had his own home waiting for him, with his own life and his own duties that had been delayed by their unplanned excursion that evening.

Charles shook his head. "No. Supper will be waiting for me at home, and I must make arrangements for some footmen to take up guard duty here." He reached over and swung open the door. "I will wish you a good night here."

Maggie looked at him for a long moment, and then she nodded and stepped down. "Until tomorrow?" she asked, and this time there was no desire hidden in her voice.

"Certainly tomorrow," Charles assured her.

She cast him a smile—fast, enigmatic—before shutting the carriage door and mounting the stairs to the entrance. Charles waited until the door opened, revealing Mrs. Pershing's trim figure silhouetted by the butter-yellow light that puddled on the pavement, and then he slid the speakeasy door aside to give Stephens the command to return to Edgington Manor and the cold rooms that awaited him there.

Chapter Eight

When Charles arrived at Edgington Manor, the house was a ghostly crescent under the light of the gibbous moon. A light shone feebly in his sister's window, but otherwise, the entire estate was cloaked in darkness. He sighed, recognizing his mother's mute rebuke for his treatment of her the night before. He could almost hear her voice, declaring that she wouldn't hold supper for him. In fact, she wouldn't show him any consideration whatsoever, which is exactly the treatment such a disrespectful son deserved.

Indeed, when he opened the front door, he was greeted by a solitary parlor maid, sitting patiently upon a bench in the shape of a gilded sphinx with two candles on the table beside her.

He thanked her coolly when she rose, but he had no hat, coat, and gloves to hand her, as he had forgotten them at the house in Chelsea in his precipitous exit. He left her standing in her halo of golden light with a puzzled expression on her face as he mounted the stairs that curved ponderously upward into the highest reaches of the house, holding the second candle before him.

With all the gaslights blazing, the manor house

seemed a palace made of congealed winter, and in his boyhood imagination, he had half convinced himself—and wholly convinced his sister—that it had once belonged to the fairytale Snow Queen, lovely and terrible. But with only a flickering candle flame to illuminate his steps, its pitiless splendor was swallowed in gloom. The images of his ancestors sneered at him from the walls as he walked down the East Gallery, and he felt a crowding solitude pressing down on him, as if he were trapped in a labyrinthine mausoleum.

He turned the corner, and he was greeted by a faintly ruddy light spilling out from his sister's doorway, which dispelled every sense of the grotesque in its utter familiarity. He approached the implied invitation suspiciously, remembering their conversation—or was it a spat?—the night before. But unless he wished to retreat to the first floor and walk its entire length to the library and his private stairs, there was nothing for it but to pass by, and his pride would not allow so ignoble a retreat.

He stepped forward, and as soon as he drew even with the doorway, Millie's expected greeting rang out.

"There you are! I have been waiting for you for *hours.*"

Stifling a sigh, Charles pasted a politely inquiring look on his face and stepped into her sitting room.

"Oh, Charles, I should be so cross with you," Millie continued. "Come, sit down! You always make me nervous when you loom so."

Charles lowered himself onto an unlikely settee, a froth of wood and brocade that looked scarcely able to stand its own weight. A covered dish sat upon the table before it, and when he lifted the cover, he discovered cold beef with a golden pudding nestled beside it. One of his childhood favorites; his sister clearly wanted to put him in a good mood, which was not a good sign. But food should never be wasted, and so he began to eat even as she continued her chatter.

"What did you tell Mamma last night?" she asked. "Whatever it was, it caused her to take to her room and declare that her heart was in too delicate a condition to bear the burden of society today, and so I was forced to miss tea with Lady Mary and Lady Elizabeth."

"You didn't go on your own?" Charles asked, in hopes of deflecting whatever aim it was she had in mind rather than out of any curiosity.

"How could I?" Millie demanded. "It was hardly a private or feminine affair. Fully fifty people were there— well, forty-eight without me or Mamma—and half of them gentlemen. If you had not sent cousin Beryl away—"

"She would still be sucking our blood as professional poor relations always do," Charles finished.

Millie opened her mouth to retort and then shut it again with a toss of her hair. Had his sister always been so affected? Charles wondered. Listening to her was like being subjected to the twitter of a caged finch, full of a great deal of pretty notes intended to draw attention to itself and very little else. Yet his sister's manner of speech was not so different from that of most of the women of his acquaintance. The sophisticated ones were arch and their words barbed, and the ingénues simply burbled, but there was a fundamental similarity to them, the former growing out of the latter with enough time and disappointments. How utterly foreign it was to Maggie's way of expressing herself, the difference between a fife's trilling and a rifle blast.

"That is not what I wish to discuss," Millie was saying. "I was telling you that I should be furious with you about upsetting Mother so, except that she had time, between her smelling salts and doses of laudanum, to begin arranging this year's house party."

Damn. Charles sat up a little straighter. The annual house party was to be Maggie's performance. His mother usually didn't begin to arrange it until March, and he had hoped to have some measure of the girl's progress by that time so that he could influence the date of the event accordingly. "When is it to be?" he asked, making his voice light.

"She thinks she wishes to spend the late spring in the country this year," Millie said carelessly, "so she intends to hold it as early as seems practicable."

"When, Millie?" Charles repeated.

She made a face at him. "Six weeks." Was that enough time? Charles wondered. It would have to be. "But that isn't what I am so excited about! She has come up with a truly daring and brilliant theme for this year. Do you want to hear it?"

Probably not, Charles thought even as he made himself say, "Of course."

"An Eclogue!" she crowed, her eyes shining. "A mythological pastoral! Can you imagine? The men shall all be satyrs and shepherds—and gods dressed up as shepherds—and the ladies shall all be nymphs and shepherdesses."

"And goddesses dressed up as shepherdesses?" Charles supplied.

"As virgin huntresses," Millie corrected primly. "And she had the most wonderful idea of whom each of us should play!"

"Let me guess," Charles said. "You are to be Diana to my Apollo."

Millie pouted. "Oh, I made it too easy, with the hint

about huntresses. But isn't it just perfect? You will be the sun, all gold and handsome, next to the pale, cold beauty of your sister the moon! Of course, Mamma will be our mother Leto."

"And our dearly departed father then is Jove. How subtle of Mother." Except that their dear father was not unfaithful with their mother but unfaithful to her . . . He'd not stand for such a plan. Games and themes were all well and good, but he would be no Apollo.

Millie continue through a list of several dozen possible activities for the party, from competitions inspired by the Olympics—which were Greek, not Roman, Charles reminded her, to her sarcastic dismissal—to role-playing Apollo's pursuits of various nymphs, a suggestion that seemed to have more than a slight bite of revenge in it for Charles' unenthusiastic response to her other ideas.

She had not forgotten their wager, dropping several hints and making too-astute predictions about the possibilities presented by the house party for the introduction of an unsuitable woman. Charles allowed these to pass without comment, steering her back to the topic of the party when she became too insistent.

At length, Charles rose and retreated to his own suite, where the gaslight bathed the white walls in a light that flattened shadow. Feeling more battered than he had any reason to feel after the events of the day, he sought the comfort of his bed immediately. But when sleep came, it did not bring oblivion, for he was haunted by dreams in which he was a lusty satyr pursuing a series of nymphs who looked remarkably like Maggie King. Whenever he thought he had caught one, she would slip through his fingers, transforming into a bird or a flower, or turning into a raving Maenad and trying to eat him alive, or, when he reached out to touch her, simply fading away until he was left with nothing but air.

The next day brought even more confusion for Maggie than the previous one had, for her lessons began almost as soon as she awoke and continued without remittance until seven o' clock at night. She was allowed no time for herself even though Sally and Nan arrived with Moll and Jo around midday to be noisily integrated into the running of the house. Maggie was so distracted by a three-way conversation among Mrs. Pershing, Sally, and Moll in the front hall that the unflappable Miss West actually frowned and rose to shut the parlor door, informing Maggie that her time was being wasted unless Maggie applied herself more conscientiously to her lessons.

And Maggie did apply herself. Forms and formalities, intricacies of grammar and subtleties of pronunciation, and the unrelentingly rapid veneer of knowledge from the stack of books that Maggie was sent plowing through— all of it filled Maggie's mind until she felt that it would burst.

Mme. Rochelle interrupted briefly for another fitting, and that was a different kind of torture. Maggie watched in incredulous amazement as a dizzying array of fabrics were draped over her thin body, pinned here and stitched there, and then snatched away again. Mrs. Ladd's singing lessons were no better than the rest, for Maggie discovered that she had been doing absolutely everything wrong and had to relearn each element of singing through a separate and painful process.

Miss West left at her appointed time, and yet there was no sign of Lord Edgington. After waiting for half an hour with her books spread in front of her, Maggie took another bath—she'd had one the night before, much to Mrs.

Pershing's bemusement, for that good lady couldn't seem to decide whether Maggie was displaying an admirable concern for hygiene or a reckless disregard for her health.

Maggie wrapped herself in a dressing gown that Mme. Rochelle had brought that day, an enveloping garment in a pale blue that the dressmaker had declared sweetly innocent without being cloying. Maggie didn't understand the differences between cloyingness and innocence and didn't care, for it was deliciously soft with only her new cotton nightdress between it and her skin. She had no desire to redress in the layers that Miss West had taught constituted respectable dishabille, and so she curled up in the center of the bed with only those two scanty layers and spread her assigned reading in front of her. She concentrated upon it, or at least she put the full force of her will into making herself concentrate upon it, for little, unwatched corners of her mind were constantly trying to skitter away, to listen for a newly familiar step in the corridor, for a particular baritone voice . . .

She jumped when the knock finally came. Charles!

"It's me," said Sally's voice.

Maggie suppressed her surge of disappointment. Perhaps he had forgotten. Perhaps he had never intended to come. "Come in."

The door opened, and Sally stepped through, blinking uncertainly. She looked small and plain in the blowsy bedroom, her green calico dress painfully faded and her pale red-gold hair scraped away from her scarred face into an unflattering bun. Maggie had never realized how thin and insignificant her best friend really was—Sally had always filled up their tiny flat just as they all had, but here, in a room that Maggie knew was merely average size, she seemed dwarfed.

"Mrs. Pershing's sending us out for clothes tomorrow,"

Sally said. "Nan and Moll are gonna get maids' uniforms, and I'm to get a dress of black silk moiré." She seemed to savor the words as her dark blue eyes went wide in her pale face. "Silk, Maggie. Can you fink on it?"

Maggie hugged her knees to her chest. "I know. I'm getting silk and lace and stuff I don't even know the names of."

Sally sighed, sitting on the edge of the bed. "That must be glorious."

"Yes," Maggie said, though she had been too overwhelmed by the chaos of the past two days and her terror of Danny to think about the dresses that were being made for her somewhere on Bond Street.

"Your Lord Edgington sent two footmen to collect us. It took both of them to drag Giles into the carriage when 'e found out 'e was being sent to some school, and they 'ad to 'old 'im down to keep 'im from jumping out even arfter it started moving," Sally continued, smiling now. "'E was howling fit to wake the dead. 'E made Jo cry, and so both of them were yelling and screaming, and people on the streets were staring at the carriage like they was finking that someone was being murdered."

Maggie chuckled. "I hope he'll forgive me."

"*I* 'ope they lock the doors at night at that school so's 'e can't run away," Sally countered. "We picked 'Arry up, too. 'E and Frankie were at the flat on Church Lane."

Maggie did not fail to note the omission. "But you didn't pick up Frankie?"

Sally sighed. "No. 'E wouldn't 'ear of coming. Said 'e don't need nothing from . . . from your toff."

Maggie suspected that his actual words were much more vulgar than that. She bit her lip and nodded. "I didn't think he'd come. But I'd still hoped . . ."

"I know," Sally said. "But 'Arry, now. 'Arry listened

real serious-like to what the footman 'ad to say about that solicitor cove, and then he smiled."

Maggie nodded, her heart contracting slightly. Harry had been a part of their strange family for two and a half years, and in that time, she could count on one hand the number of times the boy had smiled. Maggie was, what, seventeen? No, she couldn't be so young. Maybe nineteen. Harry had just turned seventeen last Christmas, and yet many times, he seemed to her almost like an old man. "That's good," she said, the words hurting her. It *was* good that he was happy, very good, and yet it was a happiness she'd never been able to give him but that the baron could grant with a carelessly written letter. It wasn't fair, part of her cried out. Her sweat and blood, the work of her life, and none of it could compare to what Lord Edgington could do with a thought and a wave. *I am sorry, Harry, that I wasn't enough,* she sent silently. Never good enough, never strong enough, never powerful enough . . .

Sally looked at Maggie askance. "You're already talking like a toff, you know."

Maggie shrugged uncomfortably. "I have to practice or I'll slip up when I shouldn't. I'm not any different than I was."

"You were always differ'nt," Sally said. "But us chavies don't mind. It's good that you're learning to be like a lady."

Maggie looked at her doubtfully. "You really think so?"

"Of course," Sally said stoutly.

"Today, I had the feeling that I was losing myself," Maggie said broodingly. "I know I'm not a lady, but I'm not sure what I am."

"You're me old mate," Sally said simply. "If acting like

a lady gets you summat in this world, your chavies will
be the last to grudge it to you. Come on. Mrs. Pershing
says I'm to brush your 'air and get you ready for bed."

Maggie laughed. "You don't need to act like that when
no one's here, Sally. We've always done for ourselves."

"If I'm to be paid for brushing your hair, bringing you
wash water, and shining your shoes, then I'm going to do
it," Sally said, her expression setting in a way that Maggie
well recognized. "Now, come on."

Maggie rose reluctantly and led the way into the dressing room, where she sat obediently at the table to let Sally
pull the pins from her hair. The heavy locks fell loose,
tumbling almost to the floor. Maggie looked at Sally in
the mirror.

"I guess it's good that I never went to the wig maker
like I talked about," she said. "I'd make a foolish lady
with a cropped head."

"It would be a right shame to cut it." Sally picked up
the brush and began to work, starting at the ends, her eyes
fixed studiously on her work. "So. You've bedded the
nob, 'ave you?"

"Sally," Maggie warned.

Sally just sighed. "I thought you would, the first day,
when 'e come to the flat. 'E gave you this look oncest or
twice, and you probably didn't know it and 'e didn't
know it, but the way you looked back . . . it sent a shiver
through me, it did. Then when you come to Bess' place,
'e looked like 'e thought you was 'is own woman."

"I don't want to talk about it," Maggie muttered. Not
with Sally, who wouldn't understand her gamble, her
hunger—for the baron but also for something more than
her narrow, precarious little life.

"I'm not going to try to scold you, Maggie," Sally said

with a note of resignation in her voice. "I just want you to be 'appy. Is 'e making you 'appy?"

Happy. The word rolled like a foreign thing through Maggie's mind. Did she feel happy with the baron? She felt desire, yes, and fear and ambition and lust and . . . something else, a strange kind of recognition as if she could see inside him a little and find something that she expected to be there. That realization was itself alarming, for how could Lord Edgington be anything except wholly unknown to a girl like her? How could he be anything but an unfathomable, unobtainable mystery? And yet the sense remained. That was not happiness, surely not, but there was something in it that seemed to be somehow related.

"Something like that," Maggie finally answered.

Sally stopped brushing, and her eyes flickered upward for a moment. "Don't let 'im 'urt you," she said. "Whatever you do, don't let 'im 'urt you."

I don't know how I could stop him, Maggie thought helplessly, but aloud she said, "I won't."

A knock came at the outer door, cutting off whatever response Sally might have made.

"I think I'm supposed to answer it," Sally said with a lopsided, self-conscious smile. She set down the brush and entered the other room. Maggie followed, her heart speeding up despite her half certainty that it was Nan or Moll or Mrs. Pershing. She watched from the other end of the room as Sally began to open the door—and bit her lip hard at the sight of the man standing there.

It's him, it's him, it's him! her senses sang even as she suppressed her reaction as fiercely as she could. He looked painfully perfect in a dark evening suit, flawless and unreal.

"Pardon me for bothering you, Miss King," the baron

said with rigid politeness, taking in her appearance swiftly. "Mrs. Pershing implied that you were studying. I had not realized that you had retired."

"Do you often come to women's bedrooms when they are studying, then?" Maggie asked automatically. Then, in the same breath, she added, "Sally, will you excuse us, please?"

With a small nod, Sally walked out, shutting the door behind her.

Lord Edgington's expression was a mixture of amusement and hunger. "I don't seem to know how to be around you, Maggie. I have never met a woman like you before."

I have met dozens of toffs like you, Maggie thought but didn't say because she knew it wasn't true. She'd never before met a nob who doubted his own honor for a moment, for one. And she had never met one who had even seemed to notice her. "Is that why you call me Maggie, Margaret, and Miss King, all three?"

He shrugged. "Miss King is what one calls a lady, Margaret is an employee, and Maggie is . . . well, I am not sure what Maggie is, exactly. You would have to tell me."

The question struck her. "I don't know, sir. Maggie is just . . . Maggie. Should I know?"

"If you should, I should probably know what I am, too, and I don't think I want that kind of enlightenment," Lord Edgington said, and Maggie couldn't tell whether he was trying to make a joke or was deadly earnest.

"You know more of me than I do of you," Maggie said, not knowing what else to say.

"Oh?" The baron's eyebrows went up.

She shrugged. "To you, I am Maggie, Margaret, and Miss King. To me, you are only Lord Edgington. I know of no other name that you have."

"My Christian name is Charles," he said. "Charles Edward Xavier Crossham, Lord Edgington."

"Charles," Maggie said, trying it out. "I like that."

"And I like Maggie," he returned, crossing the room toward her. "It sounds so straightforward. Honest."

At that, Maggie snorted. "Then maybe I do know you better than you know me."

The baron frowned stiffly, stopping an arm's length away from her. "Have you lied to me, then?"

"Not to you, not very much, at least. But I have lied." And cheated, and stolen, and murdered . . .

"Who hasn't?" He reached out, and Maggie caught her breath, but he only took a handful of her black hair and ran his fingers gently across it before dropping it again. "Your hair is astonishing. I never imagined it would be so long."

Blinking at the non sequitur, Maggie looked down at where her hair ended at her knees. "I was just telling Sally that it's a good thing I never sold it to the wig maker, as I'd considered." She pulled it over one shoulder and began to braid it efficiently, automatically. The baron caught her hand.

"I like it down," he said.

"It tangles, sir," she replied, but she didn't make an attempt to finish plaiting it. *What are you doing here?* part of her wanted to ask. *Why do you come? What are you looking for?* But the rest of her did not want to know, so she kept her mouth shut and smiled at him in a way she hoped was winsome. She shifted her hand so that it was no longer under but holding his. "I am glad you are here. I was beginning to think that you wouldn't come tonight."

"How could I stay away?" The reply was facetiously light, but the light in his brandy-colored eyes made her heart beat faster.

Wordlessly, she guided his hand, wrapped it around her waist, and stepped against him, tilting her head back in invitation. But instead of kissing her, he cupped her cheek in his free hand.

He said, "You trouble me, Maggie. You give yourself so easily."

Maggie pulled back slightly. "I've only ever given myself to you. You know that."

His lip twitched—his version of a lopsided smile. "Which is no small part of the reason why I fear that I am taking advantage of you."

"Perhaps you are being the one taken advantage of," Maggie said with no small amount of asperity. "Perhaps I am using my body to try to tie you to me, to squeeze more money out of you. I have no regrets"—*yet*—"so why should you?"

That answer clearly took him by surprise, though his only obvious reaction was the sharpening of his gaze as he went very still for a moment. "That is all this is to you? A chance for a little more money?" His voice was calm and low, and Maggie could read nothing in it.

Was it all? She wanted to be able to tell herself, brutally, that it was, and yet something in her cried out against it. "This is all it can be for someone like me," she said instead. "It is all it should be. If I should make it more, then I would be fooling myself, letting myself believe in a dream."

"And you never dream, do you, Maggie?" he asked softly.

"Do you?" she returned. "You can't believe in your own honor—do you dare to dream? The problem with dreams is that some day everyone must wake up. It's better not to sleep."

He let her go with a sigh and made a circuit of the

room, stalking slowly, like a baffled lion. He stopped in front of one of the tables that was crowded with porcelain gewgaws and picked up a china shepherdess, looking at it reflectively for such a long time that Maggie began to think that he wasn't going to say anything at all.

Finally, he began to speak, abstractedly, almost more to himself than to her. "Until I came here two nights ago, the last time I had been in this room was seven years before. My mother had just found out about the existence of this house—that my father had bought it to keep his mistress in only six weeks after their wedding. I was twenty years old and had never seen my mother weep until that moment." His expression turned ironic. "I don't think I'd ever seen her care enough about a thing to cry about it. So I stormed to Chelsea in a rage, ready to confront my father, harboring the mad idea of calling him out or striking him down or . . . something. When I arrived, he wasn't here. Only Frances was, his most recent mistress, newly moved into the house. She was beautiful, one of those rare women whose appearance is so astonishing that men will commit the grossest of errors and count them virtues if they gain her smile by it. She greeted me kindly, with bewildering generosity and even sympathy after she had extracted what I came to her for. She was vulgar, of course, and her manner was affected rather than genteel, but when she smiled, a man felt like a king. She lured me to her bedroom on a pretense, and then, quite dispassionately, she set about seducing me."

"Did it work?" Maggie asked the natural question, hoping to coax out the point of the story.

Charles shook his head, his lip curling slightly. "I may have had few scruples—I was more angry at my father for upsetting my mother than I was at any infidelity—but even I balked at that. Still, for a moment, half a moment,

I kissed her back, and I imagined a revenge upon my father of a very different kind. That madness passed quickly, and I all but bolted from the house that made my mother weep. But Frances succeeded, in her way, for after that, I was either too much of a coward or too little of a hypocrite to bring the subject up with my father."

"Why are you telling me this now? Why tell me at all?" Maggie asked, frowning at him. "You haven't got no reason for it that I can fathom."

The baron set the figurine down with an impatient motion. "It is because these rooms remind me of her. I have thought many times about why she kissed me, why she wanted me to—to *rut* with her, is the only proper word, and I finally decided that her body was the only thing she knew how to use to get on in this world. When a young man came along and threatened to take away everything she had worked for, she did not oppose him with a strength she did not possess but gave in so completely that she made it impossible for him to fight her. You aren't Frances, and yet when you speak of using your body, here in this room, and when you give so easily . . ." He trailed off.

Maggie made a face, folding her arms across her chest. "You're right. I'm no Frances. I'm not beautiful, and no man has ever given anything to make me smile. I'm not a whore—not yet, anyway—and I don't want to make no woman cry, even if she is a rich, spoiled nob. But that doesn't mean that I'm stupid enough to pretend that you've come here because you can't live without my love and are going to turn me into a princess and carry me away to a castle in the clouds. I have to keep my wits about me and look out for myself and my chavies because no one else will."

"Do you not want me, then?" the baron demanded, his face like ice.

Maggie sighed, feeling old. "You know the answer to that. I want you much more than is good for me. But I have to remember what is real." She walked over to him and placed a hand on his chest. "This is real." She tiptoed so that she could place a kiss against the bare skin of his neck, the skin hot and salty under her lips. "So is that. You, me, this night. I can't afford to believe in anything else."

He looked at her for so long that she began to fear that he would turn away. When he spoke, he said, "Fair enough." He laughed, a short, bitter sound. "I only wish I had your certainty." Before she could ask what he meant by that, he kissed her, and then there was no need to say anything else for a very long time.

Chapter Nine

A day passed, and another, the future swirling into the past like an unstoppered drain that had long lain stagnant. Charles did not know what to make of the sudden rush, for while the weeks passed like a breath, the hours from waking until sundown pressed heavy and pallid upon him, the attenuated light that filled his marble rooms tasting worn, as if it had been reused from some more energetic age and all that was left was memory. The ledgers, legislation, and parliamentary meetings that filled his days were all too familiar, and his family, also, seemed caught in a kind of endlessly repeating dance. His mother went through her usual cycles of rapprochement and rebuke while Millie teased him about his extended absences—which she had eventually assigned to an amorous cause, with disconcerting accuracy—and badgered him about his stinginess with arrangements for the house party.

Then the sun would slip wearily below the horizon, and Charles would follow it into London as the mists rose from the Thames and swirled as smoke-thick fog through the streets of Chelsea—to one particular house where the light was yellow and the rooms were small and bourgeoisie but warm. The house where Maggie would be eat-

ing her dinner with Miss West as she labored over her
newest lessons with a combination of striking ignorance
and ferocious intelligence.

He had kept her from her books for the first three
nights, but Maggie had soon asked impatiently whether it
was more important to him that she spend time with him
or that she accomplish the task he had set before her.
Ignoring her provoking stance, Charles had to admit that
she had a point. And so, reluctantly, he left her to her
books until she finished the assignments Miss West had
set before her that day, keeping himself occupied with the
daily report from Miss West and the journals, papers, and
letters that seemed to fill his life. Then he would have her
show him what she had learned that day, reviewing her
progress as she kept her narrowed eyes fixed to his midsection. Then the distance that was between them—the
distance that he worked to cultivate and maintain—would
disappear in their embraces.

Charles had half suspected that his strange fascination
with the gutter-bred girl would evaporate as soon as her
new wardrobe arrived and she had been transformed, su-
perficially, at least, into an echo of every girl that had
been thrust into his path at every ball he had ever at-
tended. And yet it had quite the opposite effect, for even
as her speech became more refined in accent and diction,
and even as she was enwrapped in book muslin, lace
berthas, crinolines, and neat kid boots, the unconvention-
ality of her mind was only thrown into sharper relief. Part
of him wondered if she could possibly ever be taken for
a lady, not because she was too coarse but because she
had an edge, a certainty and strength and definitiveness
that he had never seen emerge from the protected parlors
of the gently bred. And yet who would identify her origins, now that they were increasingly clothed in the

proper appearances and mannerisms, and who could guess where her strength had its source?

After the first week, Miss West began to take Maggie on public outings, Maggie playing the role of a chaperoned orphan of some means come to live with her bachelor great-uncle. Maggie laughingly told him of Hyde Park encounters with audacious young men who attempted to leverage chivalry into an informal introduction, and he heard in her voice the awe and gratification of a woman who was discovering that she was both fascinating and respected. He recognized the young men's attempts for what they were—not the behavior of men toward a possible illicit liaison but the actions of hopeful if not entirely proper would-be swains toward a young woman of their own circle. He could not help but feel a surge of jealousy that they excited her blushes, mixed with a sullen self-directed anger that he had not treated her with as much circumspection as the most daring of the gentlemen wastrels.

Some days when he came, her pleasure upon seeing him was dimmed by a haunted expression in her eyes, and Charles quickly learned it meant that some urchin or sturdy beggar had stopped her during her daily outing to present Danny's continuing pleasure at her progress. It infuriated Charles to see it and it frightened him for her, a strange emotion that he was not accustomed to experiencing. But one afternoon spent in Scotland Yard convinced him of the futility of pursuing official channels, for the inspector bowed and scraped and smiled, but all his assurances rang hollow and meaningless. As he had no means by which to box with a shadow on his own, there was nothing that he could do but offer her words of reassurance that she did not believe and remind her of how happy her friend Harry was and how safe—though unrelentingly rebellious until Charles promised him pocket-money of four shillings a week—the young boy Giles was. She seemed to labor under a growing sense of dread, and despite the logic that told him that no criminal would attempt to do anything to a woman protected by Lord Edgington, Charles could not manage to dismiss her fears from his mind. Even if she was safe for now, what would happen when their time together was over? What would the mysterious and villainous Danny O'Sullivan do to her then?

Even now, not all her friends were provided for. Frankie, the lanky redheaded youth who had threatened Charles at Maggie's flat, refused to be drawn into any plan for his future, steadfastly sticking to the streets, though he visited Maggie at least once a week to bring her news. Charles did not trust the boy, did not trust the fire in his eyes when he looked at Maggie, however oblivious she was to it, nor the raw hatred whenever he looked at Charles.

Charles had encountered the youth alone in the front hall very late one night, the boy leaving just as he arrived. The youth had surveyed him boldly, a sneer on his dirt-smudged face.

"God knows why, but me Maggie likes you," Frankie said abruptly. "An' if you 'urt her, I'll tear your lights out an' feed them to the dogs while you bleed from your belly, eh!"

Charles looked at him coldly, secretly moved at the loyalties the small young woman inspired. "If you are worried about someone hurting her, I think you had better look to Danny O'Sullivan than to me."

Frankie's eyes had narrowed. "And 'oo says I ain't?" With that, he had slid out into the night and dissolved into the lean shadows.

A week passed, then two, then three. Some nights, it seemed to Charles that Maggie had been fashioned out of the matter that was left over when his own soul was made—others, he felt that he would never truly understand her or her ferocious protectiveness for the strange, troubled family she had gathered about herself. Most often, though, she seemed wholly herself, compelling but inscrutable, provoking and fascinating, a powerful will encased in a body so delicate that it seemed on the verge of breaking with the task of encasing all that she was. He did not know why he went to her every night he could, and he understood still less why she came to him despite her blunt explanations that really explained nothing of what happened between them once they were alone. She was color and fire and anger and hope to him, and he did not dare question it for fear that it would disappear one morning like fairy gold.

Yet in a few more weeks, she would be gone. And then what was he going to do?

The third Thursday in the Chelsea house brought a terse note in what Maggie had come to recognize as the baron's hand:

> *Tonight I have other engagements.*
> *Apologies,*
>   *Edgington.*

Maggie sighed, both in disappointment and relief. She looked forward to his daily visits with a frightening intensity, and they always filled her with a burning joy but left her feeling hollowed out when he had gone, as if he had taken some critical part of her with him, folded up in his pocket. Then she had only a few hours to snatch sleep from the night before dawn brought another round of lessons and outings and the relentless rules that seemed to be pressing her brain into a new, foreign shape.

But at least once a week, a message like this came, telling her that Edgington could not come, the reminder of another life and another duty that Maggie was not a part of and did not comprehend. She had always assumed that nobs, being nobs, could do as they pleased, but it appeared that they had the freedom only to do as it pleased other nobs, which seemed a poor kind of freedom to come with so much wealth. She had the sense from Edgington, though never expressed, that high society was a kind of grandiose Punch and Judy show that unceasingly repeated an act that had ossified generations ago, the individual title bearers mattering no more than the identity of the hand inside a puppet.

Miss West had just left when Mrs. Pershing brought the note, and Moll was stacking the china onto a dangerously tottering pile upon her silver tray. Maggie looked at the curtains that hid the dark street from view—that hid, too, the sight of the crossing sweep upon his corner. Damn Danny. Damn Danny and his bullying, his schemes, his lies.

Maggie felt restless, trapped inside a house that had seemed so big only a few weeks before. But any prison, however large, was still a prison. She had to get out, to go somewhere that she knew, somewhere that she understood. Not to Church Lane—though Frankie was keeping up the rent there somehow, it would be the last place that would be safe for her in London tonight. But, perhaps, to a friend's flat . . . .

Maggie had not spoken to Perle Blanc since she had been installed as Edgington's . . . lover, or student, or whatever, and the few carefully worded letters with equally carefully worded replies led her to believe that the opera singer had secrets to impart to Maggie, if only she dared. Perhaps now was the time to see her and find out what those secrets were.

Maggie stood with decision, heading upstairs to her bedroom, where she changed quickly into her old petticoats and brown calico dress. She thought for a moment about stripping off her pantaloons: no street girl wore such an innovation. But she had become used to them these past few weeks, and they would be invisible beneath her skirts.

Her old clothes hung awkwardly on her now that she wore a corset of a more fashionable shape, so she loosened the laces as well as she could alone. She didn't want to ring for Sally—didn't want Sally to know of her venture until she was gone, for Maggie knew her friend would only protest and Maggie wouldn't give in, leaving Sally more angry and upset than if she had sneaked out in the first place.

Maggie felt under the mattress for the revolver, and her palm encountered the cold metal of its cylinder. She closed her fingers around it and pulled it out, fishing with her free hand for the bullets Frankie had brought her. She loaded the gun awkwardly, then slid it into her ample pocket through the hidden slit in her skirt. It lay heavily, reassuringly against her thigh.

Despite the pistol's weight, Maggie felt unaccountably light and free as she hurried back down the stairs without her encumbering crinoline swinging around her ankles. She passed the first floor without incident, but Mrs. Pershing was in the front hall when she arrived, pausing for a moment's conversation with one of the footmen Edgington had placed there on twenty-four-hour watch.

The housekeeper looked up at her entrance and raised her eyebrows. "Going out, miss?"

"Yes," Maggie said, not offering an explanation.

To her credit, the housekeeper merely tightened her lips rather than attempting to argue. Something of Nan's attack had reached her ears, and the concern which seemed to be an intrinsic part of her personality had been transformed into an unnatural vigilance. "Harwell and Thomas are on duty right now. They can go with you."

"No," Maggie said flatly. "I will—shall—be safer alone."

Mrs. Pershing's expression grew tighter, but she merely nodded curtly. "Be careful, Miss King."

"I will," Maggie said. She slid into the morning room, where she lurked in the shadows of the bow window, peering out through the crack in the curtains without touching them. Sure enough, there was the crossing sweep. The neighborhood was now as busy as it ever got, the street peppered with hackneys and the occasional omnibus, and the pavement dotted with gentleman-pedestrians in the plain, dark afternoon suits that were almost a uniform, dodged by hurrying maids sent on some suppertime errand for their mistresses. One of the men paused at the corner and spoke to the sweep . . . and, yes, after a brief exchange, the sweep started out in front of the man, pushing aside the street filth with his wide broom so that the man could walk unbesmirched behind him.

Quickly, Maggie slid through the front hall and out the door, hurrying down the stoop steps and onto the pavement before the sweep was even halfway across the street. By the time he'd taken the penny from the gentleman and turned his idle gaze back to Lord Edgington's house, Maggie was already three houses up, and the boy did not spare her a second look, just another plain maid among so many.

It was a long walk to St. James's Square, where Perle Blanc had her flat. It was full dark by the time Maggie arrived, and a foul black fog had settled damply over the city, concealing movement and muffling sound so that she almost stumbled into a bobby before his bull's-eye lantern swung her direction, the vague glow warning her of his approach just in time for her to sink unseen into a doorway.

The plate-glass doors of Perle's building gleamed a welcome, and Maggie stepped inside with a nod to the doorkeeper. The little reception room shone in scarlet and brass, ferns dangling in the corners while more delicate plants lurked under moisture-fogged Ward cases in the velvet-smothered windows.

"Right noxious night to be hout," the doorkeeper noted with his usual joviality.

"Yes," Maggie agreed. "The gas jets are almost burning green with it, eh, Ned?"

Ned chuckled appreciatively. "That they are, miss, that they are."

"Does Miss Blanc have visitors tonight?"

"No, not tonight. I hexpect you'll be the first." Ned beamed.

Maggie nodded good night, crossing the room to climb the mahogany staircase that rose up through the center of the building. Her footsteps were silent on the deep Oriental carpet, the stair rail under her hand warm with lustrous wax. There were four flats per floor here, and Perle's was on the fourth and highest; she declared she could not abide the sounds of footsteps above her.

Maggie knocked, and the maid who answered showed her swiftly through the front hall to the richly appointed parlor, bedecked in a prince's ransom of antiquities and art. Perle claimed that she had a great sensitivity to beautiful things, but those closest to her knew that her sensitivity was directly proportional to an object's monetary value. Maggie knew that every item was carefully assessed, documented, and insured. In a very real sense, Perle lived among the means for her comfortable retirement—and her source of provision for the two bastard daughters who lived with a poor but semigenteel widow in Cornwall and would soon be old enough to be sent to a good finishing school.

Perle rose from her chaise in the center of the room as Maggie stepped inside.

"Ma chérie!" she cried, opening her arms in expressive invitation. "I could scarcely believe my eyes when Lord Edgington stole you away, forgetting your shawl and bonnet! He must have swept you off your feet! And then your letters, telling me your address but scarcely anything else. *Très mystérieux!* So, are you his mistress yet? If you are, why are you still wearing those old rags?"

The parlor maid retreated discreetly, and Maggie stepped into Perle's embrace. "I am not precisely his mistress," she said. "And I'm wearing these old rags because I came alone, on foot—the baron doesn't know I am here."

Perle released her and held her at an arm's distance. "He doesn't know? Do you mean that he doesn't wish you to associate with your old friend?" Her voice held mingled reproach and understanding.

Maggie was touched. "Friend, Perle? I thought I was just another would-be protégée."

Perle made a tsking sound. "Not you, *ma chérie*. You have known me too long for us not to either be friends or enemies, and you are no enemy of mine. Now, sit with me and answer my question!" In her usual overwhelming manner, she pulled Maggie down to sit beside her on the chaise she had just vacated.

"I can't be seen associating with you now because Lord Edgington has taken me to create a hoax, not as his mistress," Maggie said. "I am supposed to pretend to be an innocent young lady of good breeding, and I will be introduced as such to his friends. If I was seen visiting you by someone who knows him . . ."

Perle looked at her shrewdly. "So that is why you now sound so fine: He is having you taught how to speak and act."

"I'm trying," Maggie said, conscious of how much she still had to learn. Three weeks from the date Edgington had given her for the house party. She was already half out of time. Could she make it? Was she capable of a transformation on such a scale, no matter how superficial it was to be?

"But he is your lover, too, no?" Perle pursued.

Maggie bit her lip and nodded.

Perle sighed in satisfaction. "And you are using a vinegar-sponge? And are washing yourself after?"

Maggie nodded again. Such knowledge was only one benefit of her long association with the opera singer. After her first two encounters with the baron, she had been protecting herself faithfully—never breathing a word of it to Edgington, though it had been difficult, at first, to take those nightly measures in secret. She did not know why, but she did not want the baron to know that she . . . calculated. She feared he'd be angry or insulted, but she must take what steps she could to keep from ending up like Nan—to keep from ending up like her own mother. "He asked me about the likelihood that I might conceive. I told him that I don't know whether it is at all likely, since I only have my courses two or three times a year. He seemed pleased."

Perle snorted. "He's no fool. But do not trust your body. You are eating better; you do not look like a little starving bird any longer. When that happens"—she shrugged—"other things can change, too."

Maggie nodded again.

"So you are his mistress, then?" Perle pursued.

"Not precisely," Maggie replied, avoiding her eyes.

"What has he given you?" The opera singer was not to be deflected.

"A wardrobe worth one hundred pounds," Maggie said. "The use of a hired carriage and a house to live in until his charade takes place. Lessons in learning to be a lady and singing instruction from Mrs. Ladd. My expenses plus two pounds a week."

"Too low, too low," Perle muttered. "You are young and pretty, *ma petite*, and you now have culture and good clothes, and he gives you no jewels, no art, no real money?"

It isn't like that, Maggie wanted to say. But it was— she knew it was. He was her patron—she was his whore. It could be no simpler than that. "Perhaps later, after the hoax. Then I won't need the lessons in deportment anymore." There would be no real after, and she knew it, but she offered the possibility to Perle like a propitiation. "And . . . he has done other things. For my chavies. Harry's to become a solicitor now, because of him, and Giles had been sent to school. He's hired Nan and Sally and even little Moll, after a fashion, as maids."

Perle was silent for a long moment, an elegantly manicured finger tapping her upper lip in troubled thought. "That is certainly worth something. Yet I can't like this," she said.

"I can't ask him for more—" Maggie began, but Perle interrupted her.

"Oh, I don't like that, either, but that isn't what I'm talking about." She sighed. "You see, Maggie, if I'd have heard you were in any trouble, I would have gotten an audition for you, and happily. But I didn't hear it in the normal way. I got a letter instead, telling me what to do."

"From Danny," Maggie guessed, her stomach tightening.

Perle shrugged her soft shoulders. "It was written on expensive stationery with a good hand. Other than that, I cannot tell you for certain. But its tone—well, it sent a shiver through me, *ma chérie*, a shiver." She rummaged in a drawer and brought out a piece of paper, giving it to Maggie as if she were only too happy for it to leave her hands.

The paper was heavy with cotton rag, discreetly bearing the crown-and-diamond watermark of one of the most expensive stationers in London. Maggie unfolded it, feeling a sick tightness in her gut, and scanned the contents quickly. In a large, elegant hand, someone had written:

The girl you know as Maggie of King Street has found herself in some difficulty, having been dismissed from her employment and unable to find another. It would please a gentleman if you would arrange for her to sing in the auditions of May 29. You will be amply rewarded.

There was no signature, and it was not Edgington's handwriting, but still, still . . .

"He didn't threaten me or anything so crude as that, *naturellement*," Perle was saying nervously. "But I was afraid that if my cooperation were to be rewarded, what would happen if I refused? I didn't mean to trick you in any way—"

"Of course not," Maggie assured the singer, making herself smile as confidently as she could even as her body went cold. "It has been good, truly. The best thing that has ever happened to me."

Perle collapsed upon the chaise with a heavy sigh, leaning back as if suddenly enervated. "And yet, the coincidences," she said. "You were sent to that audition for a purpose, and then Lord Edgington carries you away for such a strange plan. . . . Can you truly believe it an accident?" She looked at Maggie with the shrewdness of a woman who had come very far in the world by dint of her own efforts. "Why do you think that Danny O'Sullivan has a hand in it?"

Maggie just shook her head. "I think it would be better for me to keep my suspicions to myself," she said. "If it was him, I don't think he'll bother you anymore." Not Perle. She had too many friends, very important friends, for it was said that she had never left a lover without lasting tenderness on both sides.

Perle looked at her for a long moment and then shrugged. "Well, I also have your hat and your shawl." She rose and opened another drawer, from which she extracted the garments. Maggie took them with a nod of thanks. "From what you have said, you won't have much of a need for them again . . ."

"I hope not," Maggie agreed, ignoring the invitation for further confidence. "Thank you, Perle," she said instead. She started to hand back the letter, but Perle waved to her, signaling that she could keep it. Maggie slid it carefully into her pocket, where it lay beside her gun, and was shown out of the flat by the parlor maid.

Chapter Ten

Maggie wrapped herself in her shawl and bonnet before stepping out again into the fog-black night, her mind teeming with a hundred thoughts and speculations as she wove her way back toward the house in Chelsea.

She was exactly where Danny wanted her to be, just as he had said. She was certain of it now. But what role in it had Edgington taken? It was inconceivable that he had cooperated willingly, and yet Perle was right—that he had decided that day to find a woman from the opera for his schemes and that the unknown manipulator had just happened to place her in his way stretched coincidence to the breaking point. Her presence at the opera house that day was no accident, but the question now was, was Edgington's? Could it have been?

She had to escape London, escape England, go halfway across the world to a place where Danny could never reach her. If only she could do it and keep the chavies safe . . .

Maggie had no need to hide her return from the crossing sweep. Whether he kept to his post or not, she had no idea, for the fog consumed everything. Outside the terrace house, she slowed for a moment as she recognized the baron's black carriage pulled up to the curb. What was he doing there? He was supposed to be at a dinner or a ball. He wasn't going to be happy about the fact that she had gone out alone. Not at all. For a moment, she considered fading back into the darkness, but then sense took over. He already knew she had left—there was nothing to be done about it except to face him as soon as possible, before his displeasure had a chance to distill into something worse.

She advanced—and a movement in the area stairway caught her eye. She jerked back, but the man vaulted easily over the rail, landing squarely in front of her. *Bloody damn!* She fumbled in her skirts for her gun, knowing she'd be too slow. The man reached for her, cocked his head to the side . . .

And that familiar movement brought instant recognition.

"Bloody 'ell, Frankie," she snarled. "What do you fink you're doin', scarin' the life out of me?"

Frankie chuckled, leaning back against the area railing. Maggie still couldn't make out his face through the thick fog. "I can't believe I just scared the great Maggie King."

"I nearly put a bullet in you, you great oaf," she snapped, regaining control of her voice. "You wouldn't be laughing then, now would you?"

"Eh, you didn't 'ave no barker in your 'ands." Frankie shrugged.

Maggie frowned at him. "What are you doing here?"

"Looking for you." He shrugged again.

"I wasn't home. So why'd you stay?"

"It's a long walk from where I'm sleeping now to see you." He pushed off the railing, and Maggie was struck by how tall he had become. He had the full height of a man, now, though it would be several years before he lost the loose-limbed lankiness of youth. How old was he? Younger than she was, though not by much, or at least he'd seemed so when they were little more than infants in Mrs. Baker's gang of kids.

"You're still in the flat, aren't you, Frankie?" Maggie asked.

"I gave Widow Merrick the rent for the next month, but no, I ain't staying there no more." Frankie shifted restlessly. "I come back one night to find a couple of Danny's bruisers waiting for me. They never saw me, but I decided it wasn't 'ealthy there, and so I'm going underground for a bit. Out in Southwark. I just wanted to let you know that if you don't see me—well, that's why."

Maggie reached out and took his arm, squeezing it gently. "You know I worry about you."

Frankie pulled back, and Maggie dropped her hand. "You shouldn't. I do fine for myself."

"I know. But that doesn't keep me from worrying. If you would just let the baron—"

"No." Frankie cut her off. "I ain't taking nuffing from that toff."

"Well, you've taken enough from me, and me from you!" Maggie retorted.

She could sense Frankie's sneer even in the darkness. "That's different. You didn't earn none of that on your back."

She froze. "It's not like that, Frankie."

"You trying to tell me you ain't fucking 'im, Maggie?" he challenged. "Does 'is carriage come 'ere every night so's you can 'ave a nice little chat?"

"I'm saying it isn't like that," she repeated softly.

Frankie stood still for a moment, then seemed to shake himself free of whatever thought he'd had. "Damn it, mum, I know that, but I just wish—" He broke off. "I can't take nuffing from 'im, is all. I just can't, Maggie. I try to fink about you and 'im and be 'appy for you, and 'appy for 'Arry and Sally and Nan and all, but it just doesn't seem fair to me. I mean, a toff, Maggs—I can't beat no toff." His hands opened and closed in impotent frustration, and Maggie stared at him, really looked at him for the first time in—how long? Years, maybe. He was Frankie to her, had always been her Frankie, but he hadn't just gotten taller. She remembered the hidden looks he'd given her over the past few months, the moody silences, the cock-of-the-walk displays and strange tempers and disappearances. Inexplicable before, they now made a terrible kind of sense.

"You love me," she said, the words scarcely a whisper. "Frankie, why didn't you ever tell me—why didn't you say anything?"

His laugh was broken. "You really didn't know, did you, Maggs? I've been tearing me 'eart out for two years and more, and you never even guessed. 'Ow could I 'ave said summat? 'Arry, 'e loves you like 'is own pers'nal angel, but I wanted to love you as a woman, wanted you to see me as a man . . ." He stood in the darkness, his lanky, rawboned frame looming over her, still only half formed.

"Ah, Frankie." She sighed. "If I'd known . . . if I'd guessed, maybe I would have looked at you differently, too. But now . . ."

"I know, Maggs. Everyfing's different. You don't even sound the way you used to. You're a right nob now, and you got your toff. And I got the streets, still, so let me keep them and me dignity, like, by going me own way. 'E's kicked me, and that's the right truth. Don't make me eat out of 'is 'and arfter." Frankie's voice was light, but

Maggie sensed the hurt—the hurt that had been there for weeks, if only she'd been listening.

She bit her lip and offered her hand. "You'll always be me chavy," she said roughly.

"I never was afraid of you forgetting that, Maggie," Frankie said. He clasped her hand briefly and then dropped it. "Steer clear of that Danny."

"You, too," Maggie said.

And then, with a final nod, Frankie drifted into fog and was swallowed by the night.

Maggie stared after him, a hundred maybes and might-have-beens swirling through her head. She shivered as a chilly eddy tickled the back of her neck, and mounted the stoop steps.

She slipped her key into the door and turned it carefully, so that she barely felt the *chunk* of the lock through the knob. She opened the door with a breath of sound and slid into the front hall.

A single gaslight burned low near the door, revealing the neat, bare entry, its black-and-white encaustic tiles stretching along side the staircase into shadow at the back of the house. Not even the footman was on duty. Frowning, she divested herself of her hat and shawl and laid them on the hall table for Mrs. Pershing to put away in the morning. The sound of a shoe grating over tile made her freeze. She looked up into the mirror, but it revealed nothing but a short expanse of wall behind her. Her attention focused on the heavy leaded glass bowl that sat on the table beside her bonnet, and she reached toward it with her left hand as she slid her right toward the gun in her pocket.

"Where did you go, Maggie?"

Edgington. The frost in his words bit the air. She closed her eyes for a moment, breathing again, and then turned slowly to find him standing in the doorway to the morning room, resplendent in his evening clothes.

Why did looking at him make something in her chest ache? Was it because he was so handsome, so unmistakably rich, so smooth and golden, like an idol? Or was it something more—or less—than that: the mere fact that he was Edgington and she was Maggie, and his soul seemed to have hooks on it that caught and tore when it rubbed up against hers.

"Out." She answered his question with a nonanswer and the obscure feeling that she was defending herself against a hidden assault. "You weren't supposed to come tonight."

His eyebrow arched, expressing his disdain for such a reply. "The dinner ended early. I realize that you went out. That was not what I was asking."

Maggie stared at him, pushing down the urge to hug herself. "I visited Perle Blanc."

Edgington's face tightened—not in guilt, no, of that she was certain. "That must be halfway across the city."

"A third," Maggie granted him.

"You are terrified of this Danny fellow, who has, need I remind you, caused your friend to be beaten and dishonored, and yet you decide to take a solitary stroll across London, through his territory, after dark?" His expression was stonily impassive, but his voice dripped with condemnation.

"I'm safer in the street than I am here," Maggie snapped. "At least none of Danny's bullyboys knew where I was then. At least I wasn't where he had put me."

The baron seemed about to retort, but then he paused. "Put you?" he repeated, his eyes narrowing.

Maggie sighed, feeling suddenly weary. "This will take a while. Maybe we ought to sit down."

Edgington looked at her a long moment and then stepped aside, silently inviting Maggie into the doorway behind him. She slid past, an automatic response going through her at his proximity—not the flutter of uncertainty but the sweet, familiar trickle of recognition.

Edgington turned on the lights and shut the door, and Maggie sought the settee in the bow window. Without invitation, he folded himself onto the cushion next to her, moving with the grace of perfect self-assurance. He was too close, his largeness crowding her.

Maggie took a deep breath. "Perle gave me a letter from some nob telling her to arrange for me to be at the same audition where you found me."

Edgington frowned. "The letter could not have said what my purpose would be there. No one but my sister knew I was looking for a woman to play such a role."

"It didn't," Maggie said. "It just gave the date. But I was meant to go to that audition, and you did choose me. I came here, and Danny said he was pleased . . ."

"Maybe Danny intended something else," the baron said. "Maybe his plan went awry but he wanted you to think it was on course."

"Who knew that you would be at the audition? Maybe he wanted me to meet you, but he had some other idea of what exactly would happen," Maggie suggested.

"Who didn't know is a better question," he returned. "Dines and Gifford were there—as they usually are—but I go to at least eight of every ten auditions. It is scarcely a secret." His lips twisted moodily. "I like opera."

Maggie shook her head irritably. "But none of this addresses the real issue: Why would Danny—or anyone—want to put me in your way?"

The baron looked skeptical. "I'm still not convinced anyone did."

Well, I am, Maggie thought, keeping herself from snapping the retort only with effort. All her instinct from a lifetime of living with the flash mob was telling her that something was up, that there was a rum lay here, and if only she wasn't the pigeon, she could see it . . .

He looked at her for a long moment, his brows drawing together. "If you truly believe you were sent to that audition to meet me, and since I have claimed that I was not sent by anyone to meet you, then there's another, more obvious question that you haven't asked."

Maggie shifted uncomfortably. "If you were involved, would you admit it?"

Edgington did not deign that with a response, his way of recognizing her attempt at deflection for what it was. After a moment, Maggie dropped her gaze to her hands, twisted in her lap—the hands whose illegitimate talents had brought her to this moment, however circuitously. "You're starting to know me too well. Two weeks ago, that would have worked. If you are convinced that Danny really wants you here, then it is only logical to wonder if I might not have a hand in it." Edgington spoke the words evenly, calmly.

"I'm not as generous as you're trying to make me sound," Maggie muttered. "When I read that letter, for a little while, well, I did think you might have tricked me." She raised her eyes to his face again. "After all, what do I know about you? I know your name and rank, that you have a mother and a sister and a house just outside of London where you will hold a party in a few weeks, and I know various unimportant likes and dislikes. But that is all. Even though I don't know that much *about* you, I think that I know *you* better than that. Well enough to know that you are not the kind of man to involve himself in such things." His amber eyes met hers steadily, yet he did not speak. His expression became even more remote, and she cleared her throat nervously and pressed on. "I know I'm not saying it right, but I'm trying to say that most toffs in your position, they wouldn't care about a girl like me—I mean, they wouldn't care what happened to me even if I was sharing their beds. Sure, they talk about honor and being a gentleman and nobby things like that, but all that means is that they have to be nobs to other nobs. You're different. Sometimes, when I'm with you, I forget that I'm not a lady, after all." Still he sat, unmoving, silent, and Maggie added lamely, "Do you know what I mean?"

"Yes," he said. His voice was low, almost raw. "I do not deserve such faith, but yes, I understand."

Maggie stared at him, perplexed. "Why not?"

His smile was more of a grimace. "You don't think that I whored and boozed with the best of them? You don't think that I gambled and dodged my tailor's bill and used other people, used them up for my pleasure just as all my family has for as long as anyone knows?"

Maggie shook her head, denying this representation. "But you have always been sober and true—"

"I have tried to mend my ways, as the trite saying goes," he agreed. "But some ways are too broken for mending. Some deeds when done cannot be undone."

"But what could you have done?" Maggie protested.

"All the usual thoughtless transgressions that every man of my station is all but invited to commit—and worse, by association. Have you never heard that the sins of the father are visited on the sons?" Edgington asked.

Maggie shook her head, and a flicker of amusement passed through his eyes.

"How about 'blood will tell'?"

"Yes," Maggie said. "I don't believe it, though."

"Why not?" He seemed genuinely curious.

Maggie scowled at him. "My mother was a half-bob Irish whore, and from what I've heard, when she wasn't turning tricks, she was gone on gin. My father—well, I doubt my mother ever knew his name, and he couldn't have been much better. When she died in the cholera epidemic, the disinfectors carried her away and dumped her in the only scrap of ground that has ever properly been hers. Now, I may not be made for much, but I have to believe that I'm made for more than that."

The baron's eyes grew hooded for a moment as he retreated into thought. "I think," he said, sounding as if he were feeling his way through something, "I think that it must be different for me. What did your mother leave you?"

Those words hit at an old ache, one so old that she hardly recognized it as pain anymore. "Nothing. Not even a name."

"But my father left me both a title and the sullied legacy of the Edgingtons," he said. "How can I take the one and not the other? The lands come with their debts, the title with its guilt. The guilt cannot end with my father's death any more than the consequences of his life, of the lives of my grandfathers and uncles for eleven generations, have ended with their deaths. The consequences reverberate down into today, and so must the stain continue with it."

Again, Maggie was struck with the image of Edgington as the animating hand for the puppet of his rank, but now the idea seemed more sinister than absurd, a grotesque mannequin that defiled the man who unwillingly took it up. "It has to start over at some point. It would be too much of a burden for anyone to have to bear the sins of all his fathers," Maggie said. "Where would it end? After a dozen generations, a man couldn't walk under that kind of load."

"The evil that men do lives after them; the good is oft interred with their bones," Charles murmured. His lips curved upward, but his eyes were sad. Maggie just looked at him, and he explained, "I'm afraid it isn't so easy. That's what the wager with my sister is about, you know. It seems like such a strange distance from the incident that began all this to, well, the two of us sitting here now." His brow arched in acknowledgement of the irony. "I was trying to right one of my father's wrongs, or to at least mitigate it somewhat, by providing for the natural child of my governess."

"His child," Maggie guessed.

"His child but her shame," Charles said. "Miss Barrett was sent away only a year after my mother engaged her, and I never even asked why. I learned the reason when I was going through his papers a few months after his death. There was a letter from the landlady of the cheap boarding house where she had lived, informing him that Miss Barrett was dead and that her daughter would be cast out if my father did not make up the rent that was owed."

"Did he?" Maggie asked.

The baron shook his head. "He must have had a gambling debt or a new horse that interested him more. I recognized the name and, from the letter, I could infer much. But when I finally found the daughter, I learned even more."

"Like what?"

Edgington's face was tight, his tone devoid of emotion. "That the governess had not been a willing participant in her own seduction. That my father had called her a slut and tossed her out with five pounds and no recommendation when she confessed her condition and begged for assistance, declaring he had no way to know that the brat in her belly was actually his. That the young woman—barely more than a girl—had been forced to sell everything she owned and then take in washing. When she couldn't support herself and her daughter that way, she had been reduced to begging from my father, who sometimes sent her a few pounds and sometimes sent her only curses."

"Oh, Charles," Maggie said. She straightened abruptly as she realized how familiar she had just been. "I'm sorry, I didn't mean—"

"I think, perhaps, that it might be more sensible for me to consider my title an insult than my Christian name." He laughed hollowly. "I found Lily Barrett in desperate straits. She had been raised with all the education and advantages her mother could provide, but what use is a poor girl reared to be a lady?"

"What did you do?" Maggie asked.

"A certain colonel owed my father a debt he had not been able to discharge at the time of my father's death," Charles said. "I arranged to have him take Lily into his household as a distant relation with a small but not despicable dowry—which I provided—so that she could meet young men of good families, third or fourth sons of the less wealthy peers or decent gentlemen, perhaps, destined for the church or in the army, who would welcome a capable and pretty young woman with good sense, a tidy portion, and a willing acceptance of slightly straitened circumstances."

"But something happened with your sister," she guessed.

"My dear sister Millie tired of her presence and decided to be rid of her by cutting her at the Rushworths' ball and then declaring too loudly that she did not understand why a girl with no family was accepted at such an event," Charles said flatly.

"And so the wager," Maggie said. "You will pass me off as a lady . . . and she will do what?"

"Sponsor a ball in honor of Lily Barrett," he said with a cool smile. "It will be an apology and reinstatement in the same act."

"It seems like a great deal of trouble and risk," she said doubtfully.

"It is important." Charles' reply was firm.

Maggie frowned at him. "You are too good for your father's sins."

He returned her expression with a dark look. "If I were so good, why would I come here, night after night?" he demanded.

Her breath caught slightly—in trepidation and anticipation. "What do you mean?"

"A dance hall singer and a baron, Maggie," he said, cocking his head so that the light gleamed off his goldbrown hair. "It cannot sound better than a baron and a governess."

"I want you," Maggie said simply. "It makes all the difference in the world."

"But when it ends, what will become of you? I will go on with my life as I always have, but you—will you end up dying too young in some boardinghouse or workhouse because you are too proud to let me know you need help?" he pursued.

"You don't need to worry about the workhouse. If Danny gets a hold of me, I won't live that long or die that peacefully," she said cynically.

"God!" The baron was caught up short. "Is he truly so barbaric?"

Maggie scrubbed her face with her hands, fighting the urge to laugh. "He's the most powerful rogue in London! How do you think he got that way? You saw what he did to Nan, and I've told you that he kills people. Do you think I was funning you? You don't seem to quite believe in him, but he's as real as anything."

"But if you do what he wants—"

"I would live a little longer, is all, a few weeks or a few months," she finished. "But you don't need to worry about that. When this is over, I'm going. Leaving to Canada or America or somewhere—I've saved every farthing you've given me, and I'll use it to buy passage and start myself off somewhere new. I have to. Sally will come with me, and, well, now I think that Frankie might, too." Not that she could ever be to him what he wanted of her, not now, but maybe if he thought she might, he could be convinced to save himself. "If you would keep Giles in school for a few years, maybe, and find a place for Nan and Moll and Jo for a little while. Harry's already got a good new life, and he's promised to look after them just as soon as he has his first real position—"

"Maggie." Charles cut through her rush of plans. "For your sake, I will keep your Giles in school, I will even look after him on holidays though, of course, everyone will assume he is mine"—his mouth twisted wryly—"and I will even sponsor him at Oxford or Cambridge, if he chooses to pursue advanced studies, or buy him a commission in the army or navy, if he wishes. As for your Nan and her little family, I am sure I can find her some occupation until her sister and son are old enough to likewise be sent away to school and she can take on regular domestic employment."

"You would do that for me?" Maggie whispered, her throat tighening so that she could barely get out the words. "I don't expect that Nan or Giles will ever thank you for it, you know, and I don't know that I'll ever be able to repay you. . . ."

"You can repay me by not leaving," Charles said, a little brusquely.

Maggie's breath stuttered a little. "What?"

His expression was intent. "I can't let you go to America. You must stay here. Take the house, keep a carriage, make a little stockpile for yourself for your old age. I know I said I didn't want a mistress, and it was the truth. I don't want a mistress. I want you."

"I can't," Maggie blurted. "Danny, he'd never let me go. As long as I'm close to you, I'll be in danger because he'll try to use me."

"I will protect you," Charles insisted.

Maggie shook her head, even as a part of her wanted to leap for that proffered haven, however illusory. To continue to see him, night after night, week after week, to have him talk to her and listen and even, sometimes, smile. To keep his kisses, his body, his passion, heat, and sincerity. It was the stuff of a glorious dream—but as she'd told him, girls like her knew better than to dream. For girls like her, dreams never came true.

"You can't protect a mistress," she said. "A mistress is a . . . an invisible convenience, not a real person like a sister or a friend. I won't be any safer than I am now. I can't live the rest of my life looking out the window, wondering who's watching me, wondering when Danny might ask me to do something horrible for him, or else. And I can't live here knowing that he might ask and that I might do it and hurt you by it."

Charles was silent for a long moment. "Are you certain?" he finally said.

"I have to be," she said. She swallowed. "But that

doesn't mean that I don't want to thank you now. I mean, in the only way that I can."

Pain flickered across the baron's expression. "You don't have to do this. You can refuse me any night you wish. I hope you understand that."

"But I don't want to," Maggie said simply. She held out a hand to him, in mute invitation, and with a low sound, he pulled her into his arms.

Maggie had never had a homecoming, never understood what people meant when they talked about it, but she imagined that it must be something like that kiss. It surrounded her, enveloped her, and she let herself sink into it and just let go.

He kissed her again, harder, and the sweetness was splintered by desire twisting deep in her center that sent a response twanging through her body. He pressed her down on the settee, and she went, surrendering herself to the skill of his mouth and hands. In moments her dress was off, and she untied her pocket quickly and hid it and the gun in the tangle of brown calico. Her petticoats went up—

"Wait," she gasped, pushing him back. "I must go upstairs. Just for a moment. I'll be back, I promise."

His lust-darkened eyes narrowed. "Why?"

"I . . . I need to use the necessary room," she tried.

"Now?" he demanded.

"Yes," she said in a meek voice.

It didn't fool him. "What are you up to, Maggie?"

"I . . . I have to get a sponge," she stuttered, feeling her cheeks flame. She wriggled under him, trying to get free, but she couldn't budge.

"A sponge," he repeated.

"With vinegar," she said. "It helps to prevent any . . . surprises."

"A prophylactic?"

Maggie stared at him mutely.

"To prevent conception—to stop pregnancy?" he added with a note of exasperation.

She bit her lip and nodded. "It doesn't always work, but it helps," she said.

"That's why you would never allow me to—"

"Yes," Maggie interrupted hurriedly. "Please. I know you don't want a child from this any more than I do. Let me get it."

"Why didn't you tell me?" Charles demanded.

Maggie couldn't tell whether he was insulted or pleased that she took such steps. "I didn't think you would want to know. I thought you'd be happy as long as it just didn't happen."

He closed his eyes briefly. When he opened them, his expression was unreadable. "You are half undressed. I will get it. Where is it?"

"In the lap drawer of my desk," Maggie muttered, feeling even more humiliated.

He pushed off her, and she straightened against the back of the settee as he went to the door. He cast a look at her over his shoulder.

"Stay there," he said. And then he went out of the room.

Charles found a small tin box exactly where Maggie had described. He opened it to reveal a small sponge, floating in a clear liquid with the unmistakable smell of vinegar. How could he have not known that she was using . . . this? She must have been very careful. Very careful to take steps from bearing a fatherless child into the world—careful so that what was between them did not extend in its consequences to include another.

There was an entire universe of cynicism in that small box. Or was it wisdom? It was hard these days to know the difference, but at some level, it felt like an indictment. What they shared was illicit, unsanctioned, unacknowledged—so it must remain, and therefore she had, with her usual unblinking recognition of the world and its ways, taken steps to keep it that way. It made him obscurely angry—not at her but at himself and, most of all, at the world.

He replaced the lid and tucked the tin into his palm before going back down the stairs again. The house was dark and silent; anticipating a confrontation with Maggie, Charles had send the footmen on duty into the back garden and had dismissed everyone else for the night. Mrs. Pershing and Nan's little family had retired to their garret bedrooms, and if Sally were sitting up, then she, too, was waiting in her attic room for a bell to summon her.

When he reached the morning room again, Maggie was sitting on the settee, though she had stripped in his absence down to her chemise and pantaloons. She watched him with her queer unself-consciousness, as if her near nakedness were of no significance. Living three or more people to a room, he supposed, modesty had been a delicacy, like so many, that she had never had an opportunity to cultivate. He wondered, with an irrational jealousy, how many times Frankie or Harry had seen her in no more than what she was wearing now.

Breaking off that thought, he closed the door and crossed to her side. Maggie looked at him inquisitively, and he produced the tin. She took it from his hand and opened it, looking at it for a long moment before beginning to reach in—

"No," he said. She might be indifferent to her undress,

but this, he knew, would humiliate her to do in front of him.

She looked up, ready to argue, as she always was, but he shook his head to forestall her.

"No," he repeated. "Trust me. I will do it when it is time. You needn't do it now." *In front of me,* he added wordlessly, and he knew by the softening of her expression that she understood.

"Thank you," she said, an odd note in her voice. "You are so good to me."

Not good enough by half, or I'd turn around and walk out right now, Charles thought roughly, but he did not argue.

She set the tin down on the table beside her—carefully, he noted, as if it would shatter at a breath—and then she looked up at him, expectant, waiting for him to make the next move.

He should not want to. Not now, after such a painful reminder of the hypocrisy of the world and of himself. And yet, he could not look at her without wanting her. Her body was too thin, too pointed, her angular silhouette visible through the fine cotton of her chemise. Her old eyes in her young face regarded him with a kind of yearning that he knew was echoed in his own gaze, and she sat stiffly with a tension through her body that set his own blood to thrumming. She should seem almost insubstantial, and yet her spare frame radiated heat and strength and life. He wanted to give her something—something she would take from him, since she would not be his mistress—and so he stood with his hips between her knees, then slowly, deliberately, he knelt.

She blanched. "No, don't, Charles—you can't kneel, not in front of me—"

"I will do as I please," he stated. "And this pleases me."

She did not ask him to rise again.

He slid his hand up her legs across the fine cotton of her pantaloons, sliding it under her chemise to find the waistband. He loosed the tapes and then grasped the fabric firmly and pulled down. She wriggled against the cushion to help him, and in a moment, the garment was off. He shrugged out of his coat and waistcoat and tossed them to crumple on the floor, sending his necktie after, and then he grasped her hips in both his hands.

"Come forward," he ordered, and she did until she was sitting on the very edge of the settee. "Lean back." She obeyed again, though her eyes betrayed her uncertainty. "You are not going to stop me." It was more of an order than a question.

"No," she agreed hoarsely.

Slowly, deliberately, he lifted the edge of her chemise, uncovering her legs, her abdomen, her belly. He could see her stomach muscles moving under her skin with every fluttering breath. He kissed her belly, and the muscles tightened at the touch of his mouth. He turned his attention to the inside of her thigh, halfway up from her knee, and she gave a smothered gasp at the contact of his lips. Her skin was impossibly thin and delicate, stretched tight over muscle and sinew, unsoftened by curves. Too fragile, too vulnerable for such a life, for such a spirit . . . He moved upward, kissing, licking, nibbling, and the taste of her skin, the sound of her breath, the anticipation that vibrated through her body stirred an answering heat that shuddered through his body and gathered in his groin, making him ache from wanting her.

He reached the nest of curls at the juncture of her thighs. Her folds were already parted, swollen with desire. He delved into the cleft once, quickly, with his tongue, and she made a strangled, whimpering sound. The taste of her nearly undid him, hot and carnal and primally feminine.

He looked up and met her eyes as she stared down at him, her face scarlet with mortification and need. Her lips formed a silent word—*No*. But her eyes burned with a very different message, and so he lowered his head again and pushed into her hard, rasping his tongue against the nub above as he exited. She cried out again, arching her back, and he tasted her again, and again, changing his motion and rhythm to keep her unbalanced, so that she could not brace against him, could not push aside what he was doing to her or control her own reactions. Her cries turned to sobs of pleasure, and her legs tightened convulsively around him as she peaked, fast and hard, her body arching in response to an internal rhythm that he first followed, then amplified, until she was panting rawly and her pleas for more and for respite turned to wordless, half-human noises. Finally, she collapsed into bonelessness onto the settee.

Charles looked up just as her gaze came into focus again.

"I feel . . . full," she said, the words grating as they came out.

"Suffused," Charles suggested.

Maggie nodded numbly and closed her eyes as he stood and stepped away from her. He was stripping. She could hear every movement—at this moment, she almost believed that she could hear his heartbeat—but she did not open her eyes again until she felt something cold and wet press between her thighs. She gasped at the contact and closed her legs around his hand automatically, looking at him—he had the sponge, and as she watched, he placed one of his hands flat against her belly, kneeing her thighs open again, and with the other, he pushed in.

The rough sponge scraped slickly against her swollen center, its cold dampness startlingly erotic. Maggie hissed, a shuddering wave of pleasure spiking through her as it went deeper, deeper, and then stopped. "I wish . . . " She swallowed hard. "Oh, I wish you could do that again."

Charles chuckled darkly. "Another time," he promised, and she surprised herself by having the sudden urge to weep from gratefulness that he had taken a measure of such brutal practicality and made it something that seemed almost right.

He took her hand, wordlessly urging her off the narrow settee and down onto the carpet. She slid down, pulling him on top of her. His skin was hot against her body, its texture subtly rougher than her own, and even that difference seemed charged with delicious significance, sending a sliver of pure sensuous pleasure through her.

"Kiss me," she begged, and as he moved his hips between her legs, he did, arching his body so that his mouth met hers. The sponge slipped deeper into her with his first thrust, the unexpected additional sensation pulling a gasp from her. She clasped him against her as he rocked, slow and deep at first, then gradually faster, moving hotly inside her until her entire body seemed to catch fire, burning around him, her skin flushed with need—need for him, need for more. He planted his elbows at either side of her head and held her face in his hands, and his eyes mirrored the flame that surged through her, and suddenly, she was falling into them, losing herself inside the blasting ecstacy.

Heat consumed her, tossing her up into a place where she could not see, she could not hear, she could only feel, and all she could feel was her body blazing and Charles, against her, inside of her, moving in the same roaring rhythm that took up her core and shook it.

Slowly, the heat receded, leaving her panting on the carpet of the morning room with Charles slumped to one side, their breaths no longer in tandem but rasping discordantly against one another.

"Thank you," she whispered, closing her eyes.

"Do not give me the burden of thanks," Charles said, so softly she could hardly hear him. "Say instead—*It was a pleasure.*"

"It surely, surely was," Maggie agreed, yet somehow, it already felt like a farewell.

Chapter Eleven

"Charles, come down! Half the guests are already arrived!"

Charles looked up to see his sister hovering in the doorway of his study, her eyes aglow even as she pouted at him. He rose, concealing his conflicted reaction under a display of equanimity. The strange chain of events that had begun with his sister's snub of their father's bastard was now drawing to a close. He should feel satisfaction and anticipation, and he did, certainly, but those emotions were counterbalanced by a greater dread.

Despite Charles' best attempts to reassure her, Maggie had grown increasingly agitated as the weeks passed and she continued to get encouraging messages from Danny O'Sullivan. She did not chatter about her fears as other women might, but instead lapsed into stillness whenever conversation lulled, her face frozen and tight as her mind took her on paths of fruitless speculation. Though Charles was still at least half convinced she was worrying over nothing, his doubts were well watered by her fear.

And he had another source of discontent that had nothing to do with Danny, for the house party marked the beginning of the end of his connection to Maggie King. She had already bought third-class tickets to America for the day after the party was to disperse. Charles was displeased with the idea, but what could he do? Maggie was miserable in London, terrified that Danny lurked around every shadow, and she could not be convinced that becoming his mistress would afford her any protection. His only counterarguments were wholly selfish, and he had too much dignity and respect for Maggie to voice them.

"Are you coming?" Millie asked impatiently, breaking into his thoughts.

Charles realized that he'd been standing stock-still, staring into the hearth. He smoothed his face and raised a supercilious eyebrow, an action guaranteed to annoy his sister. "But of course. I am merely waiting for you to lead the way."

Millie sniffed and swished out of the room in a froth of skirts. Charles followed her mutely as she fluttered down the echoing East Gallery toward the grand staircase. Her excitement overtook her irritation within ten steps, and she burst into a flood of chatter, forgetting to be annoyed.

"The guests came all in a rush—nearly half had been at an early tea with the Ashcrofts. Why weren't you there to greet them? Lord Rushworth couldn't be moved from his country seat, as usual, but Lady Rushworth and Lady Victoria have already arrived and retired to their rooms to refresh themselves, and Lord and Lady James Ashcroft, all three of their daughters, and Mr. Weldon are having tea in the Chinese parlor with Mamma, and the Radcliffe men arrived with them here, and then Lord Hamilton came . . ."

Charles listened to the list of guests with half an ear. They were the same people who came every year, whose ancestors had come to the parties held by his ancestors.

For this annual gathering, Lady Edgington dispensed
with the usual gender balancing that dominated most society events—the number of daughters and sons that the
select group had borne was too petty a concern to factor
in this elite guest list.

Most of them leased houses on Edgington land and
lived no more than a mile away, and so the "house party"
had become little more than a conceit, an extended, ex-
traordinarily exclusive kind of dinner party that marked,
for the most fashionable circles, the start of the full swing
of the London Season. These guests knew Charles better
than anyone, not because he would have necessarily chosen them to be his bosom friends out of his entire circle
of acquaintance but because they were what his mother
called "our sort" and therefore had known him since he
was in knee breeches, if not before. Charles had never
figured out exactly what "our sort" was, for the group
was not united by equal wealth, rank, or even lifestyle or
political opinion, except that it had, by definition, been
their sort for a very long time. It was these people whom
Maggie would have to fool—people who did not merely
know all the rules and forms that she had been studying,
and a thousand besides, but who had lived them from
birth and internalized them to such a degree that they
could often ignore them without accusations of vulgarity.

Cultured voices filtered up to Charles' ears as he and
Millie reached the top of the staircase above the great
hall. But by the time Charles looked over the balustrade,
there was nothing to be seen under the high blue dome
where Europa and the bull plunged into the sea except the
dots of gray-and-white maids and the cerulean-liveried
footmen who flanked the door.

The tall doors swung wide again as Charles and Millie
began to descend the staircase. Lord Gifford entered, a

woman on his arm and Sir Nathaniel Dines trailing behind.

As she took in the unfamiliar woman, Millie's expression radiated confusion, followed quickly by realization and exultation. Charles smothered a smile of grim satisfaction.

Introducing Jane Howser into the company had been a stroke of genius. Not his, though Charles would have liked to take credit, but Dines'. The baronet had kept abreast of Charles' little social experiment. Charles had admitted in passing that he was afraid that the inclusion of any unknown woman into Millie's acquaintance at this moment would rouse the utmost suspicion for no other reason than their bet. Dines had laughed and declared that what they needed was a red herring—and had neatly produced Miss Howser for the role. Charles quickly conceded that she was perfect.

Whatever Miss Howser was—and Charles didn't ask, knowing all too well the low company Dines often enjoyed—she was not a lady. She was pretty enough, with golden curls and big hazel eyes, and her dress was expensive and did not offend the eye, but there was something about her that was a little too brassy, a little too bold. Millie could no doubt talk of colors and patterns, of the cut of her skirts and the styling of her hair, and explain exactly why each was not quite right, but even to Charles' unschooled eye, she looked more contrived than sophisticated.

"Really, Charles," Millie murmured as she reached the bottom step, "surely even you could have done better than that."

"She doesn't have to fool you," he muttered back. "Just keep your mouth shut and let the others form their own opinions."

Millie stepped forward to greet the new guests and direct them to the parlor. She gave Lord Gifford a charming welcome, probably designed as a deliberate contrast to her chilly treatment of Dines. She all but cooed over Miss Howser, who was introduced as Dines' cousin. Millie shot Charles a meaningful look over the woman's shoulder to let him know that her behavior would not be to blame if the guests did not accept the new arrival at face value.

Millie took wreaths of laurel from a waiting maid and placed one on both the men's heads, giving a third to Charles.

"I see. This year the theme is to be a bacchanal!" Gifford said, cheerfully adjusting his wreath to a rakish angle.

Millie treated him with a withering frown. "A Roman pastoral," she pronounced distinctly. She took a garland of flowers and placed it around Miss Howser's neck, matching the one she already wore. With a polite excuse and another sniff at Lord Gifford, Millie ostentatiously linked arms with the woman and bustled her away with scarcely suppressed relish. Charles did not miss the cynical glint in Miss Howser's eye as she disappeared into the interior of the house, leaving him with Gifford and Dines.

"By God, Dines, she's bloody brilliant," Gifford drawled as soon as the women had departed.

Dines smiled smugly and lifted his monocle to study his protégée's retreating form. "She shall have them all in convolutions of horror within the hour. Can you imagine how your sister will react when she meets Miss Howser?"

Gifford chuckled. "Victoria will look like she's sucked a lemon, I'll wager."

"You confided in Gifford?" Charles asked Dines,

despite the obviousness of the answer. It was better than asking *What the hell were you thinking?* which is what he truly wanted to say.

"Don't think I'm a trustworthy fellow?" Gifford's tone was light, but his blue eyes glittered. "I knew half your plans already—what harm was there in letting me help you throw a red herring into the mix?"

"You're trustworthy enough as long as it amuses you," Charles said flatly.

Gifford chuckled, relaxing. "Too true, old chap. Too true. But this should be amusing enough for anyone."

Dines shrugged. "It needed to look as if we'd taken some trouble with the pretense. Including Gifford in Miss Howser's fictional social circle reinforced that appearance."

Charles nodded, still not entirely happy. Gifford was far from steady—if things did not seem entertaining enough for him, he would gladly blow the entire scheme just to enjoy the furor it caused. He might have already known about Maggie—his presence at the audition made that unavoidable—but he was safer when he was not in the middle of things.

"Shall we take our incredibly convenient ride to the new house yet?" Gifford said, smiling slightly.

Charles shifted irritably. Was there anything Dines had not told the man? "Let's see who's arrived first."

"If most everyone is here, I will suggest it," Gifford offered in an offhand tone.

"Why not?" Charles said, fighting the feeling that all his plans were spinning rapidly out of control. To keep from snapping at the man, he turned away and strode toward the Chinese parlor, leaving the others to follow.

The room was already full. Lady Edgington was ensconced in one corner with the older women: Gifford's mother, Lady Rushworth, with his sister, Lady Victoria; Lady James Ashworth with an enormous diamond glittering at her throat; and Lady Hyde. The younger generation mixed more freely, the Ashworth girls, Hyde daughters, and Radcliffe men forming and reforming in their several groups, while the older men held aloof in a far corner behind one of the two enormous jade-colored vases that flanked the far doorway.

Against his mental tally, Charles could find only a few names missing: the Mortimers, who were almost inevitably late, Lord Grimsthorpe, and the Morels, who might or might not have been invited this year since the gossip papers was still chattering about Mrs. Morel's recent indiscreet affair. It wasn't that Lady Edgington objected to affairs on principle—not unless one of the people involved was married to her—but being exposed in front of London's hoi polloi was a demonstration of bad taste that would take her several months to forgive.

Gifford scanned the room rapidly and raised an eyebrow—had enough people arrived? Charles gave a half shrug of permission, and the other man strolled over to one of the groups of young people gathered around the spinet that dominated one wall. An affectation of one of the previous Lords Edgington, it was tuned to an Oriental five-note scale and sported inlayed and lacquered panels in the Chinese style. One of the Hyde twins was picking at it in a desultory manner, whether Lady Elizabeth or Lady Mary, Charles had no idea, while the other twin, Millie, Miss Howser, and two of the Radcliffe men stood in a half circle around it. Gifford joined them, Charles trailing after as Dines peeled off toward another group.

"I say, Miss Crossham," Gifford said in his usual manner of exaggerated boredom. "I saw quite a palace going up on the way here. Who's to have it?"

Millie dimpled. "Lord Langston. Isn't it something? He says it's to be built in the style of a Gothic abbey."

Peter Radcliffe chuckled. "I've never seen an abbey with *quite* so many buttresses and towers."

"Don't you know?" the twin standing beside him asked. "Langston calls himself a medievalist, but what he mostly does is recite *Le Morte d'Arthur* and argue about where Camelot must have really been. I would wager that when he finishes, he will have a round table, a hall of arms, and a set of clattering old armor in every corner."

"And escutcheons on every wall," the other twin added with gusto, playing a snatch of melody that she probably imagined sounded medieval, though it quickly fell into weird disharmony on the strangely tuned instrument.

"And roasting pits in the kitchen," the first one agreed.

Gifford looked around the room with an expression of ennui. "Well, it still sounds more interesting than an interminable tea with biscuits and the same dreadful gossip we've heard at every party since the Season began."

"Do you want to inspect it?" Millie offered, on cue.

Thank you, Millie, Charles sent silently.

"I would love to see it!" Miss Howser trilled, a trifle too shrilly. The twin at the piano shot her sister a covert look under her eyelashes, and both smiled slightly.

"I don't see why we can't go, if we have enough carriages," Charles said in answer to the look his sister shot him.

"Dines' barouche is still here," Gifford drawled.

"So is our town carriage," Peter put in.

"I'll have them brought around," Charles said, nodding to a footman who was posted discreetly at the perimeter of the room. "Let's find out how many of the others wish to go."

"You're going, of course, aren't you?" Millie asked,

treating him to a pretty little frown. "We need a guide, and you know that I never pay any attention to the building projects."

"Of course," Charles said evenly.

It took half an hour for the carriages to be assembled and loaded. Finally, everyone who wanted to come was aboard, and they started off.

Charles found himself squeezed in the Edgington landau between Christopher Radcliffe, who was still glowing with self-importance in his new captain's uniform, and Gifford. Across from him sat his sister and, inevitably, Flora Ashcroft, whose mother had been thrusting her at him all Season. Behind him, he could hear Dines regaling Miss Howser with some story or other in the barouche they shared with Lord Radcliffe, Miss Ashcroft, and Lord Hamilton, while the twins and Peter and Alexander Radcliffe brought up the rear in the Radcliffes' closed town carriage. The small parade rattled over the bridge that ran over the small, chilly stream immediately before the estate's gates, then turned off the side lane onto the main road that led back toward London.

This is it, Charles thought, schooling his features into an expression of impassivity. The hour of truth. He should be anxious only for Lily Barrett and her probable fate of eternal banishment from polite circles if he failed. But that alone could not account for the tightness in the pit of his belly at the thought of failure. The truth was that he wanted Maggie to be successful for reasons that had nothing at all to do with his ridiculous wager—he wanted to see her win for once against a world that always seemed to be against her, and he wanted her to be recognized among his own circle, for he suspected that she somehow didn't feel quite real in a significant way. He

did not know why acceptance was so important to him,
but it was, and so he rode in tense silence.

"What is that?" Miss Flora exclaimed softly, breaking
her usual silence.

Already? It couldn't be. Charles followed her gaze. He
had a confused expectation that she must have seen
Maggie, but instead, there was a wide ditch next to the
road in which a group of sweaty workmen were digging,
already buried up to their waists.

"Gas line," he explained, relaxing. "They must be
tying into it to lay pipe to Langston's new house." At
Flora's wide-eyed gaze, he felt an impulse to sensational-
ize. "It's dangerous work, of course, and the men are
strictly forbidden from smoking."

"What would happen if they did?" Flora asked in a
tone breathless with the expectation of the unnamed horrors.

Charles raised an eyebrow. She was so . . . childish,
really, almost unnaturally so. "They might blow themselves up. There have been gas explosions on the out-
skirts of London that have flattened houses and made
great craters in the ground."

Miss Flora's expression was awed as they passed the
workers, and she craned her head around to keep them in
view as long as possible.

"There it is!" Millie cried as a half-built house came
into sight around a bend, a grandiose exclamation in gray
limestone. Charles turned, but instead of gazing at the
house, as the others did, his attention was riveted upon a
modest, nondescript chaise that turned the corner onto the
main road in front of them.

Enter Maggie, stage right.

*   *   *

Ten minutes before, Maggie had wrapped her arms hard around herself as she sat in the shadows of the waiting coach. Across from her, Sally's eyes were wide in the darkness.

Six and a half weeks of hard work had come to this. Maggie felt like a pot-metal kettle that had been dipped in the thinnest layer of plating in hopes of being passed off as solid silver. She knew she showed through at all the edges, but what could she do about it now? She would just have to make sure she was never brought fully into the light, keeping to dim corners where gilt was hard to distinguish from sterling. She would keep up her role for a week, and then . . . she hardly knew. She and Sally would make it somehow, though she couldn't yet see her way past the pier in New York.

Her incipient charade and her uncertain future should be enough to keep her mind thoroughly occupied, but Maggie's thoughts kept skittering away from such sensible preoccupations to return again and again to the inevitable loss. Not that of Nan, Giles, Harry, and the rest but, ridiculously, the loss that she had known was inevitable all along: leaving Charles. It was really the house that she would miss, of course, she told herself. And the easy life. She would not miss Charles' backward sort of kindness, nor the incredible intensity of his attention that made her feel like the only woman in the world, nor his flashes of dry humor and rare, precious smiles, nor his face, nor his mind, nor his lips, nor his body, nor his spirit . . . She could not miss any of those things because, after all, they had never been hers, not really.

Running feet cut into her thoughts and announced the arrival of the small boy Charles had hired as a lookout. Maggie heard the child breathlessly tell the driver that the Edgington party had just come into view, and Maggie held on to the strap as the coach lurched into motion, moving out of their hiding place and toward the road.

Across from her, Sally's face was ashen, her hands clenched around her own strap. The coach swung around the corner, and an enormous crack shook them on their seats, coming from the sabotaged axle. *I hope this is going to work,* Maggie thought, gripping the strap even tighter. This part of the plan had been her own idea—slightly dangerous, but a classic confidence trick with a high rate of success.

A second passed, then two. Nothing happened except that the axle creaked. *It's not going to work . . .*

The coach picked up speed without warning, and with a second, anticlimactic pop, the axle snapped in half. Maggie and Sally were thrown against the back of the coach as it bucked and pitched to the rear, sliding to a sudden and precarious halt.

Muffled cries of consternation shook Maggie from her momentary daze. Not Sally's, she realized—the voices came from outside the coach. She pulled herself off her friend, battling her skirts to make enough room in the corner of the cab so that Sally could push herself into a half-sitting, half-stooping position.

"Are you hurt?" Maggie asked.

"Just some bruises," Sally said, wincing. "You?"

"I am fine." Maggie was silent for a moment, listening to the hubbub outside the carriage. "Do you think they're coming to help?" She studied the door that was now more than three feet upslope of them. The windows along that side of the chaise showed sky and the tops of a hedge, while the opposite revealed only that the low side of the coach was caught in a thicket of bushes. "The doors open outward. I'd have to brace against something and push, but I think we can get out of the high door . . ."

The furor was closer now, and just as Maggie was deciding how she could wedge herself against the seat and
still have room for her crinoline, the handle turned, the
door swung open, and an unfamiliar man's face appeared,
framed against the square of sky. He wore a curious circle of leaves upon his bare hair, presenting an appearance
so odd that Maggie simply stared.

"Hullo!" he said. "What have we here?"

"What is it, Peter?" came an impatient female voice.

"I want to see!" declared another.

Peter's face turned away for a moment to face his unseen interlocutors. "You selfish little things. You'd be
glad if there was a whole family of orphans here, battered
to pieces, wouldn't you?"

Indignant protests followed that remark, but the
man—Peter—was already stretching out a chivalrous
elbow. "Madame?"

Not knowing what else to do, Maggie took it, and in a
moment, she had been pulled through the opening. She
perched on the doorframe for a moment, her hoops
threatening indecency with the least movement, but the
man took her waist with a cheerful "By your leave" and
swung her lightly to the ground.

"Why, you're just a wisp of a thing!" Peter exclaimed.
"Begging your pardon, madame," he added belatedly as it
seemed to occur to him that such a comment about a
woman's person might not be entirely welcome.

He turned back to the disabled coach to retrieve Sally,
with rather more effort, but Maggie was scarcely left
without comfort, for the instant he moved away, she was
enveloped in a cloud of feminine comfort and curiosity.
Smooth faces, bright eyes, rich dresses, flashing jewels,
flower garlands: all the women—girls, actually—seemed
to have been shaped in the same mold, and Maggie had

the instantaneous, confused impression that they were the same girl, repeated across half a dozen bodies, before she realized that two of them really were twins.

"Are you quite all right?"

"Was it frightening?"

"Did it toss you about?"

"Are you feeling faint?"

Maggie had no time to answer their barrage of questions, but the following flood of introductions allowed her to pick out a few names—Charles' sister Millicent Crossham, Peter Radcliffe, and Lady Mary and Lady Elizabeth, or perhaps it was the other way around. Maggie had already met Miss Howser, but neither betrayed their brief prior acquaintance by word or deed.

Beyond the ring of women stood the men. They watched the scene with varying degrees of amusement and interest, seemingly oblivious to the silliness of the wreaths of leaves that they wore upon their heads. Charles' appearance, in particular, seemed incongruous, though his expression of light interest harmonized with the attitudes and presentation of the rest of the party. Yet it was not in keeping with anything that Maggie knew of his character, and she had the impression that she was seeing, for the first time in many weeks, Charles in the role of baron rather than as a man. Her heart still tripped slightly when her gaze met his—*I can't believe this is working,* she thought at him, then jerked her eyes away before anyone could notice the exchange.

"Ladies! If you want answers, you must give the girl a chance to speak!" This interjection came from Peter Radcliffe, who had rescued Sally and returned to the Edgington party.

The women subsided, and Maggie treated them to a smile that she hoped appeared both genuine and slightly shaken. "I am quite fine, thank you all, though I took quite a fright."

"And no wonder!" put in one young girl, a plain little thing except for a pair of astonishing blue-violet eyes.

"Where were you going?" Miss Crossham asked.

"To Baslehurst. I don't know if you've heard of it," Maggie added a little apologetically. "I hadn't until two weeks ago, but it's a village near Exeter. Very quaint, I hear."

"Alone? To a place you have never been?" one of the twins asked, her eyes sparkling imagined adventures, and Maggie recognized the voice that had wondered if she were injured.

"I was going with my maid," Maggie said, nodding to where Sally stood beside the carriage, forgotten now that she had been extracted from her predicament. "I have no one else, anymore."

"No one?" echoed the other twin.

Maggie raised a hand to her lips, as if appalled by what she had just said. "I did not mean that! I must sound like the most ungrateful creature in the world. I have relatives . . . cousins . . . in Baslehurst who have graciously invited me to live with them, so that I am not forced to live the life of a friendless spinster in the city." She sighed. "But I have never met them, nor had I corresponded with them until after my great-uncle died."

"Indeed." This response came from a tall, black-haired man on the edge of the crowd, standing beside a slighter blond gentleman who was examining her through a monocle. "There are many dangers for a young woman with no relations. Not the least of which is being stranded when one's coach breaks down."

Maggie contrived to look anxious. "My solicitor sold off my great-uncle's other effects so that I could let out his house with the other properties, but I had thought that it would be safer and more discreet to ride post in his carriage to Baslehurst and sell it after I arrived. He had been ill for so long, I suppose he had not thought to keep it up." She gave the disabled carriage a woeful look. "It appears that it would have been wiser to hire a post chaise, after all . . ." She treated the man to a distressed look.

But it was Miss Crossham who replied. "You poor thing! You simply must stay with us as a guest of my mother until you can make new arrangements."

Maggie gave her a look that was at once startled and slightly suspicious of the company's strange appearance while secretly she rejoiced inside. Charles had been right; with Miss Howser's presence to allay her suspicions about her bet with Charles, Millie was accepting Maggie's appearance at face value. "I could not presume."

"Oh, bosh," Miss Crossham said. "We're having a house party—it would be no imposition at all! And don't be afraid of our queer little costumes. They are a very old Edgington tradition. The house party was once a masque, but tastes have changed, and this is what it left. There's no harm in it."

"Edgington—you mean Baron Edgington?" Maggie asked, putting relief in her voice.

Charles stepped forward, toward the knot of women. "The same," he said. "My sister is quite correct—our mother would be delighted to have someone to fuss over." There was a trace of irony in the words, as if he were less than enthusiastic but had decided the fight was not worth the effort.

"Thank you," Maggie said meekly. "I suppose I must introduce myself, as there is no one to do it for me. I am Margaret King. My great-uncle was Tertius King. . . ." At their blank stares, Maggie sighed. "He lived a very retired life. I am not surprised you did not know him."

"Come on in our carriage," Miss Crossham said sympathetically. "Your maid can ride with Lady Elizabeth and Lady Mary while your driver finds a smith to repair your carriage."

Those ladies gave her a look that promised revenge for being separated from the current object of interest and given a maid instead, but they said nothing.

"Thank you," Maggie repeated. "I hardly know what to say."

Miss Crossham giggled, removing her garland of flowers and looping it over Maggie's head instead. "Then don't say anything at all!"

"Step forward, young lady."

Hiding her surge of queasiness, Maggie obeyed the baroness. As soon as they had arrived at the Edgington House—an enormous monument in white stone that had far exceeded her faint imaginings—Maggie had been deposited in a side parlor with Miss Crossham's promise that she would soon return with her mother. And she had.

The baroness sat in a large chair that dwarfed her thin body, two black-clad attendants standing silently behind her. She peered at the young woman with a slightly worried expression, not the skeptical intensity Maggie would have expected from a woman who was Charles' mother. She shook her head, making the jet beads glitter across her thin bosom.

"Millicent says that she found you on the road," the old woman said doubtfully, giving her daughter a nod.

"Yes, madam," Maggie said with a respectful nod. "I am afraid that my carriage had met with an accident, and your daughter was kind enough to invite me to ride with her. I mean no presumption, madam, I assure you."

The older woman looked torn. "Who was your father?"

"William King of Somerset," Maggie lied. Her surname, however false that it was, was convenient in that there were a great many dead men to claim relation to.

"I see," Lady Edgington said, and it was clear to Maggie that as she had never heard of William King, she held the entire affair in the greatest doubt. Behind her, Miss Crossham looked anxious. With a sigh and another worried look, the baroness said, "You aren't quite our sort."

"No, I am afraid that I have lived with a very retired family, madam," Maggie said humbly.

"But you seem to be of good stock—better than many of the lady's companions and poor relations who flock here," the old lady continued, and Maggie suppressed a smile as she thought of Miss Howser.

The expression of the women behind Lady Edgington grew stiff, and Maggie bit her lip at the recognition that she had just acquired enemies.

"Yet I really know nothing of your people," the baroness said, oblivious to the reaction of her attendants. She shook her head and made the jet beads dance. "You seem to be a sweet girl, from all that Millicent has told me, and you seem to have suffered unduly. I should be pleased to have you here as our guest for the space of the party. After that, I shall make some inquiries, and then we shall see."

"Thank you, madam," Maggie said, tension she had not known was there going out of her all at once.

"I suppose you will wish to revive yourself after your adventure this afternoon." It wasn't a question, but the lady's declaration couldn't have suited Maggie better.

"Yes, madam."

Lady Edgington rang a crystal bell that sat on the table beside her, and immediately, a parlor maid entered.

"Take Miss King to a room, please," the baroness instructed.

"Which one, m'm?" the maid asked. "The clean ones are all full up."

The lady hesitated. "Is the Winter Suite open?"

"Yes, m'm."

"Then put her there."

Maggie took her leave of the baroness and followed the parlor maid up a side staircase and down a long, echoing corridor until she reached a door at the very end. The maid opened it and stepped aside to allow Maggie to enter.

"Dinner is at eight, m'm," the maid said. "I'll send a housemaid to freshen the room and light a fire."

"Thank you," Maggie said absently as she stepped inside the chamber. She barely heard the maid leave.

She faced a sitting room more opulent than any she had ever been in. She had a vague memory of entering the Edgington House through a vast and richly decorated hall, and the side parlor where Lady Edgington had met her had been luxurious, but Maggie had been so preoccupied with the interview with her baroness, impending or in progress, that none of the details had made an impression upon her. But she was past the threshold now—past Cerberus, and she smiled at the thought of the thin, worried baroness being paralleled with the fierce monster she had read of in her studies—so there was nothing to keep her from taking in the fabulous appointments of the room.

There was nothing in the room that was not white. The floors were marble, the walls plaster and damask, the wood stained so that the grain formed delicate gold pat-

terns against the snowy ground. The result should have
been sterile, but Maggie had never realized how many
shades of white there could be, tinted gray and blue in the
shadows of the evening. She advanced, her footsteps hes-
itant on the thick rug. Everything about the room bor-
dered on extravagance—the incredible forms of the
plasterwork on the ceiling and walls, the rich texture of
the damask, the sinuous forms of the carved furniture. It
all created an effect that would have been overwhelming
if there had been any other color in the room.

Feeling like an intruder, Maggie explored the rest of
the suite, which consisted of another sitting room, a bedroom, and a vast dressing room. She returned to the first
room and sat, slightly dazed. She had not understood
until then what it fully meant for Charles to be the Baron
Edgington—she had not grasped how far above her he
truly was. He had told her stories of his youth, but the
vague references to the day and night nursery, the lawn
and allee and grotto, had not left Maggie with a distinct
picture of exactly what his life had been like. Now the
dizzying vastness and luxury of his home seemed like a
mockery of the time that he had spent with her in
Chelsea. The row house must be like a doll's house to
him. Just as the Chelsea house had rooms fully as large as
her St. Giles flat, this suite in the Edgington House could
swallow the Chelsea house whole.

Maggie shivered in the chill that radiated from the
stone walls and wished that the housemaid would hurry.
But not even the merriest fire would drive away the
queasiness in her belly that warned her that this entire es-
capade had been a very, very bad idea.

Three hours after Maggie's dramatic introduction into
their society, the company was still abuzz with excite-

ment that easily eclipsed Miss Howser's scandalous presence and any excitement over the tour of Lord Langston's half-built manor, even though, or perhaps because, Maggie had shown the greatest delicacy and reticence during the remainder of the outing. In Maggie's absence, the story had to be recounted to each of the guests who had remained behind at least half a dozen times. Lady Elizabeth and Lady Mary brought a laughing Fern Ashcroft into a dramatic reinterpretation of the entire scene, with one of the twins playing a swaggering, preening version of Peter Radcliffe and the other one playing an apocryphally flirtatious Maggie, improving the story, as they said, for the entertainment and edification of the others.

"Mother was perfectly welcoming. She had me put Miss King in the Winter Suite," Millie told Charles as she passed behind his chair. "She's resting now from her shock, poor thing, but she has promised to join us for dinner."

Charles reached out and caught Millie's hand before she could move away. "Above my suite?"

Millie freed herself, a small frown marring the smoothness of her face. "I did not think you would mind. It's not as if she'll be traipsing down the staircase to disturb your rest in the middle of the night."

"No, I suppose not," Charles agreed, even as his mind dwelt on images that were remarkably similar to the situation his sister had just described.

Finally, supper was called, and with it came the reemergence of the most salient subject of conversation—Maggie.

She descended the stairs just as everyone was passing through the front hall, following in the wake of an Edgington maid. The timing was perfect. Conversation

sputtered into silence, and the company drew collectively
to a halt and stared, for there could not have been a better setting to display Maggie's fragile coloring and delicate build than the great white vault of the hall.

She wore a dinner dress of stark black, the simplicity
of the single color belied by the layered intricacy of the
design. A gathered lace bertha embraced her shoulders,
dripping with faceted jet beads that glittered darkly
against her white arms. In such a costume, her painful
slenderness was transformed into ethereal sublimity, the
translucency of her skin glowing like alabaster in the pale
light of the gas jets.

She hesitated as she saw everyone looking at her, her
eyes going wide. Charles knew that the others saw maid-
enly reserve in that response, but he recognized it for the
wary distrust that it was. Before he could step forward to
offer his arm, Lord Gifford slid into place at the foot of
the stairs and Lady James' nudge propelled Flora
Ashcroft to Charles' side.

Gifford's motion seemed to bring everyone else back
to their senses, for they began laughing and talking all at
once, taking up their migration to the dining room as if it
had never been interrupted. Charles obediently offered
his arm to Miss Flora, who took it without reaction, her
eyes fixed upon the floor.

The tall, dark-haired man's arm felt wrong under her
own, but Maggie tried to hide any reaction as she allowed
him to lead her through the midst of the company. She
had to force herself not to stare at Charles to try to understand how what she knew of him and the life this house
represented fit together in one man.

Instead, Maggie cast a covert look around her, regis-
tering the wrongness of the amorphous gathering.
Weren't the men each supposed to escort a woman? But

there was Peter Radcliffe with a twin on each arm, and Miss Crossham walking next to another lady, only a few of the others progressing to the table in the proper pairs.

"Miss King," the man who had taken her arm said, "we do not much stand upon ceremony here, which is perhaps fortunate as the addition of another lady or two does not throw our hostess' plans off." He smiled at her doubtful look. "It is a very elevated company who can dispense with convention without fearing accusations of vulgarity. We set fashion, not follow it."

"I see . . . sir . . . ." Maggie trailed off, not sure how to address the man.

"Lord Gifford," the man supplied, his blue eyes glittering down at her. "I could call over Miss Crossham to introduce us, but it seems a little silly under the circumstances, don't you think?"

"Yes," Maggie said, inserting a sliver of doubt into her tone.

"I am glad to avail myself of the opportunity to get to know you better," Lord Gifford continued.

Maggie looked at him askance, catching the too-personal tone in his voice, and pulled back slightly. "Indeed," she said with all the chilliness she could manufacture.

"I know who you are," he whispered. "Sir Nathaniel Dines told me." He nodded at a man walking in front of them. His blond hair was ruffled, and Miss Howser was on his arm.

Dines, Charles' friend who had produced Miss Howser, Maggie's memory supplied. She had never met him but had known of his complicity in their plot. Maggie pursed her lips. Charles, Sir Nathaniel, Lord Gifford, Miss Howser—how many others knew?

But Lord Gifford said nothing more, and soon enough,

they were at the table. One of the older ladies declared
that Maggie should be the guest of honor and surrendered
her seat beside Charles. From the canny glint in the
woman's eyes, Maggie guessed that her motive was more
curiosity than generosity, for her move guaranteed that
she was merely two seats away from the new arrival. For
her part, Maggie was grateful for the placement; it insured that she had Charles on one side, and as Gifford
took the other, she was at least somewhat insulated from
direct scrutiny from any of the guests whom she was supposed to be fooling.

She had been so preoccupied with trying to keep up
the correct appearance that she did not have time to take
in the room until after she was seated. When she did look
around, though, it stole her breath with its magnifi-
cence—much as the front hall had upon her entrance, and
much as her rooms had, as well. The chamber was white
and glittering, the walls divided into snowy silk-hung
panels by intricate curlicues of plasterwork gilded with
silver, great mirrors alternating with enormous paintings
on some heroic theme, each of which was half again as
tall as she was. The long table seated the party of thirty
people easily, and yet it left the room far from crowded,
even with the blue-and-gold footmen who stood behind
every chair—Maggie guessed that it could hold three
times as many people with ease.

Maggie sneaked a look at Charles, not certain of precisely what she would see. He was the same man who re-
clined in unconsciously arrogant comfort at her little
table in Chelsea, and he filled the space at the head of this
table as easily as he had her smaller one, a golden god
against a field of snow, born to lord over such a company
in such a room. He looked, in short, like the Baron
Edgington.

His mother chattered gaily with her friends at the opposite end of the table, closely accompanied by the same two elderly women in plain black dresses whom Maggie had decided were companions or ladies-in-waiting or something of that sort. Lady Edgington did not often give any sign that she was directing the elaborate performance of the dinner, and yet everything that happened at the table seemed to revolve around her subtly, as if she were the timing spring in an intricate mechanism. Maggie wondered what she would think if she knew her son's low-class lover was at the table—what she would do. She shuddered.

Maggie spoke as little as she dared during dinner; though she no longer had to concentrate to eat her meal in an appropriately refined manner, she wanted to keep herself as much as possible in the background, unscrutinized. She was certain she looked more than a little uncertain, but she told herself that such would be expected from an orphan who had never been among society, however wealthy she was supposed to be and however genteel her origins.

Charles also said only a few spare sentences to her, retaining the role of munificent but taciturn host, though once, when she caught his eye when no one else was looking, he winked, slowly and deliberately. Her heart took flight as the chasm closed between them in an instant, and she smothered her smile in her wine.

Chapter Twelve

After dinner, the ladies had retired for a bare ten minutes before the men rejoined them, and Lady Edgington instantly declared a game of charades. This announcement was met with universal applause, and though four of the guests immediately declared themselves spectators, the rest, young and old alike, were soon divided into four teams and given their tableaux, devised along properly classical lines by Miss Crossham and Lady Edgington.

Maggie was greatly relieved that Charles arranged it so they were on the same team, along with Lord Gifford, two sisters with ash-brown hair, and the eldest sister's husband. The groups separated to plan their tableaux, Charles leading them swiftly to a small side parlor that glowed like a scarlet jewel box. There, Lord Gifford unsealed the slip of paper upon which the subject of their charade was written. Maggie already knew what all four of them were, for Charles had peeked before Lady Edgington had sealed them so that Miss West could assign Maggie lessons to cover them all.

" 'For the Fairest,' " Lord Gifford read. He looked up.

"We're to play Paris deciding which of the three god-desses should have the golden apple."

"But that's not Roman or pastoral," Maggie said, as if it were an automatic protest—Charles had publicly informed her of the theme of the party over dinner. Everyone looked at her, and she did not have to manufacture her flush.

"Miss Crossham has a rather generous idea of what's suitable to her theme," Lord Gifford drawled. "I only count it fortunate that we have three women to play the goddesses. Otherwise, I fear that I would surely end up as Venus-Aphrodite."

Maggie giggled dutifully at that, while over Lord Gifford's shoulder, Charles eyebrows shot up at her manufactured reaction. *What did you think? I'm an actress,* she thought, but she didn't dare grimace at him as she wanted to.

Hera's role was assigned to the elder of the sisters, Faith Weldon, by common accord, while her husband naturally became Zeus. Charles categorically refused to wear wings on his shoes, and so Paris was left to him, while Mrs. Weldon gently bullied the plain and blushing Miss Flora Ashcroft into accepting the place of Aphrodite. Lord Gifford took Hermes' role with grace, and so Athena was left to Maggie.

As soon as the assignments were made, everyone dispersed to devise their own costumes and props. Maggie joined a handful of guests who were heading to the bedrooms, and she passed Miss Flora just as the girl tried the doorknob to her room only to discover that it had been locked from within.

"Fern!" she cried in vexation, rapping upon it. "I know you're in there. Open the door!"

"You can't come in," came a voice through the wood.

"You'll see what I'm doing! Besides, I need Carey's help; if I let you in, you'll try to steal her."

Miss Flora stared at the blank door as if stymied, and Maggie hesitated. A rich girl could scarcely be an object of her pity, especially one who worried so over a trifle— her expression of distress was ludicrous, and on such a plump, healthy body, with her hands picking at a border of lace that would have cost Maggie a month's income as a dance hall singer . . . and yet Flora—the girl was so unassuming that it was hard to keep the proper "miss" in place—Flora *did* look miserable.

"Miss King."

Maggie pulled her attention away from the girl at the voice, and she turned to find Lord Gifford standing with Sir Nathaniel. "Yes, sir?" she asked, hiding her wariness.

The lord stepped forward so that he could be heard with his voice pitched low and motioned to the man behind him. "This is Sir Nathaniel Dines."

Maggie nodded. "You pointed him out before dinner." Sir Nathaniel was a clean-shaven man, impeccably dressed with artistically ruffled hair.

"We have come to offer our services to you," Lord Gifford continued. "As this is your first tableau, we thought you might desire a little guidance."

"Thank you, sir, but I think it would come as no surprise to anyone if the sheltered Miss King did not excel at charades," Maggie said, feeling an instinctive distrust of the black-haired lord's toothy smile. "And anyway, I was just about to ask Miss Flora to join me."

"Very well," Lord Gifford said, and he and Sir Nathaniel nodded and continued down the hallway.

Maggie had to approach the girl now. "Miss Flora?"

The girl turned her brilliant violet eyes on Maggie, her expression shy and startled. If she had been pretty, they would have made her remarkably beautiful, but her features were so mousy and dull that they only made the rest of her look more plain. "Yes, Miss King?"

"Why don't we look for costumes together? We can get sheets from my bed for our chitons." Maggie's smile felt stiff, but she hoped it looked inviting.

"Oh," the girl said. "That would be lovely."

When Maggie stopped at her door, Flora gave a nervous giggle. Maggie shot her an inquiring glance.

"This is the Winter Suite," Flora explained, blushing furiously. "I'm sure Lady Edgington meant to be kind to you. But there was once a most notorious courtesan installed here, the lover of a Baron Edgington who hated his wife but didn't dare remove her from her rooms on account of her money. It has a staircase connecting to the suite below, which he built for himself." The length and scandalousness of that story seemed to sap all of Flora's energy, for she shrunk into herself as she ended it. "I am sorry. I should not have said . . . it was many years ago. Lord Edgington has moved into the old baron's rooms out of respect for his mother, not wishing to dislodge her from her rooms for his sake, but there isn't a woman— hasn't been a mistress living in the Winter Suite for a hundred years or more."

Maggie pushed open the door and stepped inside, digesting the information. "Lord Edgington's rooms are directly below mine?"

"Yes," Flora said, looking miserable. "Oh, I am sorry. It is perfectly respectable, I am sure. Lady Edgington was being very kind—they are the largest apartments excepting the baroness'. You can lock the door to the stairs, if it has not already been sealed off—"

"I'm sure it's fine," Maggie said soothingly. "I am flattered to be given such apartments. Now, let me ring for my maid, and we'll see what we can find for costumes."

Maggie and Flora stripped the bedsheets for classical chitons, and then they went in search of props to more precisely identify themselves. Maggie's costume was simple enough to finish—Flora led her to a chamber she called the Hunt Room, which supplied Maggie not only with a helmet and sword but a stuffed duck that Flora tied, with a great deal of giggling, to Maggie's shoulder. Maggie was just relieved that they did not encounter Lord Gifford or Sir Nathaniel again.

"It doesn't look very owl-like, does it?" Maggie asked, surveying herself in a mirrored panel on the corridor wall. The helmet, with an iron brim several inches wide around it and a ridge down the center, didn't look like any etching of Athena that she had ever seen, and it slid down over her ears and forehead, while the officer's sword was so long that Maggie gave up trying to keep from tripping on it and held it under her arm.

Flora grinned. "It may not look much like an owl, but your intent will be clear enough with the helmet and sword. Now, take it off before someone sees it and think of what we can do for my costume! What am I to do? How does one look like Aphrodite?"

Maggie couldn't resist. "She was most often sculpted nude, was she not? But I doubt that shall suit for this occasion."

Flora gasped a little, her face flaming, and then dissolved into laughter. "Oh, their faces! I could just see Mamma . . . and Faith . . . and Papa . . . and Fern! They would be furious, for even they would realize that Lord Edgington would never have me after such a display."

"Lord Edgington?" Maggie asked, something inside of her going suddenly still.

"My family thinks to wed me to him," she said simply. "Actually, they think to wed me to practically anyone who is the least bit suitable, and they consider that he is the most likely young man at this gathering." Her expression turned cynical. "This is my first Season, but I am not pretty, and they are all afraid that I shall be on the shelf very soon. My dear family seem convinced that if Lord Edgington only notices me, he shall be smitten." Her mouth twisted. "As for my part, I have promised 'to look to like, if looking liking move,' but it is my judgment that Lord Edgington had looked at me often enough since we were children to know that I am nothing of interest to him."

Maggie didn't quite catch the full significance of all the girl said, but the tenor was clear enough. Her first thought was of impatient derision, that a person could be so simple that her life was overshadowed by the mere opinions of her family. But looking at the girl's soft, distressed face, she realize that Flora Ashcroft was sincerely unhappy, however silly the cause, and it occurred to her that unhappiness might find its outlets even in the pampered rich as much as happiness did even in the poor. To one who had never known the pinch of true hunger, perhaps the discomfort of a missed meal was felt as keenly as another would a meager month.

Maggie clasped the girl's arm. "I am sorry," she said. And she was sorry that the girl was hurt and her family insensitive. But not sorry that Charles didn't look at her—not sorry for that at all. The thought of Charles and Flora together—of Charles and any girl together—made her guts feel like they were being tied into knots.

Flora pasted a smile on her face. "Oh, it is nothing. Certainly nothing I should have burdened you with—and yet you seem just the one for listening!"

"Well, we must find you something," Maggie said uncomfortably. "Let us look around. Perhaps inspiration will strike."

It did, in time, and they rejoined their own group just as the bell was rung to call everyone to the ballroom for the start of the tableaux.

Maggie remembered little of the rest of that evening—just impressions of hilarity and decadence, luxury and ridiculousness, and in the center of it all, Charles, still and immovable like the Cynosure around which the sky turns. Standing among his own class, a little aloof from even the men who should be his peers, he seemed as distant and incorruptible as a star in a clear winter sky. He was the picture of the perfect aristocrat in his swallow-tailed evening coat, glowing cold and bright, and even his toga could not render him ludicrous. Every time she looked at him, her stomach hurt and her lungs seemed to ache, for she could not imagine possessing the power to reach across the vast expanse of emptiness that separated them in order to come up beside him.

I already knew that it was going to end, Maggie told herself. *Now I know that even without Danny, nothing between us could be real.*

After the charades, the party had gathered again to imbibe a final glass of sherry or brandy before retiring. One glass quickly turned to two, however, and it was several hours before the first of the party rose, marking the start of a general exodus. Charles kept his distance from Maggie the entire evening, and Maggie would not have dared to approach him now even if there had been no wager at risk.

Miss Crossham felt no such compunction. Her curiosity about Maggie knew no bounds, and though Maggie had somewhat coyly deflected her questions in the company of the others—in part to keep from seeming vulgar but just as much to incite her curiosity all the more—Maggie had scarcely entered her apartments to retire for the night when a knock announced Miss Crossham's arrival.

"Miss King, I just had to speak to you!" Miss Crossham bustled in and settled without invitation upon one of the low-backed, velvet-upholstered chairs, looking at Maggie with eyes that were bright with curiosity. Her disregard for propriety seemed not so much disrespectful as it was a kind of declaration of fellow feeling, and Maggie sat down warily across from her, unsure of what it might signify.

"You are a rare woman!" Miss Crossham declared. "No—a rare being, an ethereal thing, unmarked by mere mortals such as we, who must move along the earth and be contaminated by worldly things!"

Maggie bit down hard on the impulse to burst into laughter. Of all the beginnings, this was one that Maggie would have suspected least, nor could she think of a description of herself that was more staggeringly inapt. She dropped her eyes to her hands to hide her reaction, and then in a voice that she hoped Miss Crossham would interpret as muted from reservation, she said, "I have never been much in the world, but your praise is far too generous."

"Unspoilt child!" Miss Crossham exulted. "Oh, you must tell me your story in full, I am simply perishing of curiosity. What are your origins? What has your life been like, until the moment when we found you stranded upon the road?"

"I hardly know how my life could have been duller to describe," Maggie replied, firmly conquering the last impulse to titter as she met Miss Crossham's earnest gaze.

This tale was one she was more than ready for—she had practiced both the story and presentation more than a dozen times before achieving Charles' and Miss West's satisfaction. To Maggie's mind, it was a shade too melodramatic for truth, but her involvement in various confidence games in her old life told her that the baron's knowledge of his sister was likely exact.

She began. "My father was a man of property, and fortunately for me, his only child, none of it was entailed, for my dear mother died when I was an infant and he followed her not many years later. He had no siblings himself, and it fell to a bachelor great-uncle to be my guardian. He was a younger son who had built for himself some wealth by buying up houses in London and letting them out, and he enjoyed his city life to the neglect of his small lodge in the country. He believed that it would be to the detriment of my childish constitution to be denied the air and sun of the countryside, much less the companionship of other children and the presence of a motherlike figure, for I was a sad, sober child who had experienced little cheer in my father's widower household. With this consideration fixed in his mind, he approached a dear friend with the object of finding a happier situation for me, and it happened that the friend's daughter was married to a Middlesex squire and had three young boys but was not blessed with a daughter. My great-uncle skillfully managed my inheritance, both the principal and the property, and offered more than ample stipend for my upkeep, but the woman, whom I soon called Mamma, was so delighted by my company that my great-uncle had to force her husband to accept the sum."

Miss Crossham sighed, her eyes glazing over in sentimental rapture at the tale. "Oh, why did you ever leave that happy house? I think I should have never left!"

"My departure was not of my choosing," Maggie said gravely. "My great-uncle was a kind man but a stern one, and when I reached the age of twelve, he determined that I should be sent away to finishing school for my own improvement. Little did I know when I left the house of the happiest days of my childhood that it would be so different when I returned."

"What happened?" Miss Crossham demanded, her eyes wide.

It was a good thing that Miss Crossham was so well protected, Maggie thought. She was a bird ripe for the plucking. Aloud, she said, "Scarlet fever visited them in my absence and carried away the youngest son and my dear Mamma. The squire was quite transformed, and the happiness from that day disappeared from the house. When I finished my schooling, my great-uncle invited me to live with him, as it was no longer proper for me to stay in the house of my youth, for even though I regarded Frederick and Ambrose as my brothers and their father as my own dear father, I was now a woman grown and my Mamma—for so I always think of her—was several years in the ground, so there was no lady with whose company I could properly remain."

"You must have been quite terrified of your great-uncle!" Miss Crossham exclaimed.

"I was, at first, though I knew him to be a good and just man," Maggie agreed solemnly. "He lived very modestly, very modestly, indeed, for he kept only five servants and an old chaise—the one which is even now being taken to a forge for repair. When I arrived, he added two more domestics—a chaperone and lady's maid for my comfort—but he did not much change his ways and never went about in society. So I have lived a quiet life, very retired, though often my great-uncle said he wished it could be otherwise if only he were not so old. Within a few months of my arrival, he took ill, and I watched over him in his extremity. I discovered after his death that he had left the whole of his worldly goods to me to add to my own inheritance—but what was I to do with them? I had never come into society—I knew no one, could go nowhere, and so I left all his wealth and my own in the hands of his capable solicitor and wrote to my only living relatives. They are cousins of my Mamma—my real mother, you understand—who are of not mean estate, though perhaps not so high as one might wish, for the paterfamilias is the rector in Baslehurst. They agreed that they should be my new family for some small portion of my income, and so I am to be introduced into society at last, though it shall be the county gentry—not quite the society I had hoped it to be." She gave Miss Crossham a brave little smile.

"Oh, I do declare that you need not do any such thing!" Miss Crossham declared. "What, be banished forever from London to live in some pitiable rectory simply because one has a dearth of acquaintances and relatives? Never! I shall write them straight away and tell them that you do, indeed, have friends in London who would very much like to keep you with them. I knew the moment I saw you," she continued fervently, "that we would be like sisters. I told my mother as much, and she said that in such a case, we must learn more of you, and if the answer is satisfactory, we simply must invite you to stay with us."

"I am astonished, Miss Crossham," Maggie said honestly. Charles' cynical estimation of his sister had proved unerring, that she would unhesitatingly take a sentimental story from a stranger when she would not accept the company of a young woman without a tale of her past even if she were vouched for by the most unimpeachable sources. "I would very much like to spend more time in your company—and I have never had the pleasure of a sister." No, not a sister, for Sally's friendship was closer than mere blood to her, and Nan seemed more often like a wayward child than a sibling.

Miss Crossham leaned over to touch Maggie's cheek softly, and though Maggie has seen the frequent affectionate excesses of the female friends of Miss Crossham's class, she had to steel herself to keep from jerking away. "You must call me Millie, my dear sister, my own dear Margaret! I will tell Mamma at once—she will surely write the letter tonight, and tomorrow, you can enclose it in your own. We shall not send you into exile because of your misfortunes!"

"Thank you," Maggie said as Millie rose. She felt that more was required, and so she added, "This twice-motherless child has never dreamt to find such kindness in the world."

Millie smiled. "Any woman of sentiment would feel for your plight. Until tomorrow, my love!"

"Until tomorrow," Maggie said, bemused.

Millie flitted out—undoubtedly to find another of her bosom friends in whom to confide the entire story with appropriate embellishments and rapports of emotion—and Maggie closed the door behind her. She rang, and Sally appeared immediately from one of the inner rooms, her face tight with mute anxiety.

"It worked," Maggie said simply. "I have no idea how, but it worked."

Sally's expression melted instantly into delighted relief, and she hugged her friend hard. Maggie hugged back, grateful for the honesty of her exuberance. They both gloried in her success as Sally dressed her for bed.

But once Maggie was wrapped in her nightdress and

dressing gown and her hair was braided, Sally sighed as she stepped away, her expression abruptly sober.

"I didn't want to tell you when you were so 'appy," she said, "but I went down for dinner with the other servants, and when I come back, I found this on your bed." She reached into her pocket and held out a folded piece of paper almost apologetically. "I don't 'ardly want to worry you, mum, but it might be important . . ."

Maggie looked at the crown-and-diamond watermark on the heavy cream paper, her stomach sinking. She opened it, and a lock of short red hair fell out. She caught it in her palm and stared at it. *Frankie . . . No, not Frankie . . .* She swallowed hard against the bile rising in her throat and read the letter.

> *Congratulations. Instructions will arrive tomorrow.*
> *Yr mst hmbl srvt, &cetera, &cetera,*
> > *Danny*

The paper was coarse, but the hand was the same as the one on the note to Perle Blanc. Maggie stared at the words blindly for a moment, her guts twisting. She tightened her fist around the letter as if she could destroy the significance of the words as easily as she could crumple the paper. She looked up at Sally, who had read the letter over her shoulder.

"Can you get back to the city tonight?" she asked.

Sally nodded in understanding. "Frankie's still staying in Southwark?"

"Yes. You know his haunts at least as well as I do. I don't want to put you in danger, but it will take too long to go there and come back, and if Danny discovers that I decided to leave on my own . . ." Maggie let the sentence dangle.

"Frankie's me friend, too, mum," Sally reminded her. "I'll try to find him. If I had known it was so awful—"

"I know," Maggie interrupted. "I must see Charles. I have to get out of this now, before it's too late. Maybe Danny will let Frankie go if I can't be of any use to his plan because the baron won't have anything to do with me anymore."

The pain in Sally's eyes echoed the sickness in Maggie's stomach. "Good luck."

Maggie smiled thinly. "Or something like that."

Chapter Thirteen

"Edgington!"

Charles turned to find Dines and Gifford approaching, wearing nearly identical smirks on their faces. He suppressed the urge to scowl—and to punch Gifford in his arrogant mouth for the looks he had been shooting Maggie all evening.

"That was quite a show your little guttersnipe put on!" Gifford exclaimed. Charles had been walking through the ground-floor rooms toward the private library stairs to his suite while the other guests took the main staircase to the upper floors, so there was no one else to overhear Gifford's words. "I would have been wholly taken in. If I hadn't known, I might have even tried to woo her. Could you imagine? Me, courting a guttersnipe!"

Charles' fist clenched convulsively for a moment. He did not want to talk about Maggie with this man. "Since you do know, I suppose she is of no interest to you."

Gifford might be an ass, but he was no fool. He chuckled and waved a negligent hand. "Don't worry, old boy. I'm no thief. She's all yours."

Charles did not deign that with a reply. "Where is Miss Howser?"

"In, ah, her room," Dines said, his hesitation betraying that she might be in *a* room, but it was not necessarily her own. "Miss Crossham and the guests are taking her for exactly what you hope for them to do. From their reactions today, I'm sure your sister informed at least the Ashcroft sisters of your bet and of her suspicions about Miss Howser."

Charles shrugged, wanting to cut the conversation short. "I wouldn't be surprised. If you do not mind, I believe I will turn in for the night. Tomorrow will be a busy day."

Dines chuckled. "Yes, it most cetainly will."

"Good night, then." With a nod, Charles resumed his journey to his own apartments. He stepped out of the stairway into his bedroom and started toward the study to retrieve a ledger book that he needed to review that night. But when he entered his sitting room, he stopped in his tracks, for there was his mother, sitting close to the fire and nursing a glass of brandy.

"Madam?" he said, unable to find anything more coherent to say. He could not remember the last time she had entered his room. This suite, never. Even his first real bedroom after being promoted from the nursery had only been graced by her presence a handful of times.

"Hello, Charles," she said, and there was a brittle note in her voice. She sounded old. Tired. Unaccountably, it scared him.

"You wish to speak to me, madam?" he offered, sitting warily across from her.

"Yes," she said, but then she just stared at her brandy for a long time, turning the cup this way and that in the candlelight. Finally, she said, "I need to speak to you. Charles, I know you are not your father. I do not . . . mistake the two of you on any level. You look so much like him, though, that some days, I wake up angry at him, and I can't even bear to look at you, even though I know it isn't fair. Then I say things to you that I mean to say to him, and I make a muddle of everything."

"I know, Mother," Charles said quietly.

She nodded, and her jet beads rattled. "Yes, I realize that, but I've never told you, and sometimes, it's important just to say things. I have been wanting to say this for a long time, but"—she looked at her tumbler again—"I haven't been drunk enough to get up the courage until tonight." Her words didn't slur, but when she focused on Charles again, he saw the slight fuzziness to her gaze.

"I see," he said.

She nodded. "Mostly, though, when I look at you and your sister and think of your father, I hope that the three of us don't make the same kinds of mistakes that he and I did. We made so many, you know. I want things to be better for you two. I try so hard not to make one mistake that I make another that's even worse, and then it all falls apart. I spoil Millicent and smother you, and I don't know how to stop myself."

"Mamma . . ."

She smiled, and Charles realized how few times in recent years he had seen his mother truly smile. "Yes. Your mamma, always. I just wanted you to know that I am trying to be a good one." She stood, and Charles stood, too.

"You do not need to try so hard, madam," he said, feeling a pang at her words. "I don't demand so much from you."

She set down the brandy on a side table with a little shrug that was almost Gallic. "Then I will try to try less."

"And I—I will try to understand better," Charles said, "and to show a little more patience."

At that, she gave a dry laugh. "You, show patience!

The day that happens, the earth will stand still." With that, she tiptoed to plant a kiss on his cheek and drifted out of his apartments, shutting the door behind her.

Charles poured himself a drink and stared thoughtfully at the closed door, but he hadn't had a minute alone with his thoughts when a knock came from inside his chambers. Another knock located the sound more precisely— as he had expected, it was coming from the door to his private staircase. Maggie.

He smiled and unlatched it, swinging it open to reveal her standing on the tiny landing, her face ashen, even her lips bloodless.

His jaunty greeting died in his throat. He stepped out of the doorway, and she stumbled inside the room. "What's happened?"

"Danny has Frankie." The words seemed to tangle on their way out, and she swallowed hard and thrust a piece of paper at him. As he took the message in, she said, "This was in it," and held out a short lock of bright red hair.

"Are you sure it's his?" Charles asked, remembering his last encounter with the sneering young man. Whatever else Frankie was, he wouldn't make an easy victim.

"No," she admitted. "Sally's going to try to find out . . . But what can I do? Wait until Danny starts sending fingers?" Her hand closed convulsively around the lock, and she swallowed hard. "I don't know what to do. Frankie never asked to be involved in this. It's all my fault—"

"Right now, you're going to have a stiff drink," Charles said firmly. He coaxed the lock of hair from her fingers and pressed his tumbler of brandy into her hand instead. "Swallow it."

"I can't. I need to think. Alcohol makes me sleepy," she protested.

Charles frowned at her. "So much the better. If this is from Danny, he gave no directions and made no demands. Under such circumstances, I can think of nothing better for you to do tonight than to sleep well and face the morning with a clear head."

She frowned at him, but she drank obediently, coughing slightly at the first sip but then taking the rest of the glass in a single gulp.

He set the message and the lock on his dresser and took the tumbler back from her. "More?" he offered.

She shook her head. "Someone is helping Danny. Someone inside your house."

"But whom? A servant? A guest?" He wanted to scoff at the second possibility, but he couldn't quite manage to do it.

"It might be a guest, but a servant must be helping, too," Maggie said. "The note was left on my bed while everyone was at dinner. Unless there was a guest missing from the table?"

Charles frowned. "No. But a guest could easily enlist the help of almost any innocent servant without the least suspicion. And the handwriting—"

"Isn't it Danny's?" Maggie asked.

"I'm not so sure. It seems familiar to me." He looked at it for a long moment. "I don't know. It's certainly no one I've corresponded with much, but I think I may have seen it, somewhere . . ."

Maggie pulled a face as she appeared to think for a moment. "You know your guests. Who might be helping him?"

"None of the older men, certainly," he said firmly. "None of them has the spirit for getting involved in something like this on a lark, and none has the untempered vices for it to be blackmail. And none of their wives, for the same reason, nor my mother's ladies. In the younger set—well, I would dismiss the three Ashcroft sisters and Weldon out of hand."

Maggie smiled, if wanly. "I couldn't imagine a relation of Miss Flora being involved."

Charles nodded at her assessment. "The Hyde children . . . well, if they thought it was just a harmless lark, I wouldn't put it past Lady Elizabeth or Lady Mary, though I think Lord Hamilton is more sober than that. As for the Rushworths, Lady Victoria is certainly beyond reproach, but Lord Gifford—"

She wrinkled her nose. "It could certainly be him. He would probably think it was amusing."

"I agree," he said. Despite the gravity of their discussion, he felt a small surge of selfish satisfaction that she had taken such a dislike of him after his rather pointed attentions. "The Mortimers are too preoccupied with themselves for much attention to anything else. Not Millie—she couldn't keep her mouth shut. Sir Nathaniel Dines, the same as Lord Gifford, ditto Lord Grimsthorpe. Of the Radcliffe brothers, Colin and Christopher would certainly not countenance such a thing, but Peter and Alexander, if they thought it was a prank . . ."

"Lady Mary, Lady Elizabeth, Lord Gifford, Sir Nathaniel, Lord Grimsthorpe, and Peter and Alexander Radcliffe," Maggie repeated in a tone of dismay. "That scarcely seems to reduce the possibilities at all."

"Seven out of thirty, I know. What should we do?" Charles asked.

"Kill Danny," Maggie said brutally. "Throw him in the Thames or bury him in the garden—I don't care. I'll have him dead."

She was a tiny thing, standing there trembling in a frilled white wrapper. Her declaration should sound ridiculous, and yet a chill prickled the back of Charles' neck at her words. "You really would do it if you could, wouldn't you?"

She bit her lip hard enough that it went white. "I have to, Charles, if I possibly can. The chavies won't be safe until he's gone for good."

"Even if you hang for it?" Charles asked quietly.

She looked at him but didn't seem to be seeing him. "What you don't realize is that I'm already dead. I've been dead now for four years, living on time Danny's let me have. I helped him out once, and I might as well have killed myself then because Danny isn't one to owe anyone anything or to forgive you for the owing. I didn't know him then and thought he'd leave me be, but if I'd've known better, I would have shot him when I had the chance."

Charles didn't know what to say—didn't know what to think. This was still the Maggie he had always known, here in front of him, the passionate woman who sucked the marrow from life and wouldn't let go, but he felt like he was being allowed a glimpse of the other side of her determination, seeing for the first time the cruel lessons that had taught her the importance of tenacity, the deprivations through which she had learned what it was to need and why it was so important that she keep those she loved from want.

He took the tumbler from her gently and guided her to a chair that sat in one corner of the room, pulling the other up opposite her. She sat, automatically, it seemed, as if numbed to her surroundings by the violence of the turmoil within. He said nothing, merely waiting for her to come to grips with her thoughts and decide what she wanted to tell him.

"You don't know my life," she said eventually, her voice sounding hollow, as if from far away.

"You have told me many stories of it," Charles objected.

She wrapped her arms around her midsection and hugged herself hard, shrinking into the chair until it seemed to swallow her. "I have told you the truth, but I have told you the simple stories. The pretty stories." Her mouth twisted. "Even Nan's tale had a happy end—when she was all alone on the streets with a little sister and a swollen belly, she remembered her old friend Maggie and got a decent life again for her family."

"But there are unhappy stories," Charles said quietly, feeling her pain as an ache in the gut and not knowing how to make it go away.

"There are terrible stories," Maggie whispered, her eyes wide and focused on distant horrors. "When I was just a little thing, barely a child, my mother died and my brother, Bill, sold me to an autem mort—a beggar woman with a gang of beggar children. She was fair enough—gave us a patch of dry floor to sleep on and shared the food out even-like when there was enough, and she didn't much cuff the kiddies that didn't deserve it." Unconsciously, she began falling back into old patterns of speech. "But then she died and her man, Johnny, took the gang. He wanted to be a real rogue, a true flash cove, and so he didn't like the begging and sweeping and mudlarking that most of us did. We all had to learn to pick pockets, and every day he got harder on us. Eventually, he made all the big kiddies bring him a pound a week and all the littles bring six shillings—you just can't do that honest-like, you understand, but we had to do it or he'd beat us something awful."

"Why didn't you run away?" Charles asked.

"Where? To who?" Maggie spat. "One boy, Jamie, he tried to run, and when Johnny caught him, he beat him so hard the he started vomiting everywhere, and he was never right in the head again. Most of the girls were driven to selling themselves, and those who weren't tried on the most dangerous kinds of confidence games to pay him their weekly due, while the boys all went into troublemaking of one kind or another."

"You didn't sell yourself," Charles said, quietly. The words contained a silent question: *So what did you do?*

Maggie's mouth twisted. "Not until I met you, eh? No, I was littler than most of the boys, as skinny as one, too, and twice as quick. I sang sometimes, but mostly, I stole. I was a good pickpocket, but I was better at being a snakesman, slipping through windows of some untended shop or house to let the big men in at the door. That's how I got into the flash life. Then a cracksman took me as an apprentice for a while, and I learned how to crack all the locks except those new patent types. In those cases, I could lift a key and get a wax impression and have it back before the cove thought to miss it. I was a thief, Charles, and before the end, I was a whole lot worse than that."

"How?" asked Charles even as his chest tightened.

"I killed Johnny," she said calmly, her eyes clear and steady as she held his gaze. "That's how I know that I'd shoot Danny and be glad of it if it saves the chavies from him. I've already done it once."

"You're no murderer, Maggie," Charles said with certainty. "I can't believe it."

Maggie shrugged. "All Johnny's lieutenants had to kill someone for him to get promoted. That's how he got his hold over them, see, because he knew who they'd killed and could tell the peelers any time he wanted if they crossed him. If he asked you to be a lieutenant, you didn't say no because then he'd have one of his other lieutenants kill you instead. He fingered me for promotion, and I was supposed to shoot Danny, who was a new scurf then, crowding Johnny's turf. Johnny gave me a gun and stood on the bridge next to me, but when Danny came, I couldn't think of a reason that I wanted to kill a man I'd never met. But when I looked at Johnny, I saw Frankie getting old too quick and Jamie with his head smashed and Sally with a bloody nose, crying about the john that had beaten her and stolen her money. I saw Sam dying when Johnny wouldn't let him have no food after he got too sick to beg. I saw Moll coughing up blood and getting a kick in the ribs for it. And when I pulled the trigger, it was Johnny I'd shot, not Danny. I remember how his body fell over the edge of the bridge into the water below—I've seen it a thousand times in my mind, the bridge and the fog and the sudden fire at the end of the pistol, the shot so loud that it wasn't like a noise at all but almost like a silence, and Johnny, falling over with a hole in his head, falling over and over and over again . . ."

Charles took a shuddering breath, pulling himself out of the grotesque vision that she had conjured. "You didn't have a choice," he declared.

"Yes, I did," Maggie said flatly. "I could have refused. I could have chosen to die. I could have shot Danny, like I was meant to. But I didn't, and no matter how many times I see Johnny die in my mind, I can't be sorry for it. I didn't just kill him—I was glad I did it, because no one else dared to. The only thing I'm sorry about now is that I didn't shoot Danny, too, when I had the chance." She cocked her head to the side, her black eyes piercing.

"Now you know all that I am, and when you accept the full truth of it, you will hate me for it, though I don't fear any longer that you might turn me in to the police for my old sins, however black they may be."

Charles rebelled from her assessment. "I do not—cannot hate you, Maggie. You're not evil. I know you. You couldn't be. Did you take pleasure in the killing?"

She shook her head, tightening her lips.

Charles nodded, for she had given him the answer he knew that she would. "Then, however wrong I may be in the eyes of justice in this kingdom, I cannot regard you as other than an executioner—even a hand of fate. There may be no room in a civilized state for private pursuits of law, but when law looks away, then civilization is lost, and what can a just man do?"

"I wasn't thinking of justice," Maggie said resentfully. "I was thinking of Sally and Moll and Jamie and Sam."

"You were thinking of saving them," Charles corrected.

She shrugged helplessly.

"Though the killing might be wrong, you did save them."

"Not Sam. And not Jamie—he fell in with Danny and got taken up for coshing a toff and stealing his purse. If I don't get rid of Danny, not Sally or Moll, either," Maggie insisted.

"Nevertheless," he said. Her voice cut him when she insisted she was not sorry—not because she wasn't but because it was so clear that she wanted to be, that she felt she ought to be.

She gave a shaky noise that was probably intended to be a laugh. "You try to make my vices into virtues—it cannot be done. Are you going to make every theft I made into a sacrifice? Every cheat of an innocent as some sort of Robin Hood tale? I'd never heard of Robin Hood then, and I stole so that I wouldn't be beaten, and the loot didn't help the poor but made Johnny rich. There was no goodness in it."

"No more than in my own multitude of sins," Charles said firmly. "Mine might be less black in the eyes of the law, but that is only because the law was written by the rich, who would hang a child for stealing a handkerchief as they make away with the livelihoods of hundreds—and I have been as guilty as any." Maggie began to retort, but he cut her off. "I will not get into an argument about which of us is more corrupt. That isn't what is important now."

"What is, then?" she demanded, her chin rising. "If it isn't important that I killed a man, it's hard to imagine what would seem important to you."

"You do," he said simply.

She froze. "Still? But I watched you today, among all those aristocrats, and you were so perfect with them that I knew you couldn't want me, not really . . ." Her words trailed off, and then she made a noise of vexation. "Damn you," she said with feeling. "I meant for there to be a clean break now. I meant for you to know what I was, to hate me, to send me away before Danny asks me to do whatever terrible thing he wants of me." She grew more agitated. "Because I'll do it. He has Frankie, and so I have to. Then you go and ruin it with your bloody misguided generosity."

"I'm not going to send you away," Charles said stubbornly. "I won't—I can't."

Maggie pushed to her feet with a frustrated sound. "But you have to! I can't walk away now. He'll kill Frankie—"

"I will protect you," Charles insisted, standing as well.

"You can't, you idiot!" She all but snarled the words.

"I must!" he snapped back. "God, Maggie, do you think I'll just toss you onto the street after all this?"

"You would if you knew what was good for you," she returned. Her words grew savage. "There is nothing between us. There can be nothing between us—nothing honest, nothing honorable, nothing right."

Charles opened his mouth to reply hotly, then paused as he made an irritating realization. "You still try to provoke me."

"It's working, too." Maggie smirked, which made it only worse.

Charles took a deep breath, trying to keep a rein on his temper. "I am not going to throw you out. You could not make me do it by confessing the worst of your past to me, and you're not going to do it by acting like an obnoxious—an obnoxious brat." She looked startled at that insult, and Charles smiled grimly. "Am I supposed to just accept the fact that I have made things harder for you than they were before our association? Hell, am I supposed to just accept that my . . . attentions have made *you* worse than you were?"

"You didn't seem worried about that when you pushed me down onto the parlor floor and took me there," she retorted tartly.

"Which is precisely the point I was trying to make," Charles pointed out. "I corrupt everything I touch, and yet I cannot stop touching. I am going to make love to you tonight, I already know I will, and yet I should not. Knowing that, how can I not protect you as much as I can?"

Maggie rolled her eyes. "That makes no sense. Who cares about what you should or shouldn't do?"

"I do! I am supposed to," Charles said. "I ought to be . . . better, stronger than you."

Her eyes narrowed. "You are an arrogant ass," she pronounced precisely.

Charles raked his hands through his hair. "Maggie, sometimes you make me wish I could hit a woman! That is not what I meant, and you know it."

She snorted. "So much for being better."

Damn, but she was good at annoying him. How had she come to know him so well? "Maggie, no matter how wrong it was for me to seduce you, corrupt you, whatever you wish to call it, I believe—I have to believe—that there is something good in this, because I know there is something good in you. I cannot just . . . let go of it. No matter what."

She looked stymied, the fight going out of her all at once. "You insist that I am good? Still? Why?" She spoke in the same tone in which a person might ask, *Are you mad?*

Charles gave her a sardonic smile. "A dying man knows water when he tastes it." She opened her mouth to argue again, but Charles wasn't in the mood to listen to any more of her self-flagellation, so he stopped her mouth with his own. She stiffened against him for a moment, but then she seemed to go boneless all at once, her lips hungry and hot against his, the intensity of it stealing his breath, stealing his mind. He gave her everything she asked for and took even more, holding her hard against him as her mouth surrendered to his own. She tasted like herself, familiar and carnal, her body too small and frail in his arms to stand against the assaults of the world. He wanted to protect her, to place himself between her and the universe, to keep her safe and make her his. Forever.

Finally, she pulled away, and with a muffled sound halfway between a whimper and a sigh, she pressed her face against his chest and closed her eyes, clinging to him as if he had obliterated her desire to fight with him in that kiss.

"You undo me," Charles said softly, fervently. "God, Maggie. You find a corner of myself that's picked loose, you pull . . . and I just unravel."

"I don't want to *unravel* you," she protested, her eyes opening and seeking his face. "I want you, that's all, for the time we have left together, even though I know I shouldn't."

"Why does it have to end?" He spoke the words slowly, with decision.

Maggie shook her head, rocking against his chest. Her eyes were damp. "I've already told you I won't be your mistress. I can't stay here with Danny threatening my chavies. You know that."

"I'm not talking about that. What if you were to become a person Danny does not dare to coerce? Maggie, mine only—" He broke off with a bitter laugh. "I sound like an idiot. I can't do this; I don't have the words; I don't know how to make it sound like it is supposed to. I'm not even sure how it should sound, to ask a woman like you, when I feel so intensely—is there nothing that doesn't sound trite and hollow? My drink in the desert, my undoing, my life . . ." Maggie pulled back slightly, staring at him, her face blank with incomprehension. He pressed on. "I'm sure those words have been said by a thousand men, and their meaning has been wrung out of them with the use. So I will just say it bluntly: Maggie, will you marry me? Become my baroness, leave all this behind. The rector's family we paid off in Baslehurst will be only too glad to find themselves related to a peeress—"

Maggie's laughter cut him off, high and shrill and brittle. "Charles, Charles you are mad. I don't belong here. I can't own this. Just look at me! I'm the street rat you picked precisely because I did not belong. A reformed pickpocket and a dance hall singer. You're talking rot, and tomorrow, you will realize it and will repent of this stupid conversation."

"If you don't belong, then it's this place that is wrong, not you," he said.

"Your world doesn't care, Charles. For a week, it is a clever coup for me to parade as one of you. But I am a fraud, and your sister's reaction to Lily Barrett is clear enough evidence of what happens to frauds—"

"You are the most honest woman I know, damn your stubborn eyes," Charles grated.

"I am not a lady," she said distinctly. "If you ask me to become a lady, to play at it all the time, wouldn't I become a fraud, then, and lose what you care most about?"

"Maggie, the mere fact that you can say such a thing means that it is impossible for you to be anything other than yourself, whatever veneer you apply." He glared at her, and she lifted her chin at him in the exasperating way that she had. "Stop arguing for once and tell me you'll marry me."

Her gaze was sharp. "Why is this so important to you? Are you trying to rescue me, Charles? Are you trying to rescue your own conscience?"

"Of course not." Then honesty made him add, "Perhaps—perhaps that is some small part. Because I do think, in some obscure way, that you are my salvation. But if I just wanted to assuage my conscience, I would simply write you a cheque for one hundred pounds, two hundred, and congratulate myself for setting you up with a new life and be done with it. But I am not going to do that because what I want is you, here beside me, every hour that I can have you for the rest of my life."

Maggie closed her eyes, her face tight. "I do not know what to say. I do not know what I *can* say. Just—don't ask me that question now. When this is all over—you can ask me then."

The way she said *all over* sounded like *never* to Charles, and a chill passed over him. But all he replied was, "You can say yes, Maggie. That's what you can say." Then he pulled her into his arms and applied all the powers of persuasion at his body's disposal, even though he knew it would not be nearly enough.

Chapter Fourteen

"What are we to do today, Millie?" Fern Ashcroft asked as she lounged on a sofa with her sister, disconsolately paging through a book of poetry. Flora had motioned for Maggie to sit with them as soon as she had emerged from the breakfast room, and so she sat, pretending to work on a little embroidered handkerchief that Miss West had started. The weight of the revolver was heavy against her leg. She had insisted that her modiste leave a six-inch length of seam open in each of her skirts to form a slit so that she could wear a pocket between her dress and her petticoats. She'd had no clear thought in view at the time her dresses had been made except that pockets were too useful to not have, but now she was grateful for her requirement. Charles had helped her dress that morning, though he still did not know about the gun, and she had done her own hair, for Sally had still not returned from her trip into the city. Maggie tried not to be uneasy about her absence—Southwark was far away, and it was a large district to search—but she still worried.

Maggie studiously avoided Charles' gaze; she found that she could not trust herself to look upon him without betraying a lack of indifference that was inappropriate to the role as the innocent heiress. Even across the room, with all the inane, desultory conversation of a morning begun too early after an evening that had lasted too long, she could feel him like a naked flame. His anger seemed to scorch her skin and heat her soul, and she could not comprehend the casual obliviousness of the rest of the company in the presence of such a vital force. She couldn't marry him. The very idea was ludicrous. But it didn't matter, for within the week, she wasn't going to be in a position to marry anyone.

"Today, we shall be nymphs of the wood!" Millie announced. She had distributed another set of flower garlands and laurel wreaths at breakfast, and Lady Mary and Lady Elizabeth had stolen Peter Radcliffe's and their brother Lord Hamilton's crowns for their own coiffures. In response, Peter had taken those of his three brothers and Sir Nathaniel Dines and now wore all four of them atop his head and, in order to outdo the twins in all respects, had talked Maggie and Flora Ashcroft out of their garlands. This action had naturally introduced the idea for a new pastime to the twins, that of trying to knock the precarious stack of wreaths off Peter's head, much to the amusement of Lord Gifford, Sir Nathaniel, and Alexander Radcliffe. Maggie kept a sharp eye on her private list of suspects, but she wasn't sure what she expected to accomplish—it wasn't as if one of them would jump out at her and announce he was passing messages for an unknown man in London.

"I don't know about Gifford, here, but I am not feeling very nymphlike at the moment," Sir Nathaniel drawled, running a hand over his smooth chin, his blue eyes half lidded. Clinging to his elbow, Miss Howser giggled. Maggie suspected that she wasn't the only person to have not spent the night in her own room.

"Nymphs or huntsmen," Millie amended primly. "We are going to have an archery contest!"

Lady Rushworth looked up from her conversation with Lord Hyde. "Archery? Why, no one's done archery since I was a girl!"

"I thought it would be a novelty these days," Lady Edgington said with a nod to the company.

"Let us repair to the firing range," Charles said coolly, pushing himself upright from the window in which he had been leaning.

Peter Radcliffe struck a dramatic pose. "Hie you, hie you all to the coursing fields, where fiercesome bags of hay await the stings of your outrageous arrows!" With that, he pushed open the nearest French window and stalked through onto the terrace, his heroic attitude ruined when one of the twins, stifling her giggles, hurried up behind him and knocked his tottering wreaths onto the dewy ground.

That marked the beginning of a general exodus. The process took several minutes, as servants had to be called to bring gloves, hats, overcoats, and wrappers, but finally, everyone was gathered on the lawn beyond the terrace. The women held the skirts of their diaphanous morning dresses out of the damp grass as their crinolines swayed like gaudy church bells in the fresh, damp breeze.

"I do wish you had told us last night what we could have expected for the day," Faith Weldon said to Millie, her limpid eyes filled with delicate reproach. "I would have worn a dress more suitable to sport."

"That would have spoiled that surprise," Millie said airily, directing a waiting footman to distribute four bows to the company.

Maggie watched the process uncertainly. She had never drawn a bow before. But then again, neither had most of the others; she would be more exceptional if she were skilled than if she demonstrated no ability at all.

There were three targets set upon the grass at some twenty yards' distance—not sacks of hay, as Peter Radcliffe had anticipated, but stacks of bales with brightly painted paper targets affixed to them. Flora stood at Maggie's elbow, glancing at the lowering sky with patent unease.

"Do you think it will rain?" she asked.

Maggie looked up critically. The clouds were deep slate, and they moved as she watched, the hills and valleys overhead bulging and sinking as she imagined the sea might right before a storm. Such a sight was rare in London—the heavy, damp air pressed the smoke down into the streets, hiding the clouds above—but the air was thick with the taste of rain. Behind them, the great façade of the manor seemed to pulse white against the dark green of the sward and the deep gray sky, the dome of the front hall rendered insignificant by the full length and height of the structure.

To be the wife of Charles, the mistress of that . . . A pang shot through Maggie, wistfulness seasoned with the sting of impossibility and the deeper pain of hopeless longing. *Fool*, she sneered at herself. *Idiot. He's not yours to have, he never was, he never could be, and you knew it from the beginning. He knows it, too, and will come to his senses soon enough.*

She kept her face still—it felt carved, like a death mask made for someone else—and responded to Flora's anxious question. "Undoubtedly," she said. "I do hope we don't get soaked through."

Lady Edgington divided the party into four groups. No one demurred, not even Lady Rushworth's sarcastic daughter, whose pale, thin lips twisted in a kind of private smile as she grasped her weapon. They lined up in front of their respective targets, firing three arrows each in turn as Millie's own lady's maid assiduously tallied the scores and four footmen retrieved the arrows between each set.

Maggie was in the third set, following Sir Nathaniel Dines, who neatly planted the first two arrows almost precisely in the center of the target. Maggie watched as he drew his arrow back for his last shot, and right before he released, the tip dipped. The arrow sprang from the bow and buried itself in the second to outermost ring. She blinked. Had he done it on purpose? Sir Nathaniel turned around and caught her staring in confusion, and he gave her a smile and a slow, deliberate wink before handing her the bow and taking his place at the back of the group. Maggie shivered slightly, then told herself that she was being ridiculous, reading something sinister into actions that were merely odd simply because Sir Nathaniel had made Charles' list of people who might help Danny.

She stepped up to the firing line, nocked an arrow, and drew back the bowstring. She was surprised at how easy it was—she had expected it to take more strength. She aimed carefully at the target, remembering how the boys in Johnny's gang had been obsessed with knife throwing for one long winter, how she'd practiced and practiced in secret so that she could stand with the best and win their respect despite her sex and small size. . . .

She released the string, and the string made a soft zipping sound as the arrow jumped forward to land neatly at the edge of the bull's-eye. Exclamations went up around her, and she smiled as she aimed the second arrow—this time, a little farther to the left. She did not want to appear to be *too* good.

Charles was in the fifth set. His arrows formed a tighter cluster than hers, and to her questioning look, he merely answered, "I hunt," as he passed back down the line. Lady Rushworth, after overcoming an initial unsteadiness, sent each of her quarrels into a tight bull's-eye, much to the astonishment of her son, Lord Gifford. Her daughter, Lady Victoria, did not fare much worse.

As the rounds and eliminations progressed, bets and counter-bets were taken. Millie attempted to participate until she was treated to a suppressive glance from her brother. The final shots were taken to cries of glee or despair, depending upon the wagers of the audience. The favorite, Lady Rushworth, won handily. As she exchanged her bow for her cane, appearing to be calm except for two spots of color high on her papery cheeks, she simply observed that archery had been a great sport when she was a girl, and she had been the best of them all. Even so, Sir Nathaniel Dines might have beaten her if not for a stray gust of wind that tossed one arrow a few inches to the side—he took defeat in good graces, saying that if it had been thrown daggers rather than Cupid's darts, he might have been the victor yet, a remark that the twins took as hilarity though there was no hint of humor behind his glittering monocle. A chill ran up Maggie's neck as she remembered her own thoughts less than an hour before. She looked at his retreating form. Too old—he was in his thirties, surely, and no one that old could have been in Johnny's gang when Danny took over. And a baronet! she reminded herself. How silly would her paranoia make her?

The game concluded just in time, for scarcely had the company started migrating back across the lawn toward the house when the first drops of rain began to fall. The twins let out little shrieks and burst into a run, dashing with Millie, the younger Ashcroft sisters, and the Radcliffe sons back to the protection of the house. The rest of the company ignored the weather entirely, ambling across the lawn as if the vagaries of the elements were beneath their august consideration.

It seemed that the weather did show them some measure of respect, for the last of the party reached the shelter of the morning room just as the rain began in earnest.

"Oh dear!" Millie exclaimed. "I left my parasol on the field."

"Why did you bring out a parasol in weather like this?" Peter Radcliffe asked.

"You never know," she replied tartly, nonsensically. "And now they're taking up the targets," she added, looking at the group of servants struggling to load the slippery hay bales onto the cart in the raid. "They're not going to see it. They'll trample it for certain!"

"I will get it," Maggie found herself volunteering. She felt smothered, pressed in the morning room with so many wide crinolines and shoulders. Even the rain seemed like an escape in comparison.

"Oh, not you!" Millie looked horrified. "You could catch your death. Let Charles go. Or Peter."

Peter Radcliffe snorted. "So I can catch *my* death? Thank you all the same, Millie, but I think I'll decline."

"No, really, I will be fine. I was raised in the country, you know—I used to be caught out in rainstorms all the time," Maggie said cheerfully, and to head off further protests, she put action to her words, opening the long window, stepping outside, and striding across the terrace toward the targets on the lawn with her wrapper pulled tight against the rain.

"Charles, you must go after her!" Lady Edgington's voice had a note of horror in it, but Maggie didn't look back. If this act destroyed her pretence of gentility, then so much the better. Then she'd be useless to Danny, and maybe he would let Frankie go. If he had Frankie at all.

Maggie heard footsteps behind her, catching up quickly. She looked at Charles as he drew even with her. His face was cast in an expression of stern disapproval.

"What are you doing?" he demanded.

"Escaping," she said curtly.

"You are getting soaked." The rain hissed down around them, the wind blowing the icy needles into her face and causing them to trickle down the back of her neck.

"Not yet," she said, pulling the wrapper tighter.

"You will get sick," he objected.

"Then so will you." She trudged on, her head down as she concentrated on not slipping on the short, rain-slick grass of the lawn.

"You're a fool," he retorted. "Soaking yourself isn't going to help anything."

Maggie scowled. There was the parasol—a good twenty feet from where the servants were laboring. "It will get me away from the others. One of them is helping Danny, and I'm going half crazy thinking about who it might be."

"Maggie, we're going to get through this." From another man, the words might have been soft, tender, but Charles all but ground them out with an expression of the kind of determination that moved mountains.

A determination that would get him nowhere. Maggie retrieved the parasol with a sigh. "Of course we will," she lied, and then she turned and headed back toward the house, leaving Charles staring after her.

Back in the morning room, Maggie returned Millie's parasol and retired to her rooms to change out of her wet attire, avoiding all the ladies' attempts to fuss over her damp condition. She heard Charles' footsteps behind her upon entering the front hall—heard him on the stairs, continuing past his rooms on the first floor to follow her up to the second. Steadfastly, she ignored him. There was no point in speaking to him any further, for there was nothing more that could be said between them that was not a mere repetition of earlier painful conversation.

Charles caught up to her halfway down the dim corridor leading to the Winter Suite. He grasped her elbow and pulled, using her momentum to spin her around to come up against his broad chest.

Maggie opened her mouth to protest, but he gathered her firmly against him and kissed her, expertly, thoroughly, devastatingly. She could not help it—her too-taut muscles went slack, and she leaned into him, savoring the insistent rhythm of his mouth against hers, the heat and strength of his body that surrounded her as desire pooled in her center sweetly, almost like hope.

After a moment that was far too short, he pulled away, letting her go and taking a step away from her.

"You oughtn't have done that," Maggie said, saying what should be said even though she could not regret the kiss. "Someone might have seen."

"No one did," Charles said, regarding her steadily. The rain had caused his hair to start to curl against his scalp, setting his usual perfection into disarray.

She gave him a crooked smile. "Aren't you going to yell at me some more?"

"I did not yell," he said with humor and pain mingling in his expression. "Words may not be enough to change your mind, but I wanted you to remember this." His angled chin indicated their kiss and everything else that was between them. "It may be less eloquent, but I hope no less persuasive for that."

Biting her lip, Maggie nodded. "I could never forget it."

"Good," Charles said. He reached out and brushed her jawline with his thumb. "I must change clothes now. The company should start to wonder if I were gone too long."

She nodded again, saying nothing. He turned a little abruptly and walked stiffly away, his shoulders outlined against the light, and she watched him leave with a tickling tightness in her throat.

By the time Maggie rejoined the party, Charles was there, and they had been engaged in various word games for half an hour. Flora Ashroft had just won the poetry competition and was blushing as Peter Radcliffe dramatically crowned her with a wreath, making her their de facto poetess laureate. Charles had already returned to the room, and Maggie avoided his gaze as she took the seat that Millie offered her.

Lady Edgington acknowledged Maggie's arrival with a nod and announced that their next diversion would be a pastoral-themed game of anagrams. Maggie dutifully wrote the words she had memorized for the event—PHILTER TASSO ALL DAN—on the slip of paper she was given and hoped that the one she was expected to solve would be so difficult that her failure would surprise no one. When it came time to trade, Lord Gifford gave her his with a wink, and Maggie opened it.

NO SAY NULL DIVAN. Well, she should at least make a pretense of working at it. She looked at the words. No say null divan. Something about them tugged at the edge of her mind. Null divan, null*di*van, *null*divan. Nullivan . . . sullivan. Sullivan. She stared. O'Sullivan. No say null divan—Danny O'Sullivan! She looked up sharply, her breath catching in her lungs.

Lord Gifford smiled at her—there was no malice in it,

just the amusement of a school boy who had pulled a prank with repercussions he did not understand. He looked at her, and then his gaze slid sideways, to meet that of Sir Nathaniel Dines, whose monocle glinted in the gaslight and obscured one blue eye like a patch.

For an instant, she lost control of her expression. In her mind's eye, she saw his face half-obscured by side whiskers and a moustache, a hat pulled low over his slicked hair. And Danny smiled, raising a hand as if to smooth his tousled hair and pat his now naked cheeks. Danny, Danny *here*. Not Danny's goons or Danny's friends but Danny himself.

Maggie's mind reeled. He belonged here—Danny was a gentleman, as she'd suspected, but not a fallen one, no, not at all. Did the laughing Lord Gifford have any idea of what the man was, what he'd done? She stared around the room, and everything seemed to shift horribly, the cheerfulness of the guests sliding out of focus, out of tune in the presence of the coldest killer in England. The gun was leaden against her leg.

She rose abruptly, and the people nearest her glanced at her with surprised incuriosity. She saw the question in Charles eyes, and she sent him a silent, pleading look as she mumbled an excuse and pushed from the room.

Next door, the breakfast room was swathed in shadows, dull sheets of water dripping down the windows and distorting the lawn and park beyond until they were an amorphous, twisting mass of dark greenery. Maggie leaned against the wall, closing her eyes as she slipped her hand into the hidden pocket where the cold hardness of her gun lay against the taut fabric between the hoops of her crinoline.

Charles will never forgive me, she thought as her hand closed around the handle. But would it matter, anyway, when she'd so soon be dead? She had to do it. She was as good as dead already—only a fool would think that Danny had any intentions of letting her survive now that she knew his second, respectable identity. But even if it was too late for her, she could save the chavies. Strong. She must be strong for only a minute, half a minute, and then it would all be over, her life out of the power of her hands.

And Charles would be so angry.

She rehearsed the steps in her mind. Take out the gun. Cock it. Open the door a crack and peer through until she was sure she had a clean shot. Step through the doorway, raise the gun, pull the trigger, end two lives—Danny's and her own, when they hanged her. *Oh, God, Charles* . . . .

The breakfast room door creaked open. Maggie clutched at the gun convulsively, but before she could get it free, Danny was on her, his hard grip jerking her hand from her pocket and pinning her wrists to either side of her head.

She struggled against him silently, her breath rasping in her lungs, but her crinoline merely bucked and swayed when she tried to lash out with her feet, and her slight weight could do nothing against his hold. She could scream—

"Don't say nothing if you value Frankie's life." Danny—Sir Nathaniel—snarled the words from between clenched teeth. A reflection from the window glinted off his monocle. Why hadn't she seen it before? Sir Nathaniel's hair was poetically ruffled instead of sleek, and the features that were usually hidden under side whiskers and a moustache—false, she now realized— were now clean-shaven and sharply defined. But the soulless eyes that twinkled with such joyous malevolence were the same as Danny's single one, and just as frightening. "I've told a loyal man o' mine to kill him tomorrow if he don't get word not to."

Maggie stopped struggling, taking deep, ragged breaths. "What do you want, Danny?" she spat.

"Danny doesn't exist here, girl," he said, lapsing back into cultured tones, the snarl falling into a smirk without a ripple. "There is only me."

"What do you want?" she repeated. She made her eyes narrow in defiance as her heart fluttered a panicked tattoo against her chest. He was not so large as Charles, but he was still much bigger than she—a hand around her throat, half a minute, and she'd be dead. Her strengths had always been quickness and stealth. Pinned to the wall, she was as helpless as the child some people still mistook her for.

Sir Nathaniel smiled a broad, ugly smile. "I want to make the biggest flash pull in the history of the British Empire."

"Good thing the Empire isn't very old, eh? Otherwise, you'd have a much bigger job," she retorted automatically.

Sir Nathaniel ignored her rejoinder. "I misspoke," he said coolly. "I meant that *you* are going to make the biggest flash pull in the history of the Empire."

"I don't know what you're talking about." But she did know—all too well. And far too late to do anything about it. *You're going to use me. Then I'll have an accident and all the loot will disappear . . . and I can't do a bloody thing to stop it.*

"Lady Edgington. Millicent Crossham. Lady James Ashcroft. Fern and Flora and Mrs. Weldon. Lady Elizabeth and Lady Mary. Mrs. Mortimer. Lady Rushworth and, yes, even Lady Victoria. Do you know what they have in common?" the man asked coldly.

Maggie wasn't going to play this game. "Well, if any of 'em's got a wanker, someone's sure in for a surprise."

"They are ladies, my dear colleen." The endearment dripped with sarcasm. "Ladies of the best families. Ladies of the oldest families, which means that they have several hundred years of family jewels at their disposal."

"And?" Maggie said, determined to make him spell it out.

"And you will be stealing them all for me tonight," Sir Nathaniel said.

"What if they're wearing them?" Maggie demanded.

"Don't worry. They won't be. Don't you know that I've arranged everything?"

Maggie just stared at him.

"You know where the bedrooms are. You will know when it is time. The talented Miss Howser will be your assistant, and my . . . valet . . . will keep watch, so have no fear that you will not have sufficient assistance."

So much for claiming that she'd forgotten how to crack a lock—which she likely had. Miss Howser's expertise would fill in any lack there. Maggie was just along for the ride, along for the fall.

"You and Lord Gifford have it all planned out, then, don't you?" Maggie said bitterly.

Sir Nathaniel simply smiled. "Lord Gifford? I think not. He's a good boy, though; always ready for a prank. He has no idea what is at stake here—and will not, until it is far too late and he doesn't dare open his mouth."

"How do I know you aren't trying to play me for a fool, too? How do I know you really have Frankie?" she demanded. She might risk her life—lose her life—for her friend, but not for a scam.

"You'll just have to have a little faith, won't you?" the man said, an amused expression on his face. "But if that isn't enough, well, you could send a footman to the Queen's Head in Southwark. The publican will tell you quick enough what happened there two nights ago."

Two nights. Even before she had come to Edgington Manor. He had known of the plan since Charles had met him at the opera, but how had he known that the private bet between Millie and the baron would take place? And what about Lily Barrett's disgrace? Could he have arranged that, too?

"Don't think about telling your baron, either," the man continued. "He won't live to see the new year—no, not even if I'm dead, because I've left instructions. There are many accidents that can befall a young peer, especially one who is so adventurous." He chuckled. "I supposed that if the threat to your Frankie's life isn't enough, that is. Edgington wouldn't believe you anyway. We've known each other since we were boys, but you—what does he know about you except what's between your legs?"

The doorknob turned again, and Sir Nathaniel stepped away from her swiftly, spinning and striding across the breakfast room and out into the corridor. For half a second, Maggie entertained the wild idea of grabbing her gun and shooting him in the back. But she couldn't do it—that would kill Frankie and, God, Charles, too, as surely as if she'd shot them instead. She was still staring at the empty doorway in impotent frustration when Charles' voice in her ear startled her.

"Maggie. What happened?"

She looked at him. He was earnest, his brows drawn together in concern, his expression intent and devoid of the distance he displayed in the role of the baron host.

She couldn't tell him. He'd never let her steal the jewels, and she couldn't put him in the kind of danger that telling him would entail. He'd do something rash—tell Sir Nathaniel of her suspicions if he didn't believe her or challenge him directly if he did, or maybe call in Scotland Yard or something equally foolish, and that would get him and Frankie killed, which wouldn't help anyone.

"I'm fine. I felt a little light-headed for a moment . . ." She saw from his eyes that he wasn't buying that, so she added, "I'm frightened. I didn't sleep much last night and I had to see you alone again, if only for a moment." *Just stay away from me,* she said silently, but she didn't dare say it aloud, for she knew that he would not listen. It was a mistake for anyone to ever get close to her. And she made up her mind at that moment to do anything to protect him from suffering on her account, Frankie's condition be damned.

His eyes softened. "You shall marry me, you know. I am not going to let you go. You shall have as much of me as you want soon enough."

"Perhaps," Maggie said, her throat threatening to choke on that lie. "Please promise to do something for me, though."

"What is it?" he ask, regarding her gravely.

"After this week is over, find out from the colonel, the one who sponsored Lily Barrett . . . find out who might have known that you were her champion," Maggie said. Charles needed to learn the truth at some point, if only to protect himself from the viper that was his friend. But he would have to find it out on his own, when it was too late for him to do something stupid in order to save her and get himself hurt. "If he's sure no one knew then find out from her if she mentioned anything—anything at all—to her neighbors or landlady or anyone. If she did, find out who they told."

"I will do that," he said, his voice betraying his suspicion.

Maggie pressed on. "And find out from your sister whose idea it was to cut Lily, whether someone might have suggested it to her in an offhand way first, and find out if someone suggested the idea of a bet before you argued with her."

"You know something," Charles said flatly. "What is it, Maggie? Is it Gifford?" His tone was dangerous.

"I—don't know," Maggie said. "I suspect." She silently begged his forgiveness for lying. "I suspect many things, but I don't know anything yet. Please, give me a little time." Time enough so that it would be too late to stop her. "I need to find out some things. And, Charles . . ."

"Yes?" he asked, his eyes hooded.

"Promise me that whatever happens, you will take care of the chavies." Suspicious words, dangerous words, but she had to say them.

"Nothing shall happen, Maggie," he said firmly. "I will make sure of it. But I will watch out for them, nevertheless."

"Thank you," she said, even as she thought, hopelessly, *But it already has, Charles, just as I told you it would.*

Chapter Fifteen

"So much for lawn games," Millie said morosely, staring out of the window of the Chinese parlor at the steady, drenching rain. It was an hour after luncheon, and the rain showed no signs of letting up.

"We can play tomorrow, dear," Charles' mother said composedly.

"Oh, who cares about lawn games when it's raining, Millie?" one of the twins said from beside the spinet where Fern Ashcroft was trying her hand at coaxing a recognizable song from the idiosyncratic instrument.

"I love the rain," the other added with relish. "It is so delicious to be inside and warm when it is wet and cold and miserable outside." She shivered dramatically, and Lady Victoria, for once away from her mother's side, gave a secret kind of smile from her seat in another window.

"We can play cards," Flora Ashcroft offered shyly from her seat on a divan. Maggie sat next to her. After the night's rest, Maggie had ceased to be quite so much of a curiosity to the others; though Millie seemed determined that the two become the best of friends, the attention of the flightier guests had already moved elsewhere. Miss

Howser's humiliating performance in the morning games held more potential for scandal, and so Maggie was neglected in favor of whispered jokes at Miss Hower's expense, which added appreciably to Millie's smugness. For her part, Miss Howser kept up a kind of cheerfulness, two parts naïveté and one part vulgarity, that was calculated to stir up the company even more.

Charles could not enjoy the show, however. Not with Maggie sitting so pale and subdued in Flora's shadow, looking like she wanted to vomit or flee even with an expression of good-natured interest plastered to her face. He hadn't been looking toward her at the moment she jerked to her feet to leave the morning room, but he remembered that she'd had a piece of paper clutched in her hands as she plunged through the door. Another note from Danny? Sent through whom? It must have come from one of the guests, or else she wouldn't have asked him to interview Millie and Colonel Vane. The bigger question was, what did it say? Where was it now? And why hadn't she told him?

Maggie caught him staring at her and blanched, jerking her gaze away. That removed his last shred of doubt. *Damn it, Maggie, why didn't you tell me what it said?* But he knew—Danny had threatened to kill Frankie if she opened her mouth.

"Cards sound diverting to me," Charles said with decision. If he contrived to share a table with Maggie, he could talk to her without drawing anyone's attention. Maybe he could pull something of substance out of her, even in the presence of others. He summoned a servant to set up the games room as the company rose amid chatter and discussion.

The guests moved so leisurely that the tables were ready by the time they arrived. It was a simple matter for

Charles to place himself behind Maggie so that he could subtly steer her at the last moment to the table of his choosing. Flora Ashcroft joined them without seeming to notice Charles' interference, and to his surprise, Miss Howser took the fourth chair, her pert little smile not reaching her sharp eyes. Maggie's glance flickered to the woman for a moment before returning to the green baize of the tabletop, and though the exchange was too fast for Charles to read it, he had the sudden feeling that there had been a great deal of meaning in it.

He took the two packs of cards, opened them, and handed one to Maggie, across from him. "Whist?" he suggested. He meant, *Do you know how to play it?*

She understood, for a trace of her old spirit flickered across her face before she said, "Of course. Shall we play for a pound a trick?"

The other two women agreed to the conditions readily, and so Charles and Maggie shuffled their decks and handed them to Flora and Miss Howser.

"Why don't you deal?" Maggie asked Miss Howser. There was a note in her voice, too faint for anyone who did not know her well to catch, that made Charles look at her more sharply.

"Of course," Miss Howser said after an infinitesimal hesitation. She smiled at the other players and took up the cards. She seemed to hesitate again . . . and then she dealt. With a sudden suspicion, Charles watched her hands closely as the cards flicked across the table. Him, Flora, Maggie, Miss Howser, him, Flora, Maggie, Miss Howser, him, Flora, Maggie—there it was. The slight flick as Miss Howser took another card—which card?— and gave it to Maggie in substitution of her own. Charles didn't catch it again, but Maggie wore a small, grim smile by the time the woman finished dealing.

They lifted their cards—and Miss Howser's eyes widened in disbelief as Maggie's smile took on a feral edge. What was going on?

The first trick answered that question. Maggie had somehow contrived to win—contrived to make Miss Howser guarantee that she won. She did not have a perfect hand, and yet she seemed to possess an uncanny knowledge of what other people had and what they would play. She took three-quarters of the tricks neatly, the others split near evenly between him and Flora Ashcroft, leaving Miss Howser silently fuming over her single trick on the corner of the table as the first scores were tallied.

"My great-uncle was an excellent card player," Maggie announced with brittle cheer as she watched Flora deal from the cards Charles had shuffled. "He used to invite his friends Mr. and Mrs. Franklin over every Thursday, and they would spend hours over their cards. Mr. Franklin was even better than he." Her eyes flicked to meet Charles'. Frankie. She meant Frankie. He seemed to remember her mentioning something about the youth's abilities in that arena. "He was a genius at card games of all types. He taught me a little—what I was able to learn—so that I could complete their table and provide some level of challenge. But I never could beat him." She gave a cool smile to Miss Howser, who seemed to turn a little green.

The next hand was honest. It must have been, for Flora had dealt the cards that Charles shuffled. But Maggie played her hand nearly as neatly, collecting the vast majority of tricks yet again.

Flora looked at her in admiration. "I usually win at cards," she confessed shyly.

Maggie smiled back. "I'm sure you do. But you have had greater entertainment in your life than a weekly card game to look forward to. My attention was rather focused by a lack of other diversions."

Scowling, Miss Howser shuffled her pack—slowly, clumsily. Too clumsily for it not to have a crooked cause, Charles decided. Maggie looked at him, a silent challenge in her gaze.

Why should he help her? She was shutting him out, keeping secrets from him. And yet her challenge was impossible for him to not meet. He made a decision and dropped the deck, and Miss Howser hissed sharply as the cards went flying.

"Clumsy me," he said, stooping under the table to collect them even as a footman stepped forward to help. "Oh, no," he told the servant. "Don't worry about it. I have them already." He shoved the cards back together and shuffled them several times, as if absentminded, before dealing the next hand.

He gave Maggie a steady look as she raised her cards. *Trust for trust, Maggie?* She flushed and looked away.

Charles attempted to engage her in conversation several times over the course of the half hour, but though she would talk volubly—and brittlely—about her life with her imaginary great-uncle, she would say nothing of significance at all, no matter how veiled. She had collected a neat stack of pounds by the time tables were changed—mostly from the near-apoplectic Miss Howser—but Charles could not even determine why it was that she was hounding the woman.

Could Miss Howser be involved with Danny? Did Maggie know her and dislike her from her old life? She had made no indication of it before, but it was always possible. Maggie might have merely assumed that the woman would cheat and decided to give her a dose of her own medicine. It could even be some obscure sort of test of precedence in the underworld, for all that he knew.

The games finished and everyone rose to find new tables without Charles being one bit more enlightened about what Danny had communicated to Maggie and what it might mean. Maggie's winnings disappeared neatly into her pocket, and she joined another table, where she proceeded to win just as easily as before—honestly, this time, Charles hoped.

The games continued until the party retired to the Lely room for a light tea. Maggie looked as grim as she ever had, though there was a kind of bitter satisfaction in the twist of her lips. He drifted over to her side when everyone else was occupied in their own conversations.

"How much did you win?" he murmured.

"Two hundred pounds," she replied. "And not a pound of it in promissory notes, as I mentioned that I did not know for certain that I would ever be in this company again."

Charles choked on his tea. "My God. You are nearly a one-woman industry."

She cocked her head to the side. "It's only about seven pounds per person, you know. And I took no more than thirty from anyone. It's also more than I've made in the past four years together." The words were almost wistful.

"Maggie, what's going on? Really?" he asked.

Her face shuttered instantly. "Nothing."

"Maggie," he repeated warningly.

The look she gave him was filled with muted agony. "Nothing I can tell you, Charles. I swear, if I could—"

Millie sailed within earshot, and Maggie broke off, turning to the girl and shutting Charles out.

"Is this tea Darjeeling?" Maggie asked her brightly.

Charles left before he heard the reply.

*   *   *

An hour before dinner was scheduled, Charles' mother made the announcement that it was to be eaten reclining in the Roman style, and servants were produced with appropriate togas or chitons and sandals for everyone, as well as Roman-style jewelry made of cheap plated metals and low-quality paste gems.

A stir went up from the guests: surprise from those whom Millie had not yet told—in the strictest confidence, of course—and a lesser excitement from those of the party who'd already heard. Charles took his toga without comment. In return for Millie's giving up her Diana-and-Apollo scheme, he had acquiesced to the themed dinner, though he had insisted that they use divans and sofas they already owned to recline upon, however un-Roman the result may be, and that they buy used tables and cut the legs short rather than specially commissioning an entire suite of furniture.

He turned back and caught sight of Maggie standing in the corner and staring at the paste jewelry with an expression of horror. She blinked, and it was gone, but she walked quickly up to Millie and took her elbow, exchanging a few words with her before shooting a look at an oblivious Gifford.

Charles frowned and cornered his sister as soon as Maggie had left. "What did Miss King ask you?" he demanded tersely.

Millie gave him a confused look. "Only whose idea it was to have jewelry as well as costumes."

"And?" Charles prompted.

Millie shook her head. "I told her it was Lord Gifford's. I don't see as it matters," she added in a hurt tone. "I picked out the designs."

"I see," Charles said. Then, on a sudden hunch, he added, "And before you made your bet with me, did Lord

Gifford make some sort of suggestion about a bet and whether or not a lower-class woman could be passed off as a lady?"

Millie looked exasperated. "Why are you going on about that old thing? You know you've lost. No one believes in Miss Howser."

"Did Lord Gifford make any kind of reference to that effect?" Charles pursued.

"As a matter of fact, he did not," Millie said primly. "Sir Nathaniel mentioned something about it, though."

Charles blinked. Dines, too? He spotted the man across the room. Catching his eye, the baronet smiled. "Is that what gave you the idea for the bet?"

"Naturally," Millie said without much interest. "We discussed it for nearly half an hour."

Gifford. Dines. What part could they be playing in this? And what was he supposed to do about it?

Charles looked around the room, only to discover that Maggie had already retired. He cursed silently and grabbed a pair of sandals and a golden crown of leaves and took them and his robe up to his room. He called his valet, but the fabric had been cleverly—and anachronistically—tailored to create a togalike appearance without any wrapping or tucking on his part, so it was easy enough to pull on. The belt had a pouch on it, and he transferred his handkerchief into it. He looked in the mirror at his thoroughly nineteenth-century hairstyle and his silly costume and sighed, placing the golden wreath on his head at a rakish angle.

Having fulfilled the duty of dressing for dinner, he dismissed his servant and opened the door in his bedroom that led to the staircase connecting his suite with Maggie's. He left the door open, the gaslight from his bedroom guiding his steps until the first turning. He felt the rest of the way up, stopping when his outstretched hand encountered the wood of the door. He tried the handle. Bolted from the inside. He knocked.

Silence.

He knocked again, louder this time. Still nothing.

"Maggie!" he called. "I know you're in there. Open the door!"

More silence, though he swore he could feel her listening to him.

"I will knock it down," he threatened. "It's my door, and the lock is not that strong—"

He was interrupted by the sound of the bolt sliding back. He pushed against the door before she could change her mind, and Maggie sprang back so she wouldn't be hit as he shoved inside. She was nearly as pale as the white robes that she wore, her eyes like black holes in her colorless face.

Charles stifled a curse. "What the hell is going on here, Maggie? I know Sir Nathaniel Dines suggested the idea of a bet, and Lord Gifford convinced Millie to get jewelry with the costumes, but what does that have to do with anything?"

Maggie shook her head, her features pinched. "I can't tell you. I wish I could—you don't know how I wish I could—but I can't. Remember it, though. It's important."

"I need to know now." Charles growled the words in his frustration.

"I know, I know . . ." Maggie seemed to shrink into herself.

"This is about Frankie, isn't it?" he demanded, stepping forward to crowd her, remorselessly using his size to try to bully her if his words could not. "You're not telling me because Danny's threatening to do something to him if you don't . . . what? What is it that he wants you to do?"

"I don't know," she said, and he knew it was a lie even though her eyes did not waver from his face.

Charles glared at her. "He wants something from you. I know he does, Maggie, and he needs you to be here, in my house, to do it, and he wants you to do it soon. Just tell me. I can help you."

Her laugh was ragged. "Help me do what? Commit a crime? You know Danny wouldn't do this if he wanted something legitimate."

He'd guessed that Danny's plans were criminal, but what crime? Theft or murder—it had to be. Nothing less would call for such an elaborate plan. And he knew Maggie wouldn't kill without a reason, knew she'd never kill an innocent, whatever she might try to paint herself to be, so it had to be theft. "I can help you get free of him," he insisted. "Whatever he wants you to steal—"

Maggie took a jerking step backward. "I don't want to be free. Just—leave me alone!"

A sick suspicion formed in the pit of his belly. Charles closed the distance between them in a stride and grabbed her shoulders, holding her so tight that she winced and he felt the strain in his forearms. He shook her, hard enough that her head snapped back. "*Listen to me, Maggie.* Don't you dare think for one moment that I'm going to let you sacrifice yourself for him. Do you hear me?"

"I wouldn't dream that you would, Charles." Her reply was sad even as the corners of her eyes creased in pain. "Let me go. You're hurting me."

Charles stared at her for a long moment, reading resignation and determination in equal measures in her face. If he thought he could beat the information out of her, he would, he realized. Even if she never forgave him for it.

Even though he knew he would never forgive himself. Her life was in danger, he was more certain of it than he had ever been of anything, and he would do everything in his power to save it, in spite of her. But he was equally certain that she wouldn't break under anything he had the stomach to do to her. With an impotent curse, he pushed her away. She stumbled back, catching herself before she tumbled over a chair.

"Frankie will hate you for even considering this," he grated.

"I know," Maggie said, pulling herself up with a queer kind of dignity.

"I won't let you do it." He said the words flatly even as he feared the emptiness of them. He didn't even know what she was trying to do. How could he hope to stop her?

"I know you don't want me to," she agreed.

He glared at her. "I'll lock you in this room."

"I will scream, and someone will come—even gagged, even bound, there are too many people in this house not to hear me. Unless you intend to risk killing me yourself by striking me unconscious, there is nothing you can do."

She was terrified. He saw it in the emptiness of her eyes, the catch in her too-calm words. Emotion flickered across her face like a spasm—*Save me, Charles.* But then it was gone, and he knew that she wouldn't let herself be saved.

"I won't let you leave the company," he said. "You shall spend the night with me."

She nodded once, convulsively, as if she didn't believe that the night would ever come.

Damn. Damn, damn, damn, damn.

"Marry me, Maggie," he heard himself saying. "Agree, and we will announce it at dinner, and then you will be untouchable, and whatever it is Danny wants of you, you won't have to do it."

Maggie stared at Charles, her mind reeling. Could he really still want her? Knowing that she was about to betray him. Knowing that she was going to throw everything he'd ever given her away. But there was not a trace of uncertainty in him, and the full realization of his sincerity hit her like a blow to the gut. She took a deep breath. It shuddered horribly in her chest, and it was then that she realized that she was crying. *Crying.* Actual tears welling in her eyes, running down her cheeks, her breath catching and twisting into sobs. And Charles was there, gathering her up against him, kissing them away, kissing her eyes, her cheeks, her mouth, and she kissed him back hard, all her desperation turning into a hard knot of need in her belly.

She jerked at his ridiculous robes, yanking them up and off him as he stripped her in the same movement. His hands fumbled with the laces of her corset, pulling them loose, tearing the busk open and tossing the contraption aside. His drawers, her shift and pantaloons—they followed in an instant, and she pushed him hard toward the bed, the mattress striking the back of his legs and her weight sending them over. She was on top of him, starving for him. It was her last chance to kiss his mouth, to taste his body, to feel the heat of him pierce her to her core as he entered her. She slid her body across his so that her entrance was poised over his erection. Then she shoved herself down, panting, weeping, not caring for anything but him. Her need for him tore through her body, scalding her, hurting her.

"Let me save you," he was saying. "Damn it, Maggie, don't do this to us!"

She bit back a sob and kissed him hard into silence,

moving over him as he shuddered and groaned. Heat splintered through her, too sharp to be pleasure, too wonderful for pain.

"You idiot," he choked out, and Maggie found herself being pushed off him, pushed hard into the bed as he rolled over, his weight on top of her, pinning her under him as he entered her mercilessly, over and over again. Her sobs tangled with her moans and an insane, hysterical urge to laugh at the pointlessness of her grasping for him now, when there was nothing to hold on to, nothing that could be done, when even memory would be so short.

Then there was no place for her to even keep herself, and she burst into sensation, her entire body disappearing in an immolation of self. She rode the mindless blast of terrible glory, clung to it for second after second that stretched into forever, crying with the loss as it slid, inevitably, away. Maggie found herself back inside herself, tangled up again in the knowledge of her own despair and the end that would come now soon, far too soon.

Chapter Sixteen

Charles slumped into stillness on top of her. "Damn you, damn you, damn you," he repeated, like a chant or a prayer.

Maggie closed her eyes hard. "I love you. It doesn't help anything, but I want you to remember that I love you."

He raised his head, and Maggie's breath caught when she realized that his eyes were angry and red. "If you leave me, Maggie, I will never forgive you."

"I know that, too," she whispered. "Go now. We'll be late for dinner."

"No," he said, pushing off her. "I'm not going anywhere. I will stay here as you dress, and then we'll go down together."

"Someone will see us," she protested. "They'll know. . . ."

"Do you think I care about that at this point? I'm not leaving you alone." His jaw hardened.

"All right," Maggie said, knowing his efforts would be futile and yet unable to deny him that small consolation. She added, quietly, "Sally hasn't come back yet." Those words held worlds of terror. She had sent her best friend out into the night, and now maybe she was lost, too . . .

"I'm sorry," Charles said. "I . . . will dress you." His tone told her that he knew what an insufficient response that was.

Maggie nodded. She felt like a stuffed doll as Charles helped her into her clothing. She had not yet tied her pocket back on when he'd come in, and she slipped it on between her chemise and the robes' skirts. To Maggie, the shape of the revolver seemed to shout itself through the cloth of the pocket, but Charles did not seem to notice. She found a pair of sewing scissors and cut a short length of her skirt's seam open so that she could reach it easily, and still he did not react.

Charles watched in silence as she restyled her hair, and then he straightened his own with a few quick brush strokes. As he set the brush back down, a folded piece of paper on her dressing table caught his eye. He turned it over as Maggie's hand shot out to forestall him. *For my chavies,* it read in Maggie's still-imperfect hand. He opened the paper. A thick wad of pounds lay inside, carefully stacked. Her card winnings.

"Maggie . . ." he said, the evidence of her own estimation of her chances of survival making him ill.

She bit her lip. "It is a great fortune for them."

He just shook his head, not knowing what else to say. *I'm not going to let you die, Maggie. Not even for them.*

At Maggie's insistence, he escorted her from her apartment several minutes before the dinner bell was to be rung, so that no one encountered them on the way down. They stood together, mutely, in the parlor next to the dining room as the others began to gather, and then the butler appeared and announced the meal.

Five low tables were arrayed about the room, each

with two divans around three sides. The guests exclaimed and pushed into the room. Charles took Maggie's elbow and led her to a table away from Gifford, Dines, and Miss Howser, guiding her firmly to the divan next to the one he took. She sat, almost meekly, and the meal began.

Charles could never remember what was served—all the food turned to ashes in his mouth. Nor could he remember what was said nor how the company took the unconventional meal. There were pipers and a harpist, but Charles didn't know what tunes they played, and there was laughter, but he did not know whose it was or why.

But he would never forget the explosion that roared through the house like a cannon fire. The room shook, the musicians breaking off as the chandeliers swayed and shivered. A woman shrieked, and there was a burst of consternation, but before anyone could react, the flames of the gas jets grew low and orange and, one by one, flickered out.

"The gas pipe!" Charles recognized Flora Ashcroft's voice. "The gas pipe exploded!"

"Someone needs to turn off the main line in the kitchens." That was his mother, silly only when it didn't matter. "If the line is repaired and the pilot light is out, the gas will come through the open jets and smother us."

"I'll do it!" Peter Radcliffe cried. The announcement was immediately followed by a crash and a muffled curse.

"Nobody move," Charles said, his voice cutting through the growing confusion. "The servants will bring candles. Once we have light, then someone can shut off the main gas pipe. We're in no danger of exploding or smothering—no one is going to repair an exploded gas line within the hour." He reached out through the darkness to Maggie's divan . . . and his heart jerked as his hand encountered only the fabric of the cushion, still warm with the heat of her body.

No. He stood, ignoring his own order, his eyes wide, trying to see through the murky darkness. A few vague silhouettes—nothing of use. He plotted the room in his mind. The closest door was on his left and a little ahead of him. He needed a match, something to burn. He grabbed a napkin.

"Christopher," he said. Yes, Christopher Radcliffe had been sitting across from him—the man smoked a thick cigar after every meal.

"Yes?" the man's voice replied.

"Give me your box of lucifers."

There was a rustle of fabric. Slow, slow, too slow. "Here."

Charles reached out. He hit the man's arm with the first try, then followed it up to his hand, where he found the matchbox. He took it, opened it, struck one. Several people cried out at the light, and cried out again when he held it to the twisted end of his serviette. The silk caught.

"Charles?" his mother's voice called out uncertainly.

"Stay right here!" he ordered. "Everyone, stay right here." The light was faint, barely more than a candle, not nearly enough to illuminate the vast cave of the dining room. Who else was missing? He didn't know; he could only see the people at his own table, but he'd bloody well find out. Later. First he had to find Maggie, before she did something that couldn't be undone.

He grabbed the napkins from the laps of the other people at his table and shoved them into the pouch at his waist, then left the room as quickly as he dared even as the flame on the napkin torch sputtered and flared. He wished he had time to find a candle . . . but they were probably down in the kitchen. Too far.

He jogged through the shadowed rooms toward the front hall. He had no idea if he was going the right way, but he could guess. How much of a lead did she have on him? One minute? Five?

The walls glowed like damp nacre when the flame passed close, the dark shapes of furniture hulking in the shadows. He passed through the final doorway, and his footsteps echoed hollowly in the front hall. His makeshift rushlight flickered, smoke curling thickly from it. He stopped, hesitated. He stood in the middle of a tiny orb of light in the center of the vast room. The walls were distant, shadowy shapes, the ceiling invisible, the floor as white as bone beneath his feet. No flash of movement anywhere. No sound except the rush of rain on the roof of the dome, far overhead.

He closed his eyes. Where did she go? And why? He had already decided that Danny must be demanding theft of her, but the list of things someone might steal in the Edgington House was mind-boggling. Silver and art, antiquities and jewels, rare books and rare animal specimens. The list went on and on.

Think small. Think portable. Maggie had asked Millie whose idea it was to have the false jewelry. Because if everyone was wearing false jewelry, the real jewelry would stay in the guests' rooms. . . .

He started up the stairs toward the bedrooms, taking them two at a time. As he reached the first floor, the burning napkin scorched his hand. Biting back a curse, he shifted his grip quickly, yanked another napkin from his pouch, and lit it, shaking the flame out of the first before dropping it to the cold marble. A line of doors confronted him, marching down both sides of the gallery between the leering paintings of his ancestors. The flame flickered and jumped as he strode forward. He tried the first door, and it swung open at his touch. Maggie would have to be working fast. There should be open drawers, rifled boxes. But the guttering light of the napkin revealed a perfectly made bed, bare dressing table, an empty dresser top. Unoccupied. He left the door ajar and opened four more rooms until he found what he was looking for—evidence of feminine habitation, and, on the dressing table, an empty, upended jewelry box.

Charles let out a breath he hadn't realized he'd been holding. So many guesses, so many gambles—correct, so far. Now he must catch her, before she could transfer the goods to Danny. He knew she didn't expect to survive that meeting, and he was certain she had good reason to believe it. He had to stop her.

He moved faster, throwing open the doors as he went. He didn't bother to search for further signs of looting; he knew he was on the right track now. He reached his own apartments at the end of the wing without finding her. Damn. Should he check the west wing, too? But no. There would be no guests there, and whoever her contact was, Gifford or Dines or whoever, he had planned too well to be ignorant of that fact. On to the second floor, then. Charles took the shortcut through his bedroom, taking the narrow, spiraling staircase two steps at a time. He had to pause at the top and light another napkin. Four left.

He searched her own rooms first—no sign of her there. In the rooms along the upper hallway, though, he saw indications of her passage: tumbled jewelry boxes, wardrobes cast out onto the floor, and Lady James' small safe sitting on her bed with the door standing forlornly open. His dread grew with every door he opened. He was too late, too slow. How could one small girl have moved so fast? Maybe she wasn't alone.

He reached the last door in the wing and threw it open.

Nothing. Not even a traveling trunk. He entered the room, as if his presence could conjure Maggie out of thin air. How was he supposed to intercept her now? The meeting place could be anywhere. In the attics, in the cellars, in the woods, in London proper, for God's sake. . . .

A flash of movement out the window caught his eye. He reached it in two strides, hardly daring to believe his eyes. A pale white figure was toiling down the drive through the pouring rain. He put his face to the glass and cupped his free hand around it to block the light from the burning napkin. Yes, it could definitely be one of his sister's chitons. And the figure was small enough that it might be Maggie. *Bless you, Millie, and your ridiculous white costumes!* He rocked back on his heels, and just as he did, he caught a movement in the reflection of the flame on the glass that shouldn't have been there.

He started, jerking to the side, and something came whistling over his shoulder and crashed into the window, shattering it into a thousand shards that peppered his bare arms. He dropped the napkin. It sputtered on the carpet, smoldering. He ducked and grabbed for the nearest weapon. His hand closed on the back of a dainty chair in front of the dressing table, and he swung it toward his assailant. It made contact with a crack and a shock that jolted Charles' arms in his shoulder joints. The figure fell in a heap of white cloth and was still. For a moment, Charles had the confused thought that the person on the drive had somehow attacked him up here. Maggie? But the hair in the flame light was golden. Miss Howser. Miss Howser and Gifford and Dines—what were their plans?

The room grew abruptly brighter. The fire! Charles turned back to his dropped napkin to find that a small circle of carpet was alight. He snatched the napkin up by a corner and stomped out the rug. Too long—this was all taking far too long. His hands shook with impatience as he lit a new napkin, and after a moment's hesitation, he threw the old one out the window, where its flames were quickly extinguished in the rain.

Charles nudged Miss Howser's body with his sandaled foot. A long candlestick lay on the floor next to her hand. She didn't stir. Should he tie her up? Was she dead? He shook his head, trying to clear it. He didn't have time for this. He had to get a weapon, a better one than a candlestick.

He stepped back into the corridor. The Hunt Room was on the ground floor. He was only half a dozen paces from the top of the main staircase. With the flames from the napkin licking back to caress his hand, he ran for it, descending so fast that his feet slid on the fifth step and he nearly tumbled the rest of the way to the bottom.

You won't be much good to her dead, he told himself brutally, and after that, he used a little more caution. He reached the bottom and nearly barreled into Peter Radcliffe, who was emerging from a side corridor holding a candle in front of his cheerful face.

"I say, Edgington!" he exclaimed as Charles jerked the candle from his hands, dropping the napkin. "That was mine, you rotter!"

"Find another one," Charles snapped as he ducked down another corridor. Maggie was a thief now, an outlaw. He couldn't ask for help. No one else could know, or the law would kill her as surely as Danny would.

He spirited through the door of the Hunt Room. He cast about the weapons cabinets, wasting precious seconds, before discovering what he was looking for—one of the new rifles that took the premade cartridges. He jerked it off the back wall of the cabinet. Now, ammunition. He jerked open drawer after drawer in the great case

that ran the length of the wall. There they were. He leaned
the rifle against the cabinet and began shoving cartridges
into his pouch, pausing only long enough to load one into
the chamber.

He picked up his gun and looked out the front windows. He couldn't see the white figure on the drive any
longer. His chest tightened. He blew out the candle and
dropped it, took four quick strides through the darkness
to the nearest window, and swung the gunstock into it
hard. Two-hundred-year-old glass shattered, and Charles
jumped through and into the wet night.

Chapter Seventeen

Maggie stumbled again, and Danny's valet snarled a curse, jerking her back to her feet. The robes were too long, the sandals too big, and the weight of the sack made her slide whenever her foot met mud or a patch of slick grass.

He pushed her off the drive, between the double allee of trees. She paused and blinked, mopping streaming strands of hair out of her face as she tried to focus through the darkness on the path in front of her. The man cursed again, and she saw the black bar of his arm swinging at her and ducked without thinking. Her feet lost their purchase, and she went down hard, dropping the bag as her hands flew out to catch her. She was gasping against the sudden sting in her palms when the valet's kick slammed into her ribs, sending her sprawling sideways into the mud as pain exploded in her chest.

"Slut! Whore!" he spat at her. "If you lose one piece, I'll take it out o' your flesh, I will."

She lay on the ground, gasping against the pain as mud trickled into her hair. The man grabbed the sack, satisfying himself that the knot at its mouth had not come undone. Maggie had taken less than a third of the jewelry.

Miss Howser's quick fingers had dealt nimbly with locks that would have taken Maggie twice the time, even in her prime. That erased the last of her doubts. Danny hadn't wanted her talents. Danny just wanted a scapegoat. And now she was going to die.

He turned to her again, and Maggie braced for another blow. "Get up, you!"

"I can't," Maggie snapped with as much viciousness as she could muster. "Me ribs are broke."

The man burst into another long string of invective. When that failed to move her—and the threat of another kick only made her flinch—he said, "Look. I'll carry the loot. Jus' get up. Danny wants you, but I'd sooner shoot you and bring 'im 'ere den carry you."

Maggie pushed herself to her feet, every breath sending uneasy twinges of pain through her ribs. Not broken—the pain didn't quite have the stabbing quality of a broken rib—but cracked, surely. Now, though, she was unburdened while her captor had to manage the sack and his weapon, both. A small victory, a tiny one when she was giving herself up anyway, but she wasn't quite ready to surrender all hope of life yet.

She followed the man's orders and pressed on through the darkness, her feet slipping and sliding under her. The white robes were covered with filth, and they clung to her legs with every step, tangling around her feet as her revolver smacked into her thigh. Finally, she stopped and pulled off the sandals, ignoring her escort's curses. They didn't keep her toes from being stubbed, anyway, and at least this way, she had a chance of staying on her feet if anything happened.

The man slid open the cover of his thief's lantern, but that scarcely helped, for now the world was no longer a hundred shades of shadow but a wildly swinging shaft of light hemmed in by walls of blackness. Maggie muttered curses at the man under her breath as she tried to put her feet where his had just been.

They pressed through more trees, and suddenly, they were at the verge of the drive again, a pale scar across the dark park. There was the sound of rushing water, too loud to be rain. Maggie blinked through the darkness. Was that the brook that ran at the edge of the property? There should be a bridge. . . .

There was a movement in the darkness, and her perspective seemed to lurch as a closed carriage coalesced out of the shadows—its door swinging open, a man in a greatcoat stepping down.

"Hullo, Maggie."

Danny's voice wasn't loud, but it carried over the sound of the rain and the rush of the swollen brook. Maggie shivered involuntarily. Her muscles were cramping with cold.

"Where's Frankie?" she demanded. "I want to see 'im."

"Frankie isn't here right now, me dear colleen, but never you fear; he's safe enough."

"I want to see 'im, or no deal," Maggie said. She slid her hand through the slit in her skirt to the pocket where her revolver lay, damp but sound.

Light washed over her suddenly, and she blinked hard. Danny had a bull's-eye lantern, and he'd unshuttered it and turned it to shine directly in her eyes. He was hidden behind the glare.

"A little late for that, luv," he said. "It wouldn't matter even if he was here, if it makes you feel any better about it. There's nothing stopping me from shooting you and then shooting him, too, to be sure."

Maggie said nothing, her hand tightening on the grip of the pistol.

"But I'm a man of my word, I am, me colleen," he said. "I'm not going to kill him . . . if you do as I say."

"What more do you want, Danny? I'm here," Maggie said. The words came out rough and raw edged.

Danny chuckled. "Such a bold thing you are! At first, I thought I'd shoot you. Leave you on the road to be found in the morning—a thief betrayed by her own comrades, like. But then I had another idea, much more elegant. My associate here"—the lantern bobbed sideways for a second to illuminate his valet, who was standing several paces away at the side of the road— "I'm going to have him drown you instead. It's an accident that way, you see. God's own justice. The thief wandered out in the darkness to meet her comrades, and on the way back from her nefarious meeting, she fell into the stream and drowned." Danny was getting excited as he spoke, his accent slipping as he fell more and more into Sir Nathaniel's tones.

Maggie's stomach clenched, from cold or fear, she couldn't tell. "Get on wif it, den." She couldn't trust him. He wouldn't let Frankie go, and Charles, Charles might not ever be out of danger, whether she was dead or alive.

"Step down to the stream," Sir Nathaniel said, his voice laced with revolting eagerness.

I don't have a choice, Maggie told herself. *It's the only chance Charles and Frankie might have, and however slender it is, I have to take it.* She tried to fix both their images in her mind, but Charles' face grew in her imagination, eclipsing that of her old friend.

She gave a gasping, despairing laugh and stepped forward. The stream bank was slick with runoff, and her toes curled in the cold mud, trying to keep a grip as she scrambled down. She fell the last few feet, and as she pitched forward, the icy water closed over her head, and for half a second, she thought that the valet's job had already been done for him. She flailed, panicking, and she broke the surface instantly, standing up in water that didn't quite come to her waist. The force of it made her stagger, battering against her legs so hard that she had to brace herself to keep from being swept away.

Sir Nathaniel was laughing, not a sophisticated chuckle but long, loud guffaws. "My girl, you undo me! I almost didn't have to kill you at all!"

Maggie jerked as she heard another splash. It was the valet, sliding into the water near the bridge, now nearly a dozen yards from her.

"You know what?" Sir Nathaniel said suddenly. "I think I've changed my mind. I think I will kill Frankie, after all. And Edgington, too, of course, but his death shall be a work of art. It shall look just like an accident. Just like yours."

He could be lying. Maggie knew it. He wanted to hurt her before she died, to make her believe it was for nothing, but there would be no reason to harm Charles and Frankie once she was dead. Still, she slipped her hand into her skirt, backing away from the shadowy form of the approaching valet instinctively. Her revolver was soaked. Would it even work? If she shot the man, she'd be killing both the men she cared so much about. If she didn't, they might die, anyway. She froze, torn by indecision. Sir Nathaniel was laughing again, low and constant.

A crack split the air. The lantern swung as Sir Nathaniel turned toward the noise. Gunfire! It had come from the direction of the house.

Charles. The certainty of it filled her with a surge of hope and sick horror.

"Charles, no!" she shouted. "Go away! If you don't go, he'll kill Frankie." *And you, you idiot!* "Just go!"

Sir Nathaniel spat a curse, and suddenly, the lantern was arching out over the water, plunging into it, and then it was gone. "You take care of the girl. I'll get the baron."

Maggie's heart stuttered. *"No!" Not him, not Charles, no, no, no . . .* Blinded from staring straight into the lantern light, she blinked and fumbled in her pocket for the gun, yanking it out through the wet layer of cloth. Where was the valet? She held the gun in front of her, but every bush and tree branch waved in the storm-tossed night, and she couldn't separate one moving shape from another. Then—contact, hard, as the valet slammed into her, a glancing blow as he misjudged where she stood. She pulled the trigger, and the gun boomed and kicked hard in her hands. It still worked! That brief elation was extinguished as she was driven backward by the valet's weight, the frigid stream sucking at her legs. She was falling. She threw herself sideways, toward the nearest bank, and she hit the earth hard, the wind going out of her at once. More shots rang out, some close by, others from far away. She didn't have time to sort them out.

There was a huge splash as the valet lunged forward. Maggie aimed for the sound and pulled the trigger again, and this time, a scream followed the gun's explosion. The current grabbed the man and swept him close by Maggie—she could make out the outline of his body in the stream—and he splashed and cursed as he tried to regain his footing. His flailing arm met her knee and latched on. She jerked back automatically, but it only pulled him closer. She could see his face now, white in the darkness, his mouth like a great dark pit. He grabbed her sodden robes and yanked. Cursing, she hit him with all of her strength, the pistol butt striking his skull with sickening force. His grip loosened instantly, and he slid away.

Charles. Where is Charles? Maggie plunged back up the creek, fighting the current. She couldn't feel her feet anymore. Her attention was diverted by a sudden crashing in the underbrush on the opposite side of the stream. Danny's reinforcements! She raised her gun.

"Maggie! Maggie, where are you?"

"Maggie!"

It was Sally's voice, followed by Frankie's. Maggie gasped with relief, staggering against the current. "I'm here!"

"The great bloody bastard Danny didn't get me, though 'e tried hard enough," Frankie shouted.

Another shot rang out, and this time, Maggie heard the bullet fly past her. Sir Nathaniel was still alive. She plunged toward the bank again and the protection of the underbrush. "Watch out! Danny's on the bridge, and he's got a gun."

Suddenly, another lantern's light cut through the blackness from the bank where Sally and Frankie stood, dancing briefly across the edge of the stream where she was scrambling up before jumping to focus on the bridge. For an instant, Danny stood in the center of the light, his carriage several steps away, a pair of revolvers in his hands. He seemed to smile or snarl, swinging his weapons toward the source of the light, and time froze.

Then several shots rang out, the lantern light dipped, and Danny's expression turned to surprise before he slumped over onto the rain-slick boards of the bridge and lay still.

Maggie pulled herself out of the water, conscious of the sounds of several people calling her name. She should feel elated, she told herself. She should feel relieved.

Instead, she just felt numb. The lantern light bobbed and swung, and as she watched, Sally and Frankie ran out of the bushes together and onto the bridge.

"He's dead!" Maggie heard Sally say in a tone of awe. "Did you get him?"

"I don't think so," Frankie said, and Maggie saw the gun glinting in his hand.

"I did."

Maggie turned toward that voice, pitched so quietly that only she could hear it. "Charles!"

"You idiot," he said, and then he was there pulling her up, kissing her breathless, crushing her against him like he was afraid she would disappear. She kissed him back just as hard. The delicious taste of him, his wonderful heat and strength: She had almost lost them—had almost lost it all.

"Don't you ever, ever do anything like that again," he said roughly when he finally let her go.

"You shouldn't have come. It was too dangerous. You could have died!" she returned.

"How could I not?" She couldn't make out his expression, but his tone was intense with scarcely restrained emotion. "You were going to bloody well die for Frankie. Don't you think that I'd do as much for you?"

"But he was going to kill you, too," Maggie said. "He told me so. I couldn't let that happen. I love you too much."

"Do you mean that?" Charles asked, tightening his hold. He felt so warm, so safe that it made her hurt inside.

"More than anything," she said.

"God, Maggie," he breathed. "Just promise me two things."

"Anything," she said, the word choking in her throat.

"First, that you'll marry me before the month is out.

And second, that you'll never do such a damn fool thing again."

Maggie looked at Sally and Frankie, who were still standing on the bridge over Danny's body.

"I promise. Oh, I promise."

And then they kissed again, for a very long time.

Epilogue

Six months later

Where was she?

Charles frowned across the ballroom. The vast chamber was already filled to a crush, the extravagance of the ladies' sweeping skirts punctuated by the narrow monochrome columns of the gentlemen. At his elbow stood Lily Barrett, terrified and glowing at the honor of an official coming out sponsored by Lord Edgington and his new lady. But that new lady was nowhere to be found.

"Where is that wife of yours?" his mother demanded from his other side. She had suffered from a brainstorm that had left her with a droop on one side of her mouth and a personality that alternated between a confused querulousness and the gentleness and warmth that he had half forgotten from his nursery days. Today was one of the difficult days, but he merely patted her papery hand and looked over his shoulder toward her attendants.

"I do not know, madam," he said. "I will go and find her. You stay here with Miss Barrett."

She focused on the girl as he stepped away, and before

he slipped into the crowd, he heard her ask, "Are you my Charles' wife?"

He found Maggie after several minutes of searching. Her favorite haunts were empty, but he was coming down the upper gallery from checking the Winter Suite when he saw a silhouette standing where the corridor met the main staircase that led below. The figure stood with her back to him, standing at the balustrade and staring down at the guests in the entrance hall far below.

She was clad in the enormous skirts currently at the height of fashion, her hair wound intricately upon the back of her head. She was tiny, almost childlike in stature, making her look like nothing so much as a very expensive doll. She was nothing like the girl he'd seen nearly a year ago upon that opera stage . . . and yet she was, for she still carried her weight warily upon her toes, though a man who didn't know better would now simply pass it off as flightiness. She also had the same vitality, the same passion that had riveted him then. She was still his unchangeable Maggie. And she was still defying him.

He spoke when he had almost reached her elbow. Her old keenness had been dulled with the months; when they had met, he would have never had caught her so unawares. "You should be downstairs."

She started and whirled to face him, sending her skirt swaying with a susurration of silk. Her body betrayed her surprise, but her expression was closed and troubled. "I don't want to do this, Charles."

He took her elbow firmly. "I don't think that I asked."

"Of course you didn't. You never do." Maggie held her ground, glaring at him, her black eyes huge and fathomless in her pale face. Her features had filled out slightly over the past few months, the half-starved pinch relaxed with a steady supply of food.

"Yet somehow, I still get my way less that half the time." The comment was quiet, more wryly self-directed than intended for her sake.

"I don't want to go down," she repeated. She smoothed her hand down the fabric of her dress, the motion quick, irritable. Afraid.

Charles pulled her closer, and she came without resisting, her gaze softening slightly at his nearness. "Maggie," he said. "You are Lady Edgington. No one will shun you. No one will even think to, and no matter how odd a choice you might seem for a baron—well, I am an Edgington, after all." She smiled faintly at that. "Lily Barrett is already waiting below. If you do not come, people will begin saying that you disapprove of her and do not want to be her sponsor. Anyhow, you are a baroness. You cannot hide away forever, and you will never again have a chance in which the attention is diffused among so many other distractions."

Maggie looked at him for a long moment in silence and then nodded. "I suppose Lily shall only come out once."

"And, God willing, Millie shall return from her honeymoon but once, as well," Charles said. He did not mention the other distraction: This was also the Edgington family's first public appearance since the fateful house party that had left two dead. The public version of events was that Charles, Maggie, and Dines had ventured out together to stop a heist masterminded by Dines' treacherous valet, who was intercepted at the cost of Dines' life. Aside from the conspirators, only two others knew differently, and one was happy to trade her life for transportation and silence, while the other . . . well, Charles never found out exactly how much Gifford knew about Dines' plans, but he wasn't talking. Even though she understood the lie to be necessary, Maggie still looked pinched anytime someone alluded to Dines' heroism, so Charles avoided any reference to the story that he could.

Maggie looked back over the edge of the balustrade again. "When I was a little girl, I used to climb up above the stage at the Royal Italian Opera during performances and watch everyone below, imagining what it would be like to be the one on the stage."

"Now you are going to find out." He raised an eyebrow.

Maggie turned back, an expression of suppressed amusement on her face. "Perhaps I shall," she said. She glanced down again. "Look. Someone has spotted us. Since I am now an Edgington, I suppose I should begin by acting my part and living up to my scandalous new name."

She tiptoed and leaned into him, planting a kiss squarely on his mouth. It was no more than a peck, and when she drew back again, Charles treated her to a wicked smile.

"If you are going to start a scandal, you might as well do it properly," he said. With that, he pulled her into his arms and kissed her until they were both flushed and breathless. She leaned into him, the last vestiges of stiffness sliding from her. Her mouth was pliant but demanding, hot, and sweet under his, and for a moment, he had the wild urge to carry her off to their bedroom, devil take the ball.

But reason reasserted itself as she pulled away with a sigh, the smoky expression in her eyes telling him that her thoughts ran close by his.

"I suppose everyone has been thoroughly shocked now," Maggie remarked.

"Or they soon will be when they hear," Charles agreed.

Maggie's smile was feral. "Let us go down, Lord Edgington."

"Gladly, Lady Edgington."

If you like *Voices of the Night*,
you will love Lydia Joyce's
next dark, sexy romance
on sale in March 2008.

Read on for a sneak peek . . .

"Come back to bed." Emma's sleepy voice emerged from the pile of twisted blankets. "You have hours yet before the wedding."

Colin cast a glance over his shoulder as he gave his necktie a last quick tug into place. Morning light poured through the window, puddling across the bed to halo Emma's cherubic face amidst its clouds of white linen. Her lower lip protruded slightly, an artificial expression that should have looked ludicrous on a woman of thirty-five, but Colin doubted that Emma had ever in her life looked anything but exactly as she intended. Flirting, dancing, cajoling—even during lovemaking—she kept her face turned to the most flattering angle in the moonlight, her expression intense but unmarred by an unaesthetic contortion.

Predictable, cultured, and undemanding, she was exactly what Colin had always wanted in a mistress. It was a pity their pleasant affair would be interrupted by his wedding so soon.

Colin shrugged at his reflection. "I have yet to dress and shave and be jocularly ridiculed by my brothers. I know how these events go; as dreary as they are, somehow there never is as much time as one needs to prepare."

"It would be so much simpler if marriage were settled without all this unseemly to-do, parading about as if the bride and groom had single-handedly invented the institution. A few documents passed between solicitors, the appropriate signature on the appropriate blank." Emma sighed.

Colin chuckled. "*Mon ange*, you were born a cynic." He squared his shoulders and straightened his gray morning coat before crossing the room to her bedside. Emma extended round white arms to pull him to meet her upturned face—not so carelessly that she mussed his suit—and kissed him with a faultless balance of passion and decorum.

"I suppose this is good-bye," she said when they separated. Her bottom lip, kiss-swollen and still jutting out slightly, began to tremble.

"For a few months, at least," Colin agreed easily.

The lip stopped trembling. "For at least half a year, I should hope. It isn't decent that a man should hurry too quickly from a wife's bed."

"Nor a woman from her husband's?" Colin returned coolly.

Emma pulled a face delicately. "I produced Algy's heir and a spare before I took my first lover. Now we live our lives, discreet and discrete"—her smile indicated the wordplay—"and well satisfied. I would wish you better, if I thought any better were possible upon this mortal coil."

Colin laughed again. "We shall see, I suppose." It wasn't as if he had any great aversion to marriage nor any great expectations going into it, really. He assumed that it would sort itself out like his life always had.

Eton, Oxford, the usual social clubs in London and hunt clubs in the country—his life had always fallen into place without a single conscious effort on his part. He had no reason to think that his marriage would be any different.

He had decided last year that it was an appropriate time for him to wed. As the heir to a viscounty, he needed a son before he grew too old, and his cordial if distant relationship with his parents assured the stipend needed for an appropriate match. The debutantes that year were as callow and self-centered as they ever were, but this discovery scarcely put him off; after all, self-centeredness merely meant that a woman would spend more time thinking about herself than harrying him. All he demanded in a wife was an accomplished hostess with a certain warmth and physical charm, traits that abounded among the daughters of his set. So when he found himself spending more and more time at Fern Ashcroft's side, as much by chance as by design, he rapidly made the socially required hints, and upon receiving the appropriate replies, he approached her father and requested her hand.

His only regret, and that a faint one, was that the engagement coincided with his discovery of the undemanding and ever-welcoming Emma Mortimer. But the matter of a mistress, however pleasant, was no reason to change the direction of his life.

Colin looked down at Emma now and brushed a golden curl that had fallen across her forehead back to join the rest of the artfully tumbled mass. "Let's not put a time requirement to fidelity. It sounds so calculating, and you know I never calculate. Instead, I will merely say—good-bye, for now."

"I should cry, you know," Emma said, her cornflower blue eyes growing round and wet even as she spoke.

He raised one eyebrow. "Please don't. At least, not unless you intend upon pining after me until I return; if you do, I could hardly deny you the right to weep, however inconvenient. But you shall make me most abominably late if I must stay to comfort you."

Emma laughed, the dampness transforming into a merry glimmer. "Oh, you naughty thing! You know me too well. I've tried to pine before, but I simply haven't the constitution. Run along, then. I shall be here when you return, but whether or not there will still be a place for you, I can make no promises!"

"Fair enough," Colin replied, and he turned away to face his wedding day and his bride.

The aisle stretched out interminably in front of Fern, lined with familiar faces, their gazes smothering her. Distantly, she knew this should be the happiest day of her life, when her girlish dreams would finally be realized and she would emerge into womanhood on the arm of her new husband—the husband she had scarcely dared believe had chosen her. But she could muster no joy, and her smile felt more like a rictus. The heir of a viscount. It had seemed impossible that he had wanted her, impossible that she could refuse, and since Fern had never been one to attempt the impossible or even the indecorous, she had accepted. Now a stranger stood waiting for her at the end of the carpet, and the indifference of his gaze chilled her soul.

Fern's father stepped forward, and she found herself borne along in the wake of the bridesmaids and her flower-strewing nieces. The organ blast trembled in the vaulted ceiling, the vast space muddying the sound until it arrived as one great crash in her ears, and the scents of roses and toilet water crowded thick, hot, and cloying around her.

She wanted to press a hand to her roiling stomach. Instead, she tightened her grip on her bouquet and continued to smile for the staring faces, white as the orange blossoms that wilted in her grasp, and for the gray rapier figure that waited at the other end of the carpet.

Then she was there, beside *him*, standing unsupported, and the minister was speaking far too fast, the words tumbling together in her head until she could only catch fragments, like the falling shards of a stained glass window. . . .

Dearly beloved . . . a remedy against sin . . . wilt thou have this woman . . . this man . . . till death us do part . . .

The man next to her was too cold, so gray and adamantine that she might break against him just as the pieces of the minister's words broke in her ears. Fern's stomach lurched again.

"Thereto I plight thee my troth." It was her own voice, and she felt it buzzing up her own throat, but under what power, she could not say.

Then her bouquet was taken away, and her hand enfolded in a broader one, cool and strong through kid gloves, a hand that seemed to fill her world . . . and upon her finger, it slid a ring.

Kneeling, standing, kneeling, standing. Fern wanted to shout, to clap her hands over her ears, to do something to stop the torrent of words that bore her helplessly along.

And then it was over.

The clash of the organ, the clang of bells, and they flew down the aisle toward the doors that spilled light like the gates of heaven into the hot cavern of the church.

The Honorable Mr. and Mrs. Colin Barton Jonathan Radcliffe.

Oh, God, what have I done?

LYDIA JOYCE

WHISPERS OF
THE NIGHT

When four London seasons fail to find her a suitable match,
Alcyone Carter does the unthinkable and treks across Europe
to marry a foreign nobleman she's never met. But on her
wedding night, she discovers her handsome, enigmatic husband is not the man he claimed to be. Rather than live a lie,
she escapes his estate into the darkness. But her husband—
ignited by his desire and pride—risks everything to follow
her from the depths of the Romanian forests into the decadent
heart of Istanbul, where they're forced to confront the sensual
passion they've discovered—and the dire threat that could
cost them both their lives.

0-451-21897-3

**Available wherever books are sold or at
penguin.com**